Acclaim for Amy Clipston

"Clipston brings this engaging series to an end with two emotional family reunions, a prodigal son parable, a sweet but hard-won romance and a happy ending for characters readers have grown to love. Once again, she gives us all we could possibly want from a talented storyteller."

—*RT Book Reviews*, 4 1/2 stars, TOP PICK! on *A Simple Prayer*

"... will leave readers craving more."

—*RT Book Reviews*, 4 1/2 stars, TOP PICK! on *A Mother's Secret*

"Clipston's series starter has a compelling drama involving faith, family and romance ... [an] absorbing se-ries."

—*RT Book Reviews*, 4 1/2 stars, TOP PICK! on *A Hopeful Heart*

"Authentic characters, delectable recipes and faith abound in Clipston's second Kauffman Amish Bakery story."

—*RT Book Reviews*, 4-star review of *A Promise of Hope*

"[A]n entertaining story of Amish life, loss, love and family."

—*R*

D1042860

"This fifth and final installment in the Kauffman Amish Bakery series is sure to please fans who have waited for Katie's story."

—*LIBRARY JOURNAL* REVIEW OF *A SEASON OF LOVE*

"[The Kauffman Amish Bakery series'] wide popularity is sure to attract readers to this novella, and they won't be disappointed by the excellent writing and the story's wholesome goodness."

—*LIBRARY JOURNAL* REVIEW OF *A PLAIN AND SIMPLE CHRISTMAS*

"[I]nspiring and a perfect fit for the holiday season."

—*RT BOOK REVIEWS*, 4-STAR REVIEW OF *A PLAIN AND SIMPLE CHRISTMAS*

A Hopeful Heart

Also by Amy Clipston

The Amish Heirloom Series

The Forgotten Recipe

The Courtship Basket

The Cherished Quilt
(available November 2016)

The Hearts of the Lancaster Grand Hotel Series

A Hopeful Heart

A Mother's Secret

A Dream of Home

A Simple Prayer

The Kauffman Amish Bakery Series

A Gift of Grace

A Place of Peace

A Promise of Hope

A Life of Joy

A Season of Love

Young Adult

Roadside Assistance

Reckless Heart

Destination Unknown

Miles from Nowhere

Novellas

A Plain and Simple Christmas

Naomi's Gift

A Spoonful of Love included in *An Amish Kitchen*

A Son for Always included in *An Amish Cradle*

Love Birds included in *An Amish Market*
(available February 2016)

Nonfiction

A Gift of Love

A Hopeful Heart

HEARTS OF THE LANCASTER GRAND HOTEL

BOOK ONE

AMY
CLIPSTON

ZONDERVAN

A Hopeful Heart
Copyright © 2013 by Amy Clipston

This title is also available as a Zondervan ebook.
Visit www.zondervan.com/ebooks.

Requests for information should be addressed to:
Zondervan, *Grand Rapids, Michigan 49546*

ISBN: 978-0-7180-7997-0 (Mass Market)

Library of Congress Cataloging-in-Publication Data

Clipston, Amy.
Hearts of the Lancaster Grand Hotel / Amy Clipston.
pages cm.—(A Hopeful Heart; Book 1)
Includes bibliographical references and index.
ISBN 978-0-310-31998-6 (trade paper)
I. Title.
PS3603.L58H43 2013
813'.6—dc23   2013002810

Printed in the United States of America

16 17 18 19 /OPM/ 18 17 16 15 14 13 12 11 10 9 8 7 6 5 4 3 2 1

For Alicia Mey, who gave me the inspiration for this new series. Your friendship is a blessing to me!

Glossary

ach: oh
aenti: aunt
appeditlich: delicious
Ausbund: Amish hymnal
bedauerlich: sad
boppli: baby
brot: bread
bruder: brother
bruderskinner: nieces/nephews
bu: boy
buwe: boys
daadi: granddad
daed: dad
danki: thank you
dat: dad
Dietsch: Pennsylvania Dutch, the Amish language (a German dialect)
dochder: daughter
dochdern: daughters
dummle!: hurry!
Englisher: a non-Amish person
fraa: wife
freind: friend
freinden: friends

freindschaft: relative
froh: happy
gegisch: silly
gern gschehne: you're welcome
grandkinner: grandchildren
grank: sick
grossdochdern: granddaughters
grandkinner: grandchildren
grossmammi: grandmother
Gude mariye: Good morning
gut: good
Gut nacht: Good night
haus: house
Ich liebe dich: I love you
kapp: prayer covering or cap
kichli: cookie
kichlin: cookies
kind: child
kinner: children
kumm: come
liewe: love, a term of endearment
maed: young women, girls
maedel: young woman
mamm: mom
mammi: grandma
mei: my
mutter: mother
naerfich: nervous
narrisch: crazy
onkel: uncle

Ordnung: The oral tradition of practices required and
    forbidden in the Amish faith.

schee: pretty

schtupp: family room

schweschder: sister

schweschdere: sisters

Was iss letz?: What's wrong?

Wie geht's: How do you do? or Good day!

Willkumm heemet: Welcome home

wunderbaar: wonderful

ya: yes

zwillingbopplin: twins

NOTE TO THE READER

While this novel is set against the real backdrop of Lancaster County, Pennsylvania, the characters are fictional. There is no intended resemblance between the characters in this book and any real members of the Amish and Mennonite communities. As with any work of fiction, I've taken license in some areas of research as a means of creating the necessary circumstances for my characters. My research was thorough; however, it would be impossible to be completely accurate in details and description since each and every community differs. Therefore, any inaccuracies in the Amish lifestyle portrayed in this book are completely due to fictional license.

ONE

Hannah Glick pushed the cleaning supply cart down the hallway and toward the next hotel room door. She knocked three times and then called, "Housekeeping!"

She waited a few moments for a response, but the room remained silent. She pulled the master key card from her apron pocket. When she slid the key into the slot, the lock beeped and the light flashed green. Hannah pushed the door open while looking down. She stepped into the room, glanced up, and gasped when she found a tall, bare-chested man staring at her, his brown eyes wide.

"*Ach!*" Hannah cleared her throat and averted her eyes by studying a lighted sconce on the wall. "Excuse me, sir. I thought this room was empty." She stumbled toward the hallway while avoiding his own shocked look. "I'm so sorry for disturbing you. I'll come back later to clean."

Hannah rushed into the hallway and slammed into the supply cart on her way down the hall toward the vending machine room. She slipped through the door and leaned against the wall. Her hip throbbed where she'd hit the cart. She rubbed her injury while the Coca-Cola machine hummed beside her. *How embarrassing!* She'd never walked in on a hotel guest before. And the man was half-naked! The situation couldn't have been much worse.

"Hannah?" Linda Zook's voice rang out in the hallway.

"I'm in here," Hannah called.

Linda stepped into the vending machine room and raised her brown eyebrows. "You look upset. *Was iss letz?*"

"You won't believe what happened to me. I knocked on room 345 and didn't hear a response. When I unlocked the door, I walked in on a man." Hannah paused. "And he wasn't dressed."

Linda's cheeks flushed. "You mean he was . . . ?"

"*Ya*, he was shirtless." Hannah shook her head. "I've never been so embarrassed in my life. I quickly excused myself. Hopefully he'll be gone before I go back out in the hallway."

"It was an honest mistake, Hannah. He must've not heard you knock. Maybe he was in the bathroom."

"I don't know how I can face him again. He must think I have no manners at all."

"I imagine he was embarrassed too." Linda shook her head. "I can't imagine that happening to me." Her cheeks continued to flush. "I probably would have passed out from the shock of it."

"You would have." Hannah nodded in agreement. "You're flustered when a man says good morning to you."

"That's very true." Linda pointed toward the hallway. "I was just coming to see if you wanted to join Carolyn and me for a break."

"That's a *gut* idea." Hannah ran her hands over her apron and then pushed her prayer covering ties over her shoulder. "Maybe he'll be gone from his room by the time we're done." She followed Linda into the hallway. "I'll go get my cart." Hannah rushed over and pushed the cart toward the elevator while hoping she wouldn't run into the guest again.

• • •

Trey Peterson stared after the Amish woman as she hurried out of his room, bumping the supply cart on her way down the hallway. It had all happened so fast that he hadn't had a chance to react. He thought he heard a sound at the door just as he was turning off the water in the sink, and then when he stepped out of the bathroom, the door whooshed open to reveal Hannah.

When she looked up, her eyes were wide with surprise, and her cheeks were blushing as red as the roses he'd spotted in the lobby. He'd wanted to tell her that it was only an honest mistake, but she'd averted her eyes and stumbled out of his room before he could say a word.

Trey had researched the Amish culture when he'd planned to sell his New Jersey home and move to Lancaster County. He'd found it intriguing when he spotted the Amish housekeepers working at the exclusive Lancaster Grand Hotel in Paradise, Pennsylvania.

It was ironic to see the women wearing their prayer coverings and clad in their plain aprons and dresses while standing under the sparkling chandelier in the lobby. They were a stark contrast to the elaborate woodworking on the fireplace and the rare paintings.

The housekeeper who'd barged into his room had caught his eye yesterday when he had checked in. She looked to be in her mid- to late thirties, and had flame-red hair sticking out from under her prayer covering. She hadn't noticed Trey while she brushed a brown-colored feather duster over the base of a grandfather clock. Yet he found himself studying her ivory skin and bright green eyes.

And now she'd rushed out of his room horrified after walking in on him when he was shirtless. Trey shook his head and grabbed a shirt from the dresser. He pulled it on and straightened the collar.

His eyes scanned the hotel room, taking in the genuine solid cherry dressers, king-size bed frame, and tables. A large, flat-screen television sat across from the bed and in front of a leather sofa. The other side of the room held a bar with two stools, a sink, a microwave, and a small refrigerator. The room was elegant and modern, one of the nicest he'd stayed in while traveling for his bank work, but it was nothing compared to the home he'd left in New Jersey.

Trey crossed the room and picked up a framed photograph he'd placed on the dresser next to the television after he'd unpacked yesterday. He studied the image of his beautiful wife of twenty years, Corrine, and their eighteen-year-old daughter, Samantha. Sammi was the mirror image of Corrine with her light brown hair and powder blue eyes. If only he'd listened when Corrine had begged him to stay home instead of going to yet one more conference, the one in Baltimore. Then his family would still be alive . . .

Trey couldn't bear to stay in the house after carbon monoxide poisoning had taken the lives of the two most precious people in his life just over a year ago. The memories and regret still haunted him. He'd spoken with his pastor and prayed about it for months. The only choice he had was to sell the house and leave. He yearned to build a new life in Pennsylvania after his wife's love of the Amish community had called to him, like a prayer whispered in the night. By moving here and opening up a bed and breakfast, he could keep Corrine's dream alive. He'd promised to retire early from the financial industry and give her that dream, but he never got the chance. Now he *had* to do it. For her.

He placed the photograph back on the dresser and fetched his shoes from the closet. While he pulled them on, Trey thought about the Amish woman again. He hoped she had recovered from their awkward first meeting.

TWO

Later that evening, Hannah placed a basket of home-made rolls on the kitchen table. "Andrew, is your *onkel* planning to stay for supper tonight?"

Her ten-year-old son raced toward the back door. "I'll go ask him."

Hannah smiled. Andrew had followed Joshua around like his shadow ever since her husband, Gideon, passed away from a sudden heart attack four years ago. She was thankful Joshua continued running their co-owned horse business with her after his older brother's untimely death.

"What do you think?" Lillian, one of Hannah's sixteen-year-old twins, placed a platter of chicken and dumplings in the center of the table and then pushed her glasses farther up on her little nose.

"*Appeditlich!*" Hannah inhaled the aroma. "Very *gut*, Lily."

"*Ya*, it smells *gut*." Amanda, Lillian's fraternal twin, smiled. "Lillian just wants to learn how to cook so she can impress Leroy King."

"That's not true." Lillian's ivory cheeks flushed. "We're only *freinden*."

"If you're only *freinden*, then why did I see you

flirting with him at the youth gathering last night?" Amanda wagged a finger at her sister.

"We were only talking." Lillian jammed her hands on her hips.

"Girls, please stop." Hannah gave them a sharp frown. "Please finish bringing out the food. Your *onkel* and *bruder* will be inside soon."

The table was set by the time Joshua and Andrew stepped into the mudroom and shucked their boots. Joshua entered the kitchen first with Andrew in tow. Andrew gazed up at his uncle, and Hannah couldn't help but smile. A stranger could mistake the two for father and son since Andrew shared his uncle's dark brown hair and blue eyes. Andrew was also the spitting image of Gideon.

"Hannah." Joshua nodded, crossing to the kitchen. "*Danki* for inviting me to stay for supper." He revealed a bouquet of wild flowers from behind his back. "I saw these and thought of you."

"Oh, Joshua." Hannah smiled as she took the flowers. "These are lovely. *Danki*." She always appreciated Joshua's small gestures of thoughtfulness. She could just about guarantee he would bring her flowers at least once a week. She retrieved a small vase from the cabinet, filled it with water, and then placed the flowers on the table. "You know we enjoy having you stay for supper." Hannah sat at the table. "Besides, your *mamm* doesn't like you fending for yourself at home."

He rolled his eyes while washing his hands at the kitchen sink. "I cook pretty well for a bachelor." He glanced at the table. "Is that my favorite?"

"*Ya*," Amanda said, sinking into her usual seat next to Hannah. "Lillian made chicken and dumplings. She's practicing her cooking."

"I followed *Mammi's* recipe." Lillian's serious green eyes held a hint of pride.

"*Mei mamm's* recipe?" Joshua dried his hands and then sat at the head of the table as if he belonged in the seat. "That sounds *gut*."

Hannah's stomach tightened as she once again fought the urge to ask Joshua to move to another chair. That was Gideon's place, not Joshua's.

"*Ya*." Lillian nodded her head, causing her loose locks of red hair to frame her face. "I'm trying to learn her recipes."

They all bowed their heads in silent prayer before reaching across the table to grab the platters and bowls like a giant octopus stretching its multiple legs. Forks and spoons scraped the plates while conversations flew.

Joshua filled his plate with chicken and dumplings and then turned to Hannah. "How was your day?"

"*Gut*." Hannah tried not to think of the *Englisher* she'd seen without his shirt. She could never share that humiliating story with anyone other than her coworkers. "How was yours?"

"Fine." He buttered a roll while he talked. "It looks like Daniel King may work for us."

"Daniel King?" Amanda asked.

Lillian's eyebrows shot up to her hairline. "Leroy's *bruder*?"

Joshua nodded. "That's right."

"How about that?" Amanda asked her twin. "Maybe someday Leroy will work here too."

Lillian glared at her sister, and Hannah swallowed a laugh before turning back to Joshua. "That's *gut* news. I think we're ready for you to hire someone. I was looking at the books earlier. We're doing much better since the horse business started picking up this winter season. My job at the hotel has really helped our finances too."

Joshua shrugged. "*Ya*, but I wish you didn't have to work at all."

"I don't mind. I meet some interesting people." Hannah's thoughts went back to the man in the hotel room and her stomach clenched. *Interesting* didn't begin to describe all the people she met. She looked at her blond daughter. "How was your day, Amanda?"

"*Gut.*" Amanda spooned a pile of applesauce onto her plate. "The store was very busy all day. I love it when I get to meet a lot of customers. It makes the day go by so fast." She turned to her uncle, and her smile faded. "But you know, *Onkel* Josh, I can help you on the farm. I was talking to Cameron Wood, the vet who lives across the street, and he told me he's looking for an assistant. I wonder if he could pay me more money than I'm making at the store. If I worked for him, then I could learn how to take care of our horses when they're ill. What do you think of that?"

Joshua shook his head and wiped his mouth. "I think you're doing fine at the store, Amanda. Nancy's parents need your help, and we help the members of our community."

Hannah watched Amanda's shoulders hunch as

she studied her plate. She wondered why her daughter suddenly wanted to work for the neighbor instead of helping out at her best friend's family's deli.

"If we're listing our accomplishments, I finished the laundry today," Lillian said.

"I helped her fold," Andrew added with a mouthful of bread.

"You need to finish chewing that *brot* and then swallow before you speak, Andrew." Lillian scolded him as if she were his mother.

"That's *wunderbaar* that you helped your *schweschder*," Hannah said. "*Danki* for being a *gut* helper today."

"I didn't have a choice." Andrew grimaced. "She made me."

Hannah chuckled and shook her head. How she loved her children!

The conversations continued to circle while they finished supper. Once the plates were empty, Hannah and her daughters cleared the table and began cleaning up.

"*Onkel* Josh," Amanda began while scrubbing a dish, "can you stay for Scrabble tonight?"

Joshua glanced at Hannah. "What do you think?"

Hannah shrugged. "Why not? It's been awhile since we played. We can finish cleaning up after the game."

"Great!" Amanda rushed to the family room and returned with the game.

Andrew frowned. "But you can only have four players with Scrabble. What about me?"

Hannah touched his arm. "You can help me." She

wagged a finger at him. "As long as you whisper. You can't give away our letters like you did last time, okay?"

Andrew grinned. "Okay."

The family gathered around the table, and Hannah sat next to Joshua.

"I'm going to beat you this time." Joshua grinned as he picked up a tile.

"No, you aren't. You won't get away with making up words this time." Hannah laughed.

"Right," Lillian agreed. "Just having consonants and vowels doesn't make your play a word."

Amanda stood. "I should go get the dictionary."

Hannah nodded. "I agree. We have to keep your *onkel* honest."

Joshua sighed. "Now you sound like Gideon."

Hannah smiled at him as memories flooded her mind. Gideon loved playing board games, especially Scrabble. They'd spent many happy hours seated around the kitchen table playing games. She was glad Joshua liked to join them even though Gideon was gone.

Joshua rubbed his hands together. "Okay. I'm ready!"

For the next hour, they played Scrabble. Hannah enjoyed watching Andrew figure out words, and she laughed frequently as the children and Joshua teased each other.

Lillian tallied up the score. "I won." She smiled at her uncle. "And I didn't have to make up words."

Joshua shrugged as he gathered up the tiles. "Making up words is more fun."

Hannah shook her head. "You're so *gegisch*."

Joshua raised his eyebrows. "I'd like to think of myself as creative." He stood. "*Danki* for the game. It was a lot of fun." He started toward the back door.

"*Onkel* Josh!" Andrew followed Joshua to the mudroom. "I'll help you finish up outside."

Hannah watched Andrew and Joshua talk while they pulled on their boots and hats before heading outside. She couldn't stop thinking of Gideon, and her smile faded. It seemed like only yesterday her then six-year-old Andrew was trotting out to the barns behind his father.

"*Mamm?*" Amanda asked while scrubbing a dish. "Are you okay?"

"*Ya.*" Hannah dropped a pile of utensils into the frothy water.

"Were you thinking of *Dat?*"

Amanda's question stunned Hannah for a moment, leaving her speechless. "How did you know?"

Amanda shrugged. "Sometimes *Onkel* Josh reminds me of *Dat.*"

"I see the resemblance too." Lillian dried a plate. "He looks like *Dat* and sometimes he even sounds like him."

Hannah wiped the table. "*Ya*, he does sometimes." *But he's not my Gid.* The thought made tears fill her eyes. She cleared her throat. "Who's hosting the youth gathering on Saturday?"

"Katie Esh," Lillian said.

The girls discussed their friends while Hannah finished cleaning the table. She enjoyed listening to them discuss their social lives and hearing their excitement when they talked about attending singings. As she listened, she thought back to when she was their age. She also attended singings, which was where she fell in love with Gideon.

Hannah was sweeping the kitchen floor when Andrew and Joshua returned from outside.

"*Danki* for your help, Andrew." Joshua touched Andrew's head. "You're a *gut* worker."

"*Gern gschehne.* See you tomorrow!" Andrew trotted through the kitchen.

"Get ready for devotions, Andrew," Hannah called after him.

"I know!" Andrew's voice echoed from the staircase.

Joshua chuckled. "I wish I had his energy."

"*Ya*, I know." Hannah smiled. "Would you like to stay for devotions?"

"Thanks for the offer, but I need to get home."

"Okay. I'll walk you out." Hannah followed him to the porch where they stood by the steps. "Are you going to talk to Daniel tomorrow?"

"*Ya*." Joshua leaned against the railing and towered over her by a few inches. "He wanted to discuss it with his parents, but he was *froh* with the salary."

"*Gut*." Hannah folded her arms over her apron. "He's a *gut* young man. I'm certain he'll work hard for you. You've needed help for a long time."

"*Ya*." He frowned. "But I wish you didn't have to work so that we can pay him. Gideon would not be pleased that you have to be away from your *kinner*."

"Don't be *gegisch*." She dismissed his comment with

a wave. "Things are different now that Gid is gone. The girls are older. Lillian only teaches on days when I'm home, so she's here for Andrew when I'm working. I like my job, and the pay is *gut*. It's important that you have a man working with you out in the stables. The horses are our bread and butter."

"I know, but I'm certain Gideon wouldn't have approved." Joshua's eyes studied her. "You know I love your *kinner* like they were my own. I would do anything for them."

Hannah shifted her weight from one foot to the other. "I know, and the *kinner* love you too."

"If you ever need anything, you know I will be here." He stepped toward her. "Anything at all, Hannah."

"*Danki.*" Hannah took a step back toward the door. "It's late, Josh. I'll see you tomorrow. *Gut nacht.*"

"*Gut nacht.*"

Joshua headed toward his buggy, parked by the barn, and Hannah watched his lanky body move through the shadows of the early evening. Although Joshua had been a wonderful support to her and her children since Gideon had died, he didn't warm her heart as her husband had. She often sensed a longing in his intense blue eyes, but she couldn't feel more than friendship for him.

Hannah contemplated her husband and brother-in-law while she watched Joshua's horse and buggy bounce down her rock driveway toward the road. She'd grown up and gone to church and school with Gideon and Joshua. Gideon was two years older than she was and Joshua was a year younger. But it was Gideon who'd stolen her heart when she turned sixteen and joined his youth group. She couldn't resist his infectious laugh and warm smile, coupled with his sense of humor and bright blue eyes the color of the sky. He'd rented this land and the house from his parents and then asked his brother to be his business partner when he opened the horse farm.

Hannah stepped into the kitchen and locked up for the night. While snuffing out the lanterns, she thought back to her early years with Gideon. She'd married him when she was twenty-one, and the twins came along a year later. After several heartbreaking miscarriages, Hannah thought they'd only be blessed with the girls. Yet their family was complete when Andrew joined them. Hannah could still remember the joy in Gideon's eyes when they'd welcomed their son. Although he adored his girls, he'd hoped they'd someday have a son to help him run the business along with his brother. But Andrew never had the chance to help his father run the business. Gideon died when Andrew was six.

Hannah crossed the kitchen and family room and stood in the doorway to her bedroom. A wave of grief crashed over her as she studied her double bed and frowned.

"Gideon," she whispered, her voice trembling with emotion. "I'm so thankful for the life we shared and for the brief amount of time God gave you on his earth. And I'm thankful for our wonderful *kinner*. But I can't stop the loneliness that haunts me every day."

She crossed the room and touched the pillow on what had been his side of the bed. "I'm most lonely at night when I'm trapped in here with my thoughts. You took my heart with you when you left. I don't know how to fill the hole that's left where my heart used to be." She wiped an errant tear from her cheek. "I'm exhausted. It's so difficult keeping up with my job at the hotel and raising these *kinner* without you. When you were here, we had a balance. I didn't feel so scattered and unsure of myself. There are times when I'm lost, and I wish you were here to help me make decisions about the *kinner* and about our life. Sometimes I'm so confused. I'm not the same person I was when you were here. I feel as if I lost part of myself when you left. We all miss you, and we all need you. I miss you, Gid. And I love you."

She then climbed the stairs toward her children's bedrooms and sent up a prayer to God, asking him to guide her and rid her of the sadness in her heart.

. . .

Later that evening, Amanda snuggled under their quilt and looked at her sister beside her. "How's your book?"

"*Gut.*" Lillian turned the page while reading by the light of a battery-operated lantern.

Amanda yawned and rolled over to face the wall. It seemed nearly every night she fell asleep while her sister was reading a Christian novel. They were technically twins born only a few minutes apart, but their similarities ended there. For one thing, Lillian was the only one blessed with their mother's coloring. And for another, while Lillian could often be found with her nose in a book, Amanda had other interests—secret interests.

Amanda's eyes moved to her bureau where her secret book was hidden in the bottom drawer under her stockings and underwear. She'd picked up a copy of *The Veterinarian's Manual* at the bookstore located across from the deli during her lunchtime last week. She managed to hide it in the tote bag she carried to work every day and then hide it in her bureau. Amanda stole a few private moments perusing the book, but she didn't dare tell her family of her dream of going to college and becoming a veterinarian. She hadn't even shared her secret with the vet across the street because she was afraid no one would understand why an Amish girl would want to pursue a career as a veterinarian. Yet she yearned to cross to the other side of the room, grab her special book, and read alongside her sister.

Amanda heard her sister's book close and hit the nightstand. A click told her that the lantern had been turned off for the night. The bed shifted as Lillian moved under the covers.

"I wish *Mamm* didn't have to work." Lillian broke the silence between them.

"You know why she took the job. *Onkel* Josh needs help with the horses, and Andrew is too small to do the heavy work." Amanda cupped her hand to her mouth to stifle a yawn. Exhaustion gripped her after a day on her feet at the deli.

"*Ya*, but she belongs at home," Lillian continued. "Even *Mammi* said that to me after service Sunday."

"*Mammi* should understand that *Onkel* Josh and

Mamm made the decision together. Besides, I think it's *gut* for *Mamm* to get out of the *haus* and away from the memories. I've caught her crying when she thinks she's alone, and it breaks my heart. Maybe the Lord led her to the hotel so she could find some joy again. Everything happens for a reason."

"I don't know." Lillian paused. "Andrew wasn't *froh* today when I made him help me fold the laundry. I needed someone to help because I was falling behind and had to start supper. He helped me, but you should've seen his face."

Amanda smiled. "I can imagine. He'd much rather be out in the barn with *Onkel* Josh."

"Do you think Andrew might take over the horse business someday?"

"He might." Amanda yawned again. "But you never know what the Lord has in store for him." She felt herself drifting off to sleep, but her sister's voice wrenched her awake again.

"Do you think *Onkel* Josh loves *Mamm*?"

"What?" Amanda tried to decipher the implication of her sister's words. "What do you mean?"

"You heard me. Do you think *Onkel* Josh is in love with *Mamm*?"

"You mean like how *Dat* loved her?" Amanda couldn't help her grimace. The idea was preposterous.

"*Ya*, that's exactly what I mean."

"I don't know." Amanda rolled over and faced her sister through the dark. "Why would you even think that?"

"I'm not sure. It's a feeling I get sometimes. He

stares at her like he's watching a miracle happen before his eyes."

Amanda snorted. "That sounded poetic, Lily. When did you start writing poetry?"

"I'm being serious." Lillian's voice held no hint of a joke.

"I don't know. I guess anything's possible, right? Maybe *Onkel* Josh cares for her."

"Haven't you ever wondered why he never married?"

"Not really. *Mamm's aenti* Fannie never married either. Some people don't meet the right person, I guess." Amanda rolled back toward the wall. "It's late. You need your sleep."

"I miss *Dat*." Lillian's voice was soft, like an unsure child.

"I do too. But God will take care of us and guide our path. He always does. Now, go to sleep, Lillian. You have to help teach tomorrow." Amanda drifted off to sleep while contemplating her sister's question about their uncle.

THREE

Wednesday morning the elevator dinged and the door opened to the third floor with a hum. Hannah pushed the supply cart and vacuum cleaner around the corner toward the first hallway of rooms. When she spotted the man whose room she'd barged into on Monday, her stomach dropped. He was patting his pockets and his mouth formed a thin line.

Hannah turned the cart around in an attempt to slip away to the other end of the hall and avoid all contact with him. She failed to escape, however, because she was stopped mid-stride by a voice behind her.

"Excuse me. Could you possibly help me?"

When she faced him, his lips turned up in a tentative smile.

Hannah studied the man and wondered why she hadn't switched floors with Linda today to escape more uncomfortable contact with him. "*Ya*, I can help you. What do you need?"

"I've lost my room key." He shook his head. "My wife always said I'd lose my head if it wasn't attached, and she was right." He chuckled and his eyes sparkled with humor.

Hannah smiled, even though embarrassment filled

her. He was clad in a collared shirt and dress slacks, but her impure thoughts kept creeping back to the sight of him without a shirt. How would she ever erase that from her memory?

"Of course." Hannah crossed to the hotel room while keeping her eyes trained on the door. She pulled out the master card key and unlocked the door. "Have a good day." She started toward the supply cart.

"Hannah?" he asked.

"*Ya?*" Hannah studied his brown eyes, wondering how he knew her name. Of course he knew her name; it was displayed on her uniform. She touched the gold name tag pinned to her work apron and immediately felt stupid.

"I'm Trey." He held out his hand. "Trey Peterson."

She shook his hand quickly and then pulled her hand back to her side. "Nice to meet you, Mr. Peterson."

"I didn't see you yesterday."

"I wasn't here." She fingered her apron. "I work Mondays, Wednesdays, and Fridays." Why was he so interested in her name and her work schedule?

"Oh." An awkward moment passed between them. He looked to be in his early forties, and had sandy blond hair and a matching goatee trimmed neatly around his mouth. He glanced behind him and chuckled again. His laugh was warm, much like his smile. "I see the key sitting in front of the television set. My wife was right. I *would* lose my head if it wasn't attached."

"Wives usually are right." The comment escaped her lips before she could stop it, and she mentally chastised herself for the sarcastic remark.

Trey raised his eyebrows as a burst of laughter exploded from his lips. "I didn't expect a comeback like that from you."

"I'm sorry. My husband used to warn me to watch my pert remarks, so I guess we're even." Hannah looked past him and spotted a framed photograph sitting on the dresser next to the large flat screen television. The photograph featured an attractive woman standing with her arms around a teenage girl. "Is that your family?"

His smile faded. "Yes." He stepped into the room and picked up the photograph. His eyes studied it as if seeing it for the first time.

She watched him from the doorway. "You have a nice family."

"Yes, I did." He shook his head and put the photograph down next to the television. "They died a little over a year ago."

Hannah gasped. "*Ach*, no. I'm so sorry."

"Thanks." Mr. Peterson cupped his hand to the back of his neck. "Carbon monoxide poisoning. I was out of town on business." He turned back toward the photograph. "I never imagined that could happen to me. We had smoke detectors, and I thought our carbon monoxide detectors were up-to-date. I'd changed the batteries recently—or at least I thought I had. But apparently it wasn't enough."

His eyes met hers. "Some nights I can't sleep because I wonder over and over again if I could have done something if I'd been there. But I've spoken to people who insist that carbon monoxide is a silent killer. It's odorless.

Corrine and Sammi died peacefully in their sleep, and if I'd been there, I would've died too. But that gives me little comfort." His frown deepened. "I'll never understand why I was left here without them. All alone."

Hannah nodded slowly, stunned by his openness with her. "God's will is unpredictable and often takes us by surprise." She thought of Gideon and her lip quivered. She took a deep breath in an effort to stop her threatening tears. "And it can knock us down and take our breath away, leaving us wondering why. But asking why will only drive you mad. You have to accept that his will is always right, no matter how painful it is."

Mr. Peterson studied her. "You sound like you speak from experience."

"My husband died four years ago."

Trey took a step toward her. "I'm so sorry, Hannah."

The warmth in his eyes caught her off guard. Hannah cleared her throat in an effort to temper her emotions. "He had a massive heart attack. His brother found him in the pasture, but by the time the ambulance arrived it was too late. Nothing could be done." She thought back to that day in the hospital waiting room. "I felt as if the life had been sucked out of me when the doctor told us he was gone. Every dream we had and every promise we made to each other disappeared in that moment. Nothing would ever be the same. My children had lost their father, and I'd lost my life partner. It was all just gone in the blink of an eye."

"I'm so sorry." He repeated the words with just as much empathy as the first time he'd said them. "How many children do you have?"

"Three."

"How are they doing?"

Hannah shrugged. "They manage. We all miss him, but we just go on and hold fast to our faith. It's not our place to question God."

"You're right, but you said it yourself. Sometimes it's not easy."

"No, it's not—especially when I'm left alone with my thoughts late at night when I can't sleep. I keep wondering what life would be like now if he hadn't died. What if I'd walked out to the pasture to check on him that day? What if Joshua had found him a few minutes earlier and I'd called 911 a few minutes sooner?" Hannah paused when she realized she'd shared thoughts that she'd never even said aloud to family members or her closest friends. "But I hold fast to my prayers, and I pray often."

"I understand." Mr. Peterson's serious expression transformed to a smile. "I pray often. I think God's tired of hearing from me."

"I don't think God ever gets tired of hearing from his children." She spotted the time on his watch and realized she was running behind. She needed to start cleaning or her boss would scold her. She gestured toward the supply cart. "I need to get back to work. I hope you have a good day."

"You too. Thanks for rescuing me from being locked out in the hallway."

"You know you could've gotten a new key from the front desk."

"I could have, but it was nice talking to you, Hannah."

"*Ya*, it was nice talking to you too." She started toward the cart. "I hope you keep track of your key."

"I do too." He laughed. "See you later."

Hannah pushed the supply cart toward the other end of the hallway and contemplated her conversation with Trey Peterson. She couldn't fathom the pain he'd endured when he found out that his wife and daughter had both died from carbon monoxide poisoning. How would Hannah have coped with losing her whole family at once? The thought caused her to shudder.

She knocked, announced herself, and unlocked the door to an empty room. She pushed the vacuum cleaner into the room while she thought about Mr. Peterson. She wondered how he managed to keep a smile on his face despite his pain. She assumed that his prayers and faith were his strength.

Hannah clicked the on button and the vacuum cleaner roared to life. She pushed the machine back and forth, dragging the suction over the tan carpet. She wished the noise would silence her thoughts and her curiosity to know more about Mr. Peterson's life and spiritual journey after losing his wife and daughter.

. . .

After bowing her head in silent prayer, Hannah glanced across the break-room table toward her coworker Ruth Ebersol. "How's your day going?"

The older woman shrugged and pushed back a lock of graying brown hair that had escaped her prayer covering. "It's the usual. Messy rooms and dirty carpets."

"*Ya*, the same every day." Hannah pulled out her sandwich and apple. "Where is everyone else?"

"I think they're on their way." Ruth took a bite of her homemade bread. "Did you have a *gut* morning?"

"*Ya*." Hannah thought about her conversation with Trey Peterson while chewing her turkey sandwich.

Ruth's mild stare intensified. "You look like you have something interesting to share."

Hannah sipped her cup of water while considering what to share with Ruth. Although she'd worked with her friend for almost six months, she didn't know how Ruth would react to her conversation with an *Englisher*.

"Now I'm intrigued." Ruth smiled. "Did you walk in on another half-naked hotel guest?"

"I can't believe you're bringing that up again." Hannah shook her head. "I never should've confided in you and Linda."

Ruth chuckled, and her chubby cheeks turned red. She wiped her eyes with a napkin. "Don't be *gegisch*. We all make mistakes. When I first started here years ago, I recleaned an empty room that I'd cleaned the day before after the guests had left."

"Oh, no!" Hannah laughed. "I bet it was very clean after the second run through, *ya*?"

"Absolutely." Ruth tapped the table for emphasis. "Now, what happened to you today? You look as if you're bursting at the seams."

"If I tell you, then you have to promise to keep it a secret. It's about the guest I walked in on the other day."

"The *Englisher* without a shirt on?"

"That's the one. I saw him today in the hallway. I was hoping to avoid him, but he was standing outside his door because he'd lost his key. I unlocked his room, and then we had an unexpected conversation." Hannah shared what she and Mr. Peterson had discussed. While she talked, she frequently glanced toward the door and hoped her other coworkers wouldn't walk in.

Ruth continued eating her bread and cheese while Hannah repeated the conversation from earlier in the day.

Once Hannah was finished talking, Ruth wiped her mouth and shook her head. "I'm sorry to hear Mr. Peterson lost his family. That's a tragic story. So *bedauerlich*."

"I know. I thought my pain was daunting, but he lost his whole family. I can't stop thinking about it."

Ruth tilted her head. "What's got you so interested in this man? Is it that he lost his family or is it something else?"

"It's something else." Hannah paused while gathering her thoughts. "I'm surprised he was so easy to talk to. I've never met an *Englisher* like him."

"*Englishers* have the same losses we have. We're all human and we're all God's *kinner*."

"I know." Hannah bit into her sandwich. "I want to know more about how he's coped with losing his family. I think we could help each other if we talked about our loss and how we've dealt with it."

Ruth's lips formed a thin line. "You know that's not a *gut* idea, Hannah."

"I just want to talk to him. He seemed like he wanted

to share more with me, but I needed to get back to work. I don't even know where he's from or what brought him to Lancaster County."

"Don't think about him for another moment, Hannah. We're not supposed to get *too* friendly with the hotel guests, and it's inappropriate for you to be alone with a man, especially an *Englisher.*"

"I'm an adult, Ruth. I just want to talk to him. If we talked in a public place, it wouldn't be like we're meeting in secret."

"It's still not a *gut* idea." Ruth leaned forward and touched Hannah's hand. "I know Gideon has been gone for four years, but you're still vulnerable. You need to guard your heart. You may mistake friendship for something deeper and that's not *gut*, especially since he's *English*. Be careful, *mei freind.*"

Hannah studied Ruth's grimace and sighed. She knew Ruth was right, but she couldn't shake the feeling that Mr. Peterson's story could somehow help her deal with the loneliness that haunted her daily.

The break-room door slammed open and Linda Zook and Carolyn Lapp stepped in with their lunch bags swinging from their arms.

"*Wie geht's?*" they called in unison as they sank into chairs at the table.

While her friends, who were both in their early thirties, joined in the conversation, Hannah tried to push her thoughts away from Mr. Peterson.

"How are you doing today?" Carolyn unpacked her homemade bread and cheese.

"We're doing fine," Ruth said between bites of her

sandwich. She smiled at Carolyn. "You should come to church in my district Sunday. A bachelor from Ohio is visiting his *bruder's* family. I think you'd like him."

Hannah laughed. "Ruth, you're always trying to play matchmaker. I'm certain both Linda and Carolyn will find the right man in the Lord's time."

Carolyn grinned. "I wouldn't mind finding someone special and having a family of my own." She nodded at Linda. "What about you, Linda? Do you want Ruth to find someone for you too?"

Linda's cheeks flushed as she studied her turkey sandwich. "I don't know. I haven't really thought about it. I wouldn't even know what to say to a bachelor."

"Sure you would." Ruth smiled at her. "You'd just tell him your name and ask him about his home in Ohio. You'd find things to talk about."

Linda shook her head. "I don't think I can do that. I always get tongue-tied when I'm around men."

"I don't." Carolyn lifted her cup of water. "I always seem to find something to say."

Hannah chuckled. "*Ya*, you do have the gift to gab."

"I can't wait to get married. I would love to have a big family." Carolyn beamed. "I think twelve *kinner* like my parents had is just right."

Hannah shook her head. "Your parents were blessed."

"*Ya*." Ruth laughed. "They were blessed with patience too."

While Carolyn talked about her family, Hannah wondered if she would see Trey Peterson again.

· · ·

Trey steered his BMW down a winding Lancaster County road. He glanced out the window at the patchwork of lush farmland dotted with large white farm homes and thought of Corrine. His wife loved vacationing in Amish country and visiting the shops. She had dreamt of selling their house in New Jersey and living in Lancaster County. She'd talked of owning a bed and breakfast so she could help other visitors enjoy the area. He smiled as he remembered a map she'd once sketched, almost entirely by memory, pointing out the best stores to visit for the most authentic Amish trinkets and foods.

Corrine had constantly begged Trey to stop working so much and traveling so often. Although he made a generous salary, his frenetic career path was to the detriment of their time spent together as a family. He missed out on many of Samantha's school events because of his demanding schedule. Corrine wanted him home more, and opening a bed and breakfast was the compromise they'd reached. Once the business was open, Trey would find a less demanding job near their new home, enabling him to work less and enjoy more time with his wife. Samantha was getting ready to go off to college, making it the perfect time to sell their house and start over in Pennsylvania.

As Trey thought of his wife, he smiled. He'd loved Corrine since the day they'd met in college, and he wanted to keep her memory alive through those unrequited plans. Once he'd lost Corrine and Samantha, he couldn't bring himself to return to his high-powered corporate job in New York City. He blamed his obsession with the job for the reason he wasn't home the night they'd died. He had to leave his old life and start anew. He took the early retirement and headed toward the place Corrine had loved the most. Coming back to Lancaster was the best way for him to hold on to Corrine and some of their best memories as a family.

If he could only find the perfect site for Corrine's dream to come true . . . He kept her hand-drawn map secure in his briefcase, and he looked forward to the day he'd copy it and hand it to his first bed and break-fast guest.

Trey had contacted a local Realtor last week, but this morning he decided to go out looking for property alone. He knew the area well after all of the dozens of visits he'd made with Corrine over the years, and lately conversations with strangers were uncomfortable at best and usually stymied. Once Trey shared that he'd lost his family, an awkward silence hovered like an ominous dark cloud. Trey frequently found himself trying to fill the deep chasm of silence with meaningless comments about the weather or sports scores he'd spotted in the morning paper. So instead of enduring another painful conversation, he'd canceled his appointment with the Realtor. Being alone was what he needed today.

Trey steered around a bend in the road and spotted a vast farm. He noticed the plain green window shades, which was the first clue for Corrine when she was look-ing out for Amish homes, and his thoughts turned to Hannah Glick. He'd expected sympathetic platitudes followed by an awkward silence after he'd told Hannah about his loss, but instead she'd surprised him.

In fact, Hannah was nothing like he'd expected when he'd first met her Monday. He thought she'd be friendly but demure like the other Amish women he'd met during his vacations in the area. Instead, she was funny and more outspoken than he'd expected. But what had shocked him the most was that she understood his grief more than anyone he'd ever spoken to and even shared a glimpse of her own struggles after losing her husband. She was the first person who'd offered him more than the promise of prayers since he'd lost Corrine and Samantha.

Trey went around another bend and spotted a large, three-story home with a "for sale" sign in the front yard. He studied the whitewashed home, taking in the white split-rail fence surrounding a small pasture. A row of red barns sat behind the house. Would this be the location Corrine would've chosen to build her dream? Warmth filled his soul, and the answer to the question seemed to be a resounding *Yes!* as he wrenched open the car door. He walked toward the front porch steps and felt as if he were walking toward his new life.

FOUR

Hannah sat on the hard wooden bench at the bus stop a half block from the Lancaster Grand Hotel the following Wednesday afternoon. The driving rain pounded the top of the partial glass enclosure, and the wind whipped her dress like a flag fluttering from a pole. She shivered and smoothed her apron over her legs while peering down the street in hopes of spotting the bus that would take her to the warmth of her home.

She'd planned to leave work on time, but after Linda called in sick, Hannah finished her required housekeeping duties and then pitched in to help Carolyn complete Linda's rooms. Hannah had called her daily driver, Phyllis Houser, hoping she could schedule a ride later in the day, but Phyllis was booked with another family and then planned to leave to go out of town. Since she had no other choice, Hannah trekked through the raindrops to the bus stop at the end of the day.

A pickup truck sped past the bus stop and splashed through a large puddle, causing cold water to rain over Hannah, soaking her dress and feet.

"*Ach!* Where's that bus?" She brushed her hands

over her wet dress and hoped the bus would arrive soon without throwing more rainwater her way.

"Hannah?" a voice called.

She looked up and found Trey Peterson calling to her from inside a dark-colored sedan. She rested her tote bag on her lap in an effort to shield her wet dress. She hoped she didn't look as bedraggled as she felt. She wondered when she would stop finding herself in embarrassing situations with the *Englisher*. "Hi, Mr. Peterson."

"Can I give you a ride somewhere?"

"Oh." Hannah cleared her throat and considered accepting a ride from him. She knew members of her community would frown on her if they saw her alone with a man, especially one who wasn't Amish. But she wanted to get out of the rain and home to her family. She worried that her children were concerned about her since she should've been home two hours ago. She'd left a voicemail message for the twins on the phone in one of their barns, but she had no way of knowing if they had checked for messages.

Mr. Peterson frowned. "I'm sorry. Apparently I've asked you something that isn't appropriate."

Hannah made a quick decision, stood, and heaved her bag onto her shoulder. "I'd appreciate a ride home."

"Hop in." Mr. Peterson leaned across to the passenger side and pushed the door open.

She climbed into the car and placed her bag on the floor before buckling the seat belt. "Thank you for stopping."

"You're welcome." He merged into traffic. "Today

isn't the best day to get caught in the rain." She shivered, and he nodded toward the door. "You can turn on the seat heater. It's that button by the window opener."

"Your car has a seat heater?" Hannah pushed the button. "How fancy." She glanced around the vehicle, noticing the sweet-smelling leather interior and a dashboard full of gauges. The inside of the car seemed much more expensive and complicated than Phyllis's plain van. She assumed Mr. Peterson must be well off financially if he owned such a luxurious vehicle. "This is a nice car."

"Thank you. It was Corrine's favorite. I couldn't bring myself to get rid of it." He smiled over at her. "Where are we headed?"

She told him her address and explained the easiest way to get there. The rhythmic whoosh of the windshield wipers filled the silence as Mr. Peterson steered through another intersection.

Hannah enjoyed the comforting heat radiating through the seat and tried to ignore the feeling of her soggy dress clinging to her legs. She settled into the seat and allowed her body to relax. "This is much better than waiting for the bus on that wooden bench."

"I was driving by and saw you sitting there in the cold rain and felt bad for you. No true gentleman would've left you there." He gave her a sideways glance. "Do you always take the bus?"

"No, I normally get a ride home, but I had to stay late because my coworker called in sick. I helped another coworker finish her work."

"Is your coworker okay?"

Hannah nodded. "*Ya*, she's fine. I think she has stomach flu."

"I'm sorry to hear that. Stomach flu isn't fun."

Hannah looked over at Mr. Peterson and marveled at his thoughtfulness.

"I haven't bumped into you since last week. It's a good thing I haven't lost my key again because I'd have to go to the front desk to get my room unlocked." Mr. Peterson smiled. "How have you been?"

"I've been fine. Just busy at work and at home. How about you?"

He shrugged. "I'm okay. I've been out looking around."

She wondered why he was visiting Lancaster County, but she knew it wasn't her business. He merged onto a side road and zoomed past farmland Hannah knew like the back of her hand. Without missing a beat, he turned onto another road heading toward her farm.

She pushed back the ribbons on her prayer covering. "You seem to know your way around."

"You could say that." Mr. Peterson kept his eyes on the road. "I've made many trips here over the years. This was Corrine's favorite vacation spot, and I have to admit it's one of mine too."

"Really?" Hannah angled her body toward him. "So, you're a seasoned tourist? Where are you from?"

"New Jersey. Corrine started coming here as a child and fell in love with the area and the Amish culture." He glanced at Hannah and then looked toward the road again. "It was our dream to move here and open a bed and breakfast. We'd talked about doing it for a long time. I was going to retire early so I could spend more time at home and less time working and traveling. She wanted to share her love of Lancaster with others. Unfortunately, things don't always work out as you plan, but I have to make that dream come true even though she's gone. It's the best way I can think of to keep her memory alive."

"That is wonderful." Hannah studied his profile. It was obvious he loved his wife deeply. "That's a beautiful way to remember your wife."

"Thanks. I spent all day searching for the perfect place. I found one I like last week. I just had a feeling about it when I saw it. My Realtor says I need to keep my options open and not jump on the first one, but I keep thinking that's the one." He told her where the property was located, and Hannah nodded.

"I know where that is. It's a little bit of a buggy ride from my farm, but it would be a quick trip in a car. I know the area. It's very nice."

"Do you think it would be a good location for a bed and breakfast?"

Hannah nodded. "*Ya.* I think it would work well."

"I just keep wondering if I'm making the right decision. I'm doing this in memory of Corrine and Samantha. I've done a lot of research but I still have a lot to learn about running a bed and breakfast. I can cook, but I'm no chef. I've worked in finance for years, but I've never run a business like this. I'll have to hire someone to help me. I know I can't do it all on my own." He shook his head. "My sister thinks I'm crazy, but it feels right in my heart."

"Have you prayed about it?"

"Oh, yes. Like I told you before, God is probably tired of hearing me mull things over and worry about all of this. But everything fell into place when I made the decision. My house sold quickly, and I was able to retire with full benefits since I'd started at the bank right out of college. It all just felt meant to be."

"It must be God's plan then." She pointed toward the next intersection. "Turn here." The rain dissipated to a light drizzle as the car bumped through a pothole.

"But what if I'm making a huge mistake? How can I be certain it's God's plan?"

Hannah studied him. His chocolate brown eyes were locked on the road ahead, but his lips formed a thin line, as if he were pondering her words. She wondered why he put so much stock in what she had to say. What did she know about God's plan? Her life was nothing like she'd expected when she'd vowed to cherish Gideon and stand at his side as his helpmate for the rest of her life. She'd never imagined she'd become a widow at the age of thirty-four. She'd survived, however, with the help of her community and her strong faith.

She found him looking at her and knew he expected an answer. "I think if you're praying and feeling peaceful about your choices after the prayer, then it's God's plan. Have you spoken to your minister about it?"

Mr. Peterson nodded. "He told me to pray and follow my heart."

"It sounds like your minister is very wise. You need to have faith in your choices." Hannah pointed. "Turn here. My farm is on the right."

Mr. Peterson steered the car down the road, and Hannah directed him into her long rock driveway. He parked near the first barn and then turned to her. "You must think I'm crazy for asking your thoughts on my choices. You don't even know me."

Hannah shook her head. "I don't think you're crazy. I've been there myself many times. Just taking the job at the hotel was a difficult decision. I know in my heart that Gideon wouldn't be happy if he knew I was working outside the home, but I had to learn to make choices I believed were right for my family because Gid was gone."

He nodded slowly. "I know what you mean. Losing your spouse forces you to make decisions you never thought you'd make, such as retiring at forty-five and moving to Amish country alone."

"*Ya*, that's true." Hannah lifted her bag. "Thank you again for the ride." She pushed the door open.

"*Mamm!*" Amanda trotted toward the car, the ribbons on her prayer covering bobbing off her shoulders. "You're home." She took Hannah's bag and smiled at Mr. Peterson. "Hi. I'm Amanda."

"It's nice to meet you." He smiled at her.

"Mr. Peterson is a guest at the hotel. He found me soaked at the bus stop and offered me a ride." Hannah climbed out of the car. "I'm thankful he came along when he did."

"*Ya*. It was a heavy shower, but passed quickly." Amanda pointed toward the house. "Why don't you stay for supper?"

"Oh, I don't want to impose." Mr. Peterson shrugged.

"I'm just happy I could help your mother out. She helped me out last week when I locked myself out of my room."

"You're not imposing, right, *Mamm*?" Amanda raised her eyebrows. "Lily and I made Dutch Country meat loaf. I got your message, and we planned everything so it would be ready for you."

"*Danki*." Hannah looked toward the barn and spotted Joshua's buggy. It wouldn't be proper for Mr. Peterson to stay if he was the only man, but having her brother-in-law there would make it appropriate. "*Ya*, that's a *gut* idea, Amanda." Hannah turned to Mr. Peterson. "Please stay and meet my family."

"What sane man would pass up Dutch Country meat loaf?" He climbed out of the car and rubbed his hands together. Mr. Peterson's smile was wide. "I'd love to stay and meet your family."

"*Wunderbaar*." Amanda hoisted Hannah's bag up on her shoulder and started toward the house. "I'll set another place at the table."

Mr. Peterson motioned toward Amanda. "She's lovely."

"Thank you." Hannah smiled. "I'm blessed. Amanda and Lillian have been my strength since I lost Gid. I couldn't manage it all without them."

"How old is she?"

"Sixteen." Hannah started up the porch steps and opened the door.

"How old is Lillian?"

"Sixteen." When Mr. Peterson raised his eyebrows in confusion, Hannah smiled. "Twins."

"Oh!" He laughed. "I see."

"Please come in." Hannah made a sweeping gesture as they stepped into the mudroom. She looked up at Mr. Peterson and realized this would be the first time she'd had an *Englisher* over for supper since Gideon passed away.

FIVE

Trey followed Hannah through the mudroom to a large kitchen. A long wooden table sat in the middle of the room and the warm scent of homemade bread filled his nostrils. *Corrine would've loved to have been in this Amish home with me!*

"I'm finally home." Hannah crossed the room to the table where a young boy with dark hair and blue eyes sat smiling up at her. She mussed his hair and then pointed toward where Trey stood in the doorway. "*Mei freind* Mr. Peterson gave me a ride when he found me at the bus stop."

A teenage girl with glasses and hair the same shade as Hannah's, as well as Hannah's big green eyes, brought a large pot to the table and then gasped. "*Mamm!* What happened to you? You're soaked."

Hannah ran her hands over her apron. "I was drenched when a car drove through a puddle at the bus stop."

"You should go change." The redhead gestured toward the doorway. "Go on. Amanda and I will finish setting up for supper."

Hannah turned to Trey and gave him a warm smile. "Please make yourself at home. I'll be right back."

Amanda straightened the utensils at the far end of the table. "Come in, Mr. Peterson, and have a seat." She gestured toward the people around the room. "This is my brother, Andrew, and my sister, Lillian. She's my twin, but I'm five minutes older."

Lillian rolled her eyes. "She likes to remind me of that every chance she gets." Her lips formed a tentative smile. "Welcome to our home."

Although the teenagers were twins, they looked nothing alike. Besides the difference in their coloring, Amanda was taller. Her arms were rail thin, and her face was also slim. Lillian, on the other hand, seemed to take after her mother. Her face was rounder and her arms weren't as thin. But Lillian wasn't overweight; she was more "normal" looking, as Corrine used to say.

Amanda brought over a pitcher of water and gestured toward a man sitting at the head of the table. "This is my uncle Joshua."

"Nice to meet you." Trey shook the man's hand.

"*Ya*." Joshua nodded, but his smile didn't reach his eyes. He had the same dark hair and blue eyes as Andrew.

Andrew patted the seat next to him. "You can sit by me."

"Thanks." Trey sank into the chair next to the boy. "What grade are you in?"

"Fifth." Andrew nodded toward Lillian. "Lillian teaches in my school."

"Really?" Trey looked over at Lillian. "You're a teacher?"

"Not full-time." Lillian brought drinking glasses to

the table. "I'm hoping to become a full-time teacher. I'm an assistant, so I work two days a week."

Hannah entered the kitchen clad in a blue dress. "I feel so much better. That rain was terrible." She looked at Lillian. "Everything smells *appeditlich*. What can I bring to the table?"

Trey leaned over to Andrew. "What did your mom say about how everything smells?"

Andrew lowered his voice as if telling a juicy secret. "She said it's delicious."

"Thanks. I may need your help if she uses Amish words during supper."

Andrew winked. "Don't worry. I'll help you."

Trey chuckled to himself.

Amanda sank into a chair beside Trey and her sister sat across from her.

Hannah sat across the table from Trey. "Let's give thanks."

The family bowed their heads, and Trey followed suit. He waited for someone to say a prayer. When the room remained silent, he looked up and found everyone sitting with their eyes closed. Trey closed his eyes and silently thanked God for the opportunity to eat supper with Hannah and her family. Soon a chair squeaked and utensils scraped plates. Everyone seemed to talk at once. Andrew discussed school with Amanda while Lillian asked Hannah about her day.

Trey smiled and filled his plate while listening to the conversations swirling around him. It felt so good to be surrounded by a family again. He'd missed the conversations, the confusion, and the happiness for so long.

He added applesauce to his plate and then looked over at Joshua and nodded a greeting.

Joshua returned the nod while chewing. "What do you do for a living?"

"I'm recently retired. I've worked in corporate finance at a bank for many years." Trey cut up his meat loaf while he spoke. "I'm relocating and want to open a bed and breakfast."

"Oh." Joshua's dark eyebrows knitted together as he frowned.

Trey shifted in his chair and wondered if Joshua thought he had overstepped his bounds by staying to supper. Were Hannah and Joshua a couple? Had Trey given the wrong impression by giving her a ride home?

"You're opening a bed and breakfast?" Amanda's eyes were wide with interest. "I talked to a woman in the store yesterday who owns a bed and breakfast. She was telling me that she has visitors come from as far away as California. Can you imagine traveling from Pennsylvania to California? I've always wanted to go to California. I've heard it never rains there."

Lillian grimaced. "I think you're talking about Southern California where it's dry. But it has to rain sometime or nothing would ever grow."

"That's true." Amanda tapped her chin. "Anyway, I think it would be fun to own a bed and breakfast and meet people from all over the country and maybe even the world. This woman was telling me she even had a couple come visit from Canada. Wouldn't it be fun to talk to someone from Canada? I'd love to go there too."

Lillian shrugged. "I guess so."

Trey couldn't stop his smile. The girls were as different as night and day.

"Where are you going to open your bed and breakfast?" Amanda buttered a piece of bread and popped it in her mouth. "I imagine there are plenty of pretty houses around here to consider, *ya*?"

"There are." Trey described the three houses he'd visited and liked while Amanda listened with her eyes still wide.

Hannah and her daughters discussed the pros and cons of the locations of each of the homes with Trey while Joshua began a conversation about horses with Andrew.

When the women switched the topic to friends and relatives who lived near the homes Trey had perused, Trey looked at Joshua. "You have horses?"

"*Ya*." Joshua nodded while cutting up another piece of meat loaf.

"This is a horse farm." Andrew took some bread from the basket in the center of the table. "My *dat* and *onkel* Josh started it a long time ago."

"That's really interesting." Trey sipped his water. "What kind of horses do you have?"

Andrew squinted while thinking. "Belgians, standards, Dutch Harness, and Dutch crosses." He turned to his uncle. "*Ya?*"

Joshua nodded again without smiling. "*Ya*, that's right."

"Do you sell them to private owners?" Trey wondered if Joshua was always like this or if the unfriendliness was only directed at him.

"Mostly at auction, but a few to private owners." Joshua spoke between bites.

"I bet it's a lot of work." Trey noticed a look pass between Joshua and Hannah, and he wondered if he'd hit a nerve. "But I'm certain it's a labor of love, right?"

"*Ya*, it is." Joshua kept his eyes on his plate.

"My grandparents had horses. I used to love visiting them and helping my grandfather in the stable." Trey smiled at Hannah. "I'd love to see your horses sometime."

"*Ya*." Hannah looked at Andrew. "Maybe you can give Mr. Peterson a tour sometime."

"I'd like that." Andrew beamed.

Trey turned toward Joshua and found his frown deepening. *What's with this guy?*

Amanda reached for the bowl of applesauce. "What kind of horses did your grandparents have?"

Trey told them about memories of his grandparents' farm during the rest of the meal.

After dessert, Trey walked with Hannah to the porch. "That meal was delicious. Wait. How do you say it in your language?"

She held a lantern. "*Appeditlich*. I'm glad you enjoyed it."

"Your daughters are wonderful cooks. That chocolate cake was delicious too." He leaned on the porch railing. "I really had a nice time. Thank you for inviting me. It's been a long time since I've had a good home-cooked meal."

"It's the least I could do after you rescued me from the wet bus stop." Hannah gestured toward the barns

behind the house. "You'll have to come back for a tour
sometime when it's light out and not raining."

Trey pulled his keys from his pocket and they jingled
in response. "I'd like that. You have a lovely family." He
wanted to ask her about Joshua's unfriendliness, but he
knew he shouldn't. He wondered if all Amish men were
reserved. Perhaps it was part of their culture.

"Thank you." Hannah set down the lantern and then
leaned against the railing. "Gideon and I were blessed
with wonderful children." She looked out toward his
car. "I guess I'll see you in the hallway when you lose
your key."

He chuckled. "I have a feeling that will happen
again." He held out his hand and she shook it. "Thank
you again. Have a good evening."

"Good night."

Trey jogged to his car and climbed in. He spent the
ride back to the hotel thinking about Hannah and her
family and wondering if he'd ever be able to be a part
of a family like that again.

. . .

Josh stood inside, a little way from the open back door,
and watched while Trey Peterson and Hannah said
good night. He gritted his teeth as Hannah smiled
and laughed with the man. If only Gideon could see
her now. He would never approve of such behavior. To
make matters worse, Peterson studied Hannah with an
intensity that had caused Josh's stomach to roil during supper. The *Englisher* hung on every word Hannah

spoke. The whole situation was completely inappropriate and made Josh very uncomfortable.

"*Onkel* Josh?" Andrew sidled up to him. "Do you want to go check on the animals with me before you leave?"

"*Ya*." Joshua tousled Andrew's hair. "That's a *gut* idea." How he loved that boy. He loved all of Gideon's precious children. "Let's head outside now before it gets any darker." He turned to the girls, who were washing dishes. "I'll see you tomorrow."

"*Gut nacht*," they called in unison.

Joshua grabbed a flashlight and followed Andrew out to the porch, where Hannah was waving at Trey's fancy car as it sped away down the driveway.

"Your *freind* was nice, *Mamm*." Andrew walked over to his mom.

"*Ya*, he is nice." Hannah smiled down at him. "I think he liked supper." She turned to Josh. "Are you two heading out to check on the animals?"

"*Ya*." Josh motioned toward the porch steps. "Want to walk with us?"

"That sounds nice." She picked up the lantern from the porch railing and followed Andrew down the steps.

Armed with a smaller flashlight, Andrew ran ahead of them toward the row of barns. Josh looked up and silently marveled at the clear sky and bright stars.

"It's a *schee* night," he said. "There's no sign of the rain from earlier. Spring is upon us."

"It's warming up nicely during most afternoons, but it's still cold at night." Hannah shivered and rubbed her hands over her arms. "I should've grabbed my sweater."

Josh pointed back toward the house. "Would you like me to run in and get it?"

"Don't be *gegisch*." She rubbed her arms. "I'll be okay."

"I don't mind at all."

"*Danki*, but I'll be fine."

"I'll go check the horses!" Andrew ran into the barn.

Josh started after his nephew and then stopped. He wanted to talk to Hannah about Trey Peterson. He couldn't stop wondering why she'd opened her home to a stranger. He had to say something before his frustration devoured him.

He faced Hannah and found her eyebrows knitted together while she studied him. She looked adorable with her ivory skin and green eyes shining in the light spilling out from the lantern.

"Joshua?" She took a step toward him. "*Was iss letz?*"

He paused while choosing his words carefully. Although seeing her talk and laugh with the stranger upset him, he didn't want to come at her with accusations and cause her to be upset with him. He longed to draw her to him, not push her away. "I was surprised that you brought home an *Englisher* for supper tonight."

"I explained why he came home with me. I was soaking wet at a bus stop, and he stopped out of pity. He gave me a ride home."

"But why would you let a man you don't even know give you a ride home? You could've been hurt."

"I could've been hurt?" Hannah tilted her head. "What do you mean?"

"You don't know him." He enunciated the words as frustration boiled within him. "He's a hotel patron, *ya*?"

Hannah nodded.

"Therefore, you don't really know him. He's not even Amish, Hannah." Josh shook his head and wondered how he could get through to her. Was she blind? Didn't she see Josh cared about her? "I don't understand why you would get in the car with Mr. Peterson and invite him into your home to meet your family if you don't really know him."

Hannah frowned. "Amanda invited him to stay for supper. I thought it would be okay since you were here."

Josh studied her and contemplated how she felt about him. He thought it was obvious he was worried about her and wanted to take care of her and the children. Would she ever see what was right before her face?

"*Onkel* Josh!" Andrew jogged up beside him. "All of the horses are *gut*. I checked all of the barns."

"*Wunderbaar*." Josh placed his hand on Andrew's shoulder. "You're a *gut* helper."

"I can't wait until I'm done with school and can help you run the farm. We'll be *gut* partners, right?"

"*Ya*, we will be, Andrew." Josh glanced at Hannah and found her gazing down at her son with a smile. He could always spot the love in her eyes when she looked at her children. He'd noted a similar intensity when she looked at his brother, and he'd give anything for her to look at him the same way.

They walked back to the porch, and Hannah touched Andrew's back. "Run along and get ready for devotions. I'll be in shortly."

"Okay." Andrew looked up at Josh. "*Gut nacht, Onkel*."

"I'll see you tomorrow, Andrew." Josh watched his nephew hurry into the house. "He's a *gut bu*."

"*Ya.*" Hannah folded her arms over her apron. "Sometimes I look at him, and I see Gideon."

"I do too." Josh gestured toward the buggy. "I better head out. *Danki* for supper." He started toward his buggy.

"Joshua! Wait."

He turned back toward her.

"I can tell you're upset." She fiddled with her apron. "But Mr. Peterson is a nice person. He locked himself out of his room last week, and I unlocked the door for him. We struck up a conversation, and I found out that he lost his family. His *fraa* and his *dochder* died in their sleep from carbon monoxide poisoning last year. He was out of town when it happened."

"That's *bedauerlich*." Guilt caused his shoulders to hunch. How could he think such terrible things about a man who'd lost so much?

"Mr. Peterson and I have a lot in common since he lost his family like I lost Gideon."

Josh's stomach tightened. "I've experienced loss too, Hannah. I lost my *bruder*. He was my best *freind*."

"*Ya.*" She took a step toward him. "I know you have, Joshua."

"Mr. Peterson is *English*, Hannah. He's not like us."

She shook her head. "You don't understand."

"*Ya*, I do understand." He paused to choose the right words for fear of causing her to be on the defensive and ignore him. "I'm concerned about you. You've been through a lot, and you're vulnerable."

She stood up straighter and glowered. "No, I'm not vulnerable. I'm in complete control of my feelings. Mr. Peterson is just a nice person. That's it, Joshua. There's nothing else going on here."

Josh lifted his hat and raked his hands through his hair while he groped mentally for something to say to warn Hannah. "Just promise me you'll be careful." He wanted to tell her that he was certain the *Englisher* had feelings for her and that it made his blood boil to see that man look at her with longing in his eyes. But he couldn't form the words.

An awkward silence hung between them for a moment like a thick, dense fog.

Hannah blinked and then shrugged. "I will."

"*Gut nacht.*" He mumbled the words, which she repeated.

Josh started toward his buggy. His footsteps were heavy with regret twisting around his heart. Why couldn't he tell Hannah how he felt about her? He'd held his feelings at bay for more than twenty years— ever since he'd laid eyes on her at a singing. Never once had he expressed his disappointment when Hannah noticed Gideon instead of him. He'd quelled his envy, but he never found another woman to take Hannah's place in his heart. Josh watched from afar as Hannah and his brother fell in love and then married. He rejoiced with them when their children were born.

Josh climbed into the buggy and waved to Hannah as he guided the horse down the rock driveway toward the main road. He reflected on Gideon as he made his way toward his home located on his parents' farm a couple miles up the road. When his brother died unexpectedly, Josh vowed to take care of Gideon's family. Being a father figure to the children seemed an easy task, but he struggled with how to handle his relationship with Hannah. He wished he had his brother's confidence. If he were like Gideon, he would've already told Hannah he loved her and asked her to be his wife. Instead, he stared at her like a coward, praying that the Lord would make the words burst forth from his lips.

His thoughts turned to Trey Peterson and his stomach soured. Watching Hannah interact with the *Englisher* had filled him with dread and foreboding. Josh needed to find a way to win Hannah's hand. He needed to show her that he loved her. He had to learn how to be confident and tell Hannah how he felt before it was too late.

SIX

Friday morning, Hannah pushed her cart toward the supply room and hummed to herself. When she opened the door, she heard the sound of someone sobbing amid the shelves of towels and toiletries.

"Hello?" Hannah called as she stepped into the large walk-in closet. "Is someone in here?"

"Oh." Ruth stepped forward and wiped her red, puffy eyes with a crumpled tissue. "I'm sorry. I thought I was alone."

"Oh, Ruth." Hannah touched Ruth's arm. "*Was iss letz?*"

"I was just thinking of my son." Ruth leaned on a stack of towels.

"What happened to your son? Is Solomon hurt?"

"No. My son Aaron. He left fifteen years ago." Ruth shook her head. "I miss him so much. Sometimes I get emotional. I came in here to pull myself together."

"You have a son who left the community?" Hannah tilted her head in question. "I didn't know that."

"*Ya*, he did. He left before we joined your church district. I'm sorry I never told you about him before, but it was too painful to talk about. I can't believe it's been that long. He went to an ex-Amish community in Missouri, and I haven't heard from him since. I still worry about him every day, and some days are more difficult than others."

"I'm so sorry, Ruth." Hannah touched Ruth's arm again. "I honestly had no idea."

"*Ya*." Ruth sighed. "Aaron was only fifteen when he went off on his own. He said the Amish life was too restrictive." A tear trickled down her cheek. "I miss him so much. Our family isn't complete without him."

Hannah frowned. "I'm certain you miss him terribly."

"I just wish I could hear from him. I want to know that he's okay. I don't even know if he's still alive."

"Have faith that he's alive and well." Hannah hugged her. "I hope you hear from him soon. I will keep Aaron in my prayers."

"*Danki*." Ruth held Hannah tight for a moment. "I'm so thankful for your friendship."

Hannah nodded. "I'm thankful for yours too. May I get you something to drink?"

"No, *danki*." Ruth shook her head. "I'm going to just stay here for a moment and get myself together."

"Okay. I'm going to stow my cart here and go get something to drink. I'll be back to check on you." Hannah stepped out into the hallway and started toward the kitchen.

"Hannah!" a voice called as she made her way through the lobby.

She turned and found Mr. Peterson walking toward her from the elevators. "Hi, Mr. Peterson. How are you?"

"I'm well, thank you." He nodded toward the tables and chairs located across the lobby from the desk. "Would you have a cup of coffee with me?"

Hannah paused. She considered what impression her having a cup of coffee with a guest would make, but she decided a quick break wouldn't be a problem. Her boss encouraged the staff to be both friendly and professional when they interacted with guests. Having coffee was certainly being friendly while still being professional. "That sounds nice. I was just about to take my break."

"Wonderful." He poured two cups of coffee from the dispensers near the front desk and Hannah followed him over to a table at the far end of the sitting area. "How's your day going?"

"It's going fine." Hannah sat across from him and added cream and sweetener to her coffee. She thought of Ruth and hoped she was feeling better. She really must go check on her after her break. "How's your day?"

"I was just heading out to run a few errands." He sipped his coffee. "I enjoyed supper last night. Thank you again for inviting me to meet your family."

"You're welcome. I had a nice time too." Hannah yearned to hear about Mr. Peterson's move to Lancaster County. "Tell me more about your plans for the bed and breakfast."

He rubbed his hand over his goatee and paused. "Well, I was thinking I would possibly offer Amish country tours if the guests are interested, or I would at least give them a map of the area with recommendations for the most authentic places to visit."

"What about meals?" Hannah gripped her coffee cup while she imagined herself creating a menu for a bed and breakfast. "I think guests would love to have at least one Amish meal." She sipped her coffee and found it warm and sweet, just the way she liked it.

"Oh." Mr. Peterson raised his eyebrows. "That's a great idea."

"I think it would work well. Tourists love to have authentic Amish food. They want to have the whole experience when they come to visit."

"What would you suggest serving the guests?"

Hannah began counting off the options on her fingers. "When I used to host meals I normally made homemade chicken pot pie, corn or peas, potatoes, pie and cake, and a fruit salad. I sometimes would make beef with carrots or ham instead of the chicken pot pie. Oh, and homemade bread." She found him studying her with an intense expression that caused her stomach to quiver. "You don't like my idea?"

"Actually, I love it." A wide smile spread across his face. "It sounds like you've given this some thought."

Hannah shrugged. "I guess I've always thought about doing something like opening a bed and breakfast."

"You have?"

"When I was a child, my mother hosted dinners almost every week, except for during the dead of winter. Tourists would pay a fee to eat a meal in our home, and we always made a traditional Amish meal. I loved meeting the tourists and telling them about my faith and my life in Lancaster." She glanced around the lobby. "I enjoy working here, but I had more interactions with visitors when they came to my childhood farm. I like meeting and talking to people. Working in a bed and breakfast would give me the chance to do that again. It's sort of my dream to work in a place like that."

"That's really great. I bet you met some interesting people from all over the country when you hosted dinners." Mr. Peterson sipped more coffee. "What else would you recommend?"

"Have you thought about how you'll decorate the bed and breakfast?"

"No, not really." He glanced around the room. "What do you think of this hotel's décor?"

Hannah frowned. "It's very fancy. I like a plainer look, but that's probably because of my upbringing."

"So how would you decorate the bed and breakfast?" His expression was eager.

"Well." Hannah looked toward the main lobby entrance. "I like the grandfather clock here. It has a beautiful elegance, but it's not too fancy. I think the chandelier is obviously too much for a country bed and breakfast." She pointed toward candles at the far end of the lobby. "I like simple candles. They are always lovely to have."

Mr. Peterson nodded slowly as if taking in all of her suggestions. "What about the paintings?"

Hannah considered the impressionistic paintings hanging near the elevators. "I prefer simple nature scenes. They remind me of God's glorious creation." She contemplated the guest rooms. "I would also use Amish-built furniture. I prefer the traditional look rather than the modern furniture in the hotel rooms here."

Mr. Peterson grinned and then reached over and took her hands in his. His hands were warm and comforting. She didn't feel uncomfortable; in fact, she felt at home. It was as if his touch was natural and familiar. Her pulse raced.

"Hannah, I love your ideas." He leaned forward and gazed into her eyes. "I can see the bed and breakfast coming to life while you talk."

She nodded, her senses spinning with the enjoyment of his touch.

"I'm really surprised to hear that you've dreamt of owning a bed and breakfast." He released her hands and sipped his coffee. "I thought you loved the horse farm."

Hannah blew out a sigh. "I do love the farm, but it was never my dream. It was always Gideon's dream, and I wanted him to be happy. He was the head of the household, and he had good business sense. He made a decent living running the farm, and I never considered doing anything else. But that all changed when he died. I realized that I had dreams too." She rested her chin on her hand. "But it's not a reality. I can't open a bed and breakfast."

"I'm going to need your suggestions when I'm ready to start decorating the bed and breakfast."

"I'd love to help."

"I still want to come by your farm in the daylight so I can get a tour."

"You'll need to do that soon." She glanced at the clock and gasped. "Oh, dear. I need to get back to work. It was nice seeing you."

"I enjoyed our coffee break." He winked at her. "Have a great day, Hannah."

"You too." Hannah started toward the supply closet and felt as if she were walking on clouds. She could feel a strong friendship and also an attraction developing between her and this man. The feelings both excited and scared her. How could she develop feelings for an *Englisher*? She pushed the thought aside and went to check on Ruth and retrieve her supply cart.

· · ·

Hannah stepped out onto the porch the following morning and waved when she spotted Trey's shiny car bouncing up the rock driveway. She wiped her hands on her apron and walked quickly down the stairs to where his car came to a stop.

"Mr. Peterson!" She stood by the car as he pushed open the door. "What a surprise."

He climbed from the car while holding up a white box. "Good morning! I brought donuts."

Hannah took the box from him. "Thank you."

"You'd mentioned yesterday that I should come by for a tour of the farm, and I figured there's no time like the present." His smiled faded and he clasped his hands together. "I hope this is a good time. I wanted to call first, but I realized I didn't have your number. If it would be better for me to come back later, I can."

"No, no." Hannah waved off the comment. "Now is just fine."

"Hi, Mr. Peterson!" Andrew rushed over from the first barn. "You came back to see the horses."

"Hi, Andrew." Mr. Peterson pointed toward the box. "I brought donuts for everyone."

"Donuts!" Andrew looked back toward the barns. "Let me go get Amanda and Lily. They were feeding the chickens." He ran back toward the barns yelling, "Amanda! Lily! Come and get some donuts!"

Mr. Peterson grinned and shook his head. "He's a very enthusiastic boy."

"*Ya*, he is." Hannah motioned toward the house. "Would you like to come in and sit down? I can make some coffee to go with the donuts."

"Oh, no thank you." Mr. Peterson touched his belt. "I ate too much at the breakfast buffet this morning. I brought the donuts for the kids, really." He grimaced. "But you're welcome to one. I didn't mean to imply that you weren't welcome to enjoy a warm, fresh donut."

Hannah shook her head. "I appreciate the offer, but I think I'll save mine for a treat later in the day."

Andrew hurried back from the barn with his sisters in tow.

Amanda smiled. "Good morning, Mr. Peterson. Thank you for bringing us donuts."

"You're welcome." Mr. Peterson gestured toward the box. "I thought everyone could use a donut on a Saturday morning."

Lillian nodded at him. "Thank you." She mumbled her response, and Hannah wondered why her daughter was being so cold and unfriendly to their guest. She made a mental note to discuss it with her later.

Andrew rubbed his hands together. "Can we take a break and have a donut?"

"Of course, but you need to wash up first." Hannah handed the box to Amanda. "Be sure he washes up."

"I will." Amanda led her siblings up the steps toward the kitchen.

Hannah made a sweeping gesture toward the row of barns and stables and the lush pasture. "Would you like that tour?"

"I'd love it." Mr. Peterson scanned the area. "This is a beautiful farm. How long has this farm been in your family?"

"Gideon's parents have owned it for a long time. They inherited it when my mother-in-law's parents passed away. They had tenants on this land until Gideon and I were married. We moved in, and his parents helped him and Joshua start the horse farm." She motioned toward the stables. "We have twenty-nine box stalls. We normally have anywhere from forty to fifty horses here at one time."

"Wow." Mr. Peterson glanced into the stable at the horses lined up in the stalls. "Aren't they gorgeous?"

Hannah nodded. "They are. Gideon loved his horses. He once told me he loved me almost as much as he loved those animals." Mr. Peterson raised his eyebrows, and she laughed. "He was joking with me."

"Oh, I was hoping it was a joke. It sounds like Gideon had a good sense of humor."

"Oh *ya*. It was the best. He loved to laugh almost as much as he loved being with his horses." Hannah started toward the pasture. "There they are. That's Gideon's dream alive and well."

They walked together toward the pasture, and Mr. Peterson smiled. "Those are certainly Dutch Harnesses."

Hannah motioned toward the pasture. "You're familiar with the breed?"

"Oh, yes. My grandparents had Dutch Harnesses. My grandpa said he felt a connection to his family back in Holland by keeping the breed alive." He leaned on the split-rail fence facing the horses inside the enclosure. His eyes suddenly rounded, and he gasped again. "Oh, wow. That horse right there." He pointed toward a chestnut gelding near the front of the herd. "That one there. He looks just like Snickers. I can't believe it. What are the chances that I'd see another Snickers?"

Hannah raised her eyebrows. "Was Snickers a horse you once knew?"

"He was my favorite horse at my grandparents' farm. He and I seemed to really relate to each other, as crazy as that sounds."

"It's not crazy. I understand what you mean. That's actually Andrew's favorite horse, Huckleberry."

"Huckleberry?" Trey grinned. "That's a great name. I adored Snickers. He was my buddy, especially one summer I spent at my grandparents' farm. My father was in the navy, and my parents were in the process of moving across country. They sent my sister and me to stay with my grandparents so they could get settled before they brought us to our new home. It was one of the best summers of my childhood."

"Really?" Hannah studied Mr. Peterson's broad smile. He seemed caught up in the moment and the happy memories.

"My sister, Christy, and I did chores on the farm,

and we loved it. We were exhausted and tan by the end of August, but we really bonded with our grandparents and the animals. I wished I could bring Snickers home with me, but we couldn't exactly keep him in the backyard in a subdivision."

Hannah shook her head. "No, that wouldn't work too well."

Trey studied the horses. "Aren't they the most beautiful animals you've ever seen? They're huge, massive animals, but yet they're so graceful." He rested his chin on his fist while leaning on the fence. "Brings back wonderful memories of the time I spent at my grandparents' farm."

"*Ya.*" Hannah smiled. "They are a great paradox. How can something so big and powerful be so graceful? It's the Lord's work. Only God can create something so beautiful."

"That's true." Mr. Peterson was silent while he continued to stare at the horses.

Hannah turned back toward the house and spotted her children heading back to the barn. "I guess they finished their donuts."

"Are they working in the stables?"

"*Ya.* Andrew must be content to let me give you the tour." Hannah pushed the ribbons from her prayer covering back over her shoulders. "There's always work to be done. The horses get their hay and their oats in the morning and then their stalls need to be shoveled. We do that morning and night."

"I imagine that takes awhile with all of the horses you have here. My grandparents had about two dozen at one time, and it took a good part of the day to care for them."

"*Ya*, it is a lot of work. That's why we need to hire someone to help Joshua. The children help as much as they can, but Joshua really needs someone here all the time, even though he disagrees."

Mr. Peterson raised an eyebrow. "He doesn't think he needs help?"

"He doesn't like seeing me have to work so I can help pay the salary."

Mr. Peterson turned toward her. "What do you think?"

"I like working. I love being around the hotel guests and meeting new people, but Joshua thinks Gideon wouldn't like it." Hannah paused while she considered sharing her true feelings with him. It baffled her that the truth seemed to always spill out from her lips when he was around. "To be honest with you, I believe Joshua thinks Gideon would be disappointed in him somehow."

"Do you think he's right?"

"*Ya*," Hannah shook her head. "But I'm doing what I feel is best for our family, the family I was left alone to care for."

Mr. Peterson nodded slowly, as if taking it all in. "I think Joshua wants to help you raise that family."

Hannah tilted her head. "What do you mean?"

"I got the feeling he's a little possessive of you and your children." Mr. Peterson grimaced and raised his hands as if to apologize for his honesty. "I don't mean to overstep my bounds. It was just a feeling I got Wednesday night during supper, but I could be wrong."

Hannah pondered his words for a moment. The idea made sense when she thought about how strangely Joshua had acted Wednesday night. He said he was worried about Hannah and warned her to be careful with Mr. Peterson. "You could be right."

Mr. Peterson looked beyond the pasture. "Is that a pond?"

"*Ya*. We have our own pond."

"Can we walk down there?"

"Of course." Hannah fell into step with him as they walked the fence line toward the pasture. She looked up at the bright blue sky and fluffy white clouds. "It's a perfect day."

"Yes, it is." Mr. Peterson smiled down at her. "There's nothing like a farm. My grandfather made his money in real estate and retired young. His dream was to have his own farm and raise horses. Sometimes, when I visited there, I'd pretend I lived there and I'd tell my parents I didn't want to go home."

"I bet your parents didn't like hearing that."

"No, they didn't." He paused for a minute. "You know, I'd forgotten about that until just now. I think something about being here has really affected me. I feel a sense of peace I haven't felt in a long time. It's as if being here with your family and your horses has brought me some relief from my grief that I haven't been able to find anywhere else."

"I'm glad that visiting here has helped you. I know I had a difficult time finding things that would help me right after I lost Gideon. The best therapy I could find other than the Bible was sitting here." Hannah pointed toward a bench next to the pond. "Why don't we sit for a moment?"

"That sounds wonderful."

Hannah sank onto the wooden bench next to him and breathed in the warm spring air. She watched a mother duck and her fuzzy ducklings swim across the pond. Their little quacks made her smile. "This is my favorite time of year."

"It's mine also." Mr. Peterson nodded. "I think I could just stay here all day and nap in the warm sun."

Hannah contemplated his comments about Joshua. She wondered what Joshua had done to demonstrate his possessiveness. "I hope Joshua didn't make you feel uncomfortable Wednesday night."

Mr. Peterson shrugged. "I didn't really feel uncomfortable." He paused. "Okay, I did feel uncomfortable. It was as if I'd walked into another man's home uninvited."

"Really?" Hannah shook her head. "I'm sorry. I never wanted you to feel unwelcome."

"It's not your fault at all. And I was okay. I can handle a little hostility."

"Hostility?" Hannah gasped. "I had no idea he behaved that way. I noticed he was rather sullen, and it seemed as if something was bothering him during supper."

"Maybe I shouldn't come here again." He stood.

"No." Hannah touched his arm. "You can stop by anytime. It's my home, not his."

Mr. Peterson sank back down onto the bench. "This

is really a beautiful place. Paradise is the perfect name for this community. It's the perfect mix of nature and modern life. It's paradise."

Hannah nodded. "I can't imagine living anywhere else. What was the house you shared with your wife like?"

"Corrine and I had a nice house in the suburbs of northern New Jersey. The area had really good schools, which was a big draw. Actually, that's why we wanted to live there."

He picked up a stone from the ground and tossed it into the pond. A ripple moved rhythmically across the small body of water. "Sammi loved school. She played flute in the band and spent a lot of time with her friends. It was rare that I saw her without her cell phone stuck to her ear. Sometimes I'd get frustrated and even a bit envious of the attention she gave her friends, but I know that was normal teenage stuff." He stared over the pond. "It was a good life. It was a *really* good life."

Hannah nodded. "It sounds like you had a wonderful life."

"I did, but I did grow tired of my job over the years— the commute into the city, the phone ringing nonstop, the stress of running here and there. I had missed out on so much with my family because of my job. And Corrine begged me to quit and make our family the first priority. She told me I was a workaholic, and I know she was right. I had this misguided belief that it was my duty to make as much money as I could for us. I did make a nice salary, and I put a lot of money in the bank. But I did it to the detriment of my family. I forgot what was important, and that was family. It's nice to live a comfortable life, but it means nothing if you can't share it with your family."

Hannah could see the regret in his eyes, and she felt sorry for her friend.

"We were going to move to Lancaster so I could get away from that job and spend more time with Corrine and Sammi. I wanted to make up for the time I'd lost. My daughter was looking into colleges close by so we could see her often." He paused and shook his head. "But I made the decision to retire too late. I know I messed up. I should've quit the first time Corrine accused me of being a workaholic. I was too blind to see all of the mistakes I'd made. Now I'd give anything for five minutes with my family again. Just five more minutes to look into my wife's and my daughter's eyes and tell them how much I love them."

The words spoke directly to Hannah's heart. She too would give up nearly anything to look into Gideon's eyes again and tell him how much she loved him. She sniffed and wiped her eyes. "I understand."

Mr. Peterson smiled at her. "I didn't mean to make the mood gloomy." He stood. "Let's walk back and check on the children. Maybe I can help them with their chores."

Hannah looked at his expensive-looking trousers and collared shirt before shaking her head. "I don't think you're dressed to work in the stables."

He folded his arms over his chest. "So you don't think I can do manual labor?"

"I didn't say that. I just said you weren't dressed for it." She stood and they fell into step while walking back toward the stables.

He glanced down at his shirt. "Maybe I'll dress appropriately and help next time I come."

"I think the children would like that. They would appreciate the help."

"Does Joshua come to help on weekends?"

"*Ya.*" Hannah nodded. "He should be over soon. He had to help his parents with a few chores this morning. He has breakfast with his parents on Saturdays and then does a few things around the house for them before he comes here."

They talked about the weather and the beautiful horses as they approached the clearing near the stables. When Hannah spotted her mother-in-law standing with the twins on the house porch, she raised her eyebrows. It was rare that Barbie came to visit on a Saturday. She hoped nothing was wrong.

"What a surprise. My mother-in-law is visiting." Hannah picked up the pace as they moved toward the house. "You'll get to meet Barbie."

They approached the porch, and Barbie turned to the girls. "Why don't you both go inside and start getting ready for lunch?" The girls disappeared, and Barbie's expression transformed to a glower as she peered down at them.

Hannah forced a smile. "*Gude mariye*, Barbie. What a surprise to see you today."

Barbie lifted a chubby arm and motioned toward the stables. "I decided to ride over with Joshua. I thought

I should see what was going on over here." Her eyes moved to Mr. Peterson and then back to Hannah.

"Oh." Hannah cleared her throat. "Barbie, this is Mr. Peterson. He's from New Jersey and looking for a place to open a bed and breakfast."

Mr. Peterson climbed up a few steps and held out his hand to her. "It's nice to meet you, Mrs. Glick."

Barbie clicked her tongue and looked back at Hannah. "I think you should consider getting ready for lunch, *ya*? Or will you delay lunch since your children have gobbled up a box of donuts mid-morning? It seems that they may have ruined their appetites for a *gut* lunch."

Hannah clenched her jaw and took a deep breath. She'd gotten accustomed to her mother-in-law's sharp comments over the years. When Hannah married Gideon, Barbie seemed to enjoy sharing her opinions on how to run a household. After the twins were born, Barbie's opinions transformed into criticisms of how Hannah was raising her children. Hannah learned to simply ignore Barbie's words and go about her business instead of trying in vain to defend herself. Yet having to endure Barbie's condescending remarks in front of a guest was nearly more than Hannah could endure.

"Oh, look at the time." Mr. Peterson studied his wristwatch as if he'd just discovered it. "I better get going. I'm supposed to meet my realtor in thirty minutes. Thank you for showing me around the workings of an Amish farm." He smiled up at Barbie. "It was nice meeting you, Mrs. Glick."

Barbie's lips formed a thin line.

Hannah turned to Mr. Peterson. "I'll walk you to your car." They moved in silence to his waiting vehicle. "Thank you for coming to visit today."

"You're welcome." he opened the door. "I had a good time. Your farm is lovely."

"Thank you." Hannah glanced back at the porch where Barbie stood watching with her arms folded over her wide midsection. She then looked back at Mr. Peterson. "I'm sorry Barbie was rude to you." She nodded toward the house. "I better get inside."

"I'll see you Monday." He climbed into the car. "Have a good weekend."

"You too." Hannah waved as he drove off and then she headed back to where Barbie was waiting on the porch, her foot tapping disapprovingly against the railing. Hannah climbed the steps. "I have a feeling you want to talk to me."

Barbie glanced back toward the house and then stepped toward Hannah. "Why would you bring an *Englisher* to your home? What impression do you think this gives your *kinner*, especially your *dochdern*?"

Hannah frowned. "Did Joshua tell you that Mr. Peterson came for supper Wednesday night?"

"Of course he did. I wanted to talk to you about it, but then I found you walking alone with the man this morning. What are you thinking, Hannah? Your *dochdern* are at a very impressionable age. You should want them to grow up with the right morals. You may give them the wrong ideas about being alone with a *bu*."

"I'm not teaching them anything bad, *Mamm*. He gave me a ride home Wednesday after finding me soaking wet in the rain at a bus stop. Amanda invited him to stay for dinner, and I felt it was okay since Joshua was also here. Today he came to see the farm, and I gave him a tour of the property. It was all completely innocent."

Barbie shook her head. "I don't think you're being a *gut* example for your *kinner*, Hannah. You're telling them it's okay to become friendly with strangers and invite them into your home."

Hannah felt frustration boiling inside her, but she needed to keep calm. She'd realized early in her marriage that arguing with Barbie was useless. Besides, she needed to respect Barbie, who was the only mother she had since her own mother had died ten years ago. "We need to remember what Scripture says: 'Love your neighbor as yourself.' Mr. Peterson is a nice man who offered me a ride in the rain."

Barbie lifted her chin. "It's inappropriate, Hannah. You know I'm right. I'm going to make your *kinner* a proper lunch. I'm glad I stopped by so I could make sure they're eating right." Her mother-in-law marched off into the house, slamming the door behind her.

Hannah lowered herself into a rocking chair and blew out a cleansing breath. She knew it was best to stay out of Barbie's way when she took over the kitchen. Although she resented Barbie's criticism of how she was raising her children, she was thankful her children had a grandmother in their lives since her parents and husband were gone. Families were full of complicated, intertwined relationships that somehow translated into love and support.

She rocked back and forth while staring up at the glorious blue sky. A strange excitement skittered through her as she reflected on her short visit with Mr. Peterson. She was thankful for his friendship. Although they were from different worlds, they shared similar experiences. He understood her better than most of the people close to her. She looked forward to seeing him again and wondered if he had enjoyed their visit as much as she had.

SEVEN

Josh stood in the stable doorway and watched Trey Peterson drive off in his flashy car. He glowered as Hannah waved to the *Englisher* and then went back to the porch. Why would Hannah welcome this man into her home, a home Gideon had built? It didn't make any sense at all. He hoped she wasn't unhappy with her life. He groaned at the thought of watching Hannah, the woman he'd always loved, walk away from everything they believed in.

"*Onkel?*" Andrew held out a shovel. "Are you ready to clean the stalls?"

"*Ya.* I'm coming."

Josh turned back to the porch, where Hannah and his mother were speaking. He deduced from their frowns that his mother was speaking her mind. It was his fault she had insisted on coming by this morning to give Hannah a stern lecture. He'd stopped in to check on his parents last night after supper, and when his mother asked what was wrong, he spilled the news about the *Englisher* Hannah had brought home. His mother was appalled, and she insisted on coming with him this morning to tell Hannah what a poor example she was setting for her children.

"*Onkel?*" Andrew studied him from one of the stalls. "Did you come here to work or stare at the *haus*?"

Josh shook his head and grinned while crossing the stable. "You sound just like your *dat*."

"Oh *ya*?" Andrew flashed a toothy grin. "You didn't do your chores when you worked with *Dat* either?"

Josh laughed. "You're lucky I like you, or you'd be in trouble." He grabbed a shovel and gloves and then began working in the stall next to Andrew.

"You should've come earlier. Mr. Peterson brought us donuts."

Josh stopped shoveling and wiped his sweaty brow with his arm. "He brought donuts this morning?"

"*Ya!*" Andrew's voice radiated with excitement. "They were so *gut*. I should've saved one for you, but I couldn't help myself. I ate most of them. I love the ones filled with cream the best. Although, the chocolate covered ones are *appeditlich* too."

Josh's stomach churned as it had when he'd seen the *Englisher's* car in the driveway. Was the man using food to try to bribe the children into liking him? Jealousy stabbed him in the chest.

"Lillian said I shouldn't eat so many because I'd get a stomachache, and she was right." Andrew's words carried over the neighboring stall. "But I couldn't let them go to waste, you know? *Mamm* is always watching her weight, so I knew she wouldn't eat any. I was doing her a favor by finishing them. And a little stomachache was worth it. How often do we get fresh donuts for breakfast?"

Josh smiled despite his disgust with the *Englisher*. "You're a smart *bu*, Andrew."

"I'm just like you. *Mamm* says I look like *Dat*, but I think I look like you too. I bet some people think I'm your son, right?"

"Right." Josh began to shovel again while thinking about his nieces and nephew. He longed to fill in as their father, and even more, he wanted to be their stepfather. If only he could distract their mother from the *Englisher* who was trying to worm his way into her life.

. . .

Trey set his car keys and phone on the counter in the hotel room's kitchen area and dropped onto the leather sofa. He lifted the television remote and scanned the channels without giving much thought to the content. He settled on a police drama and stared at the screen while contemplating his day.

After the unwelcome encounter with Hannah's mother-in-law, he'd left the farm and met his realtor at another home. Although it was a beautiful house with six bedrooms and a vast amount of land and barns, he still liked the first house he'd found better than the rest of them. The other homes were nice, but they didn't have the charm or character of the first home he'd found.

The first home had appealed to him from the moment he'd laid his eyes on it. He was drawn to the sweeping porch that spanned the front of the house, the row of red barns behind it, the fenced-in pasture, and the little pond at the back of the property. Suddenly it hit him—the first house he'd looked at reminded him of Hannah's and his grandparents' farms. Perhaps he was searching for the warmth and comfort of his childhood, when everything was easy and he didn't have to worry about the future.

His iPhone began to ring. He pushed up from the sofa and grabbed it from the counter where he'd left it. "Hello?"

"Hey, little brother." Christy's voice sang through the speaker. "How are things in Amish country?"

"They're fine, thanks. How are you?" Trey fetched a can of Coke from the little refrigerator and popped it open before returning to the sofa.

"I'm fine. Brett's at a conference in Raleigh and the kids are asleep. It's nice and quiet here. I thought I'd give you a ring since we haven't talked in a couple of weeks. How's your search for the perfect bed and breakfast going?"

"It's going pretty well." Trey hit the mute button on the remote control, silencing the television. "I found a place I really like, but my Realtor is still dragging me all around the area to look at others so that I'm certain before I make an offer."

"Oh." Christy chuckled. "Trying to get a bigger commission I suppose, huh?"

"Maybe." He sipped his drink. "I visited an Amish farm today."

"Really? How did that happen?"

"I sort of became friends with an Amish woman."

"How did you befriend an Amish woman? Don't the Amish keep to themselves?"

"She works as a housekeeper at the hotel, and we keep running into each other." He shook his head while thinking of the first time he met Hannah. "A few of the times were a little embarrassing. I guess you could say it was sort of meant to be that we'd become friends."

"What do you mean by embarrassing?" She asked the question slowly, sounding intrigued.

Trey told her about each of their encounters, beginning with the day Hannah walked in on him when he was shirtless and ending with Hannah soaked at the bus stop. "She invited me to stay for supper Wednesday night, and I met her family. She has three kids, twin teenage girls and a little boy."

"What does her husband do?"

"He ran a horse farm with his brother. He died of a heart attack four years ago."

"Oh, no. So she's lost her spouse too. I can see why you became friends. You have a lot in common."

"Exactly. I went back to visit her today so I could see her horses. She raises Dutch Harnesses along with a couple of other breeds."

"She has Dutch Harnesses? That's incredible!"

"I know." Trey smiled. "Do you remember Snickers at Grandma and Grandpa's farm?"

"Of course I do. Snickers was your horse. He followed you around like a puppy."

"That's right. Hannah has this horse named Huckleberry. He's chestnut colored with the same four white feet and white blaze between his eyes. You wouldn't believe it, Christy. Going to Hannah's farm is like stepping back in time. While I was there, I felt more at peace than I have in a long time."

"That's really nice. I bet Corrine would've loved to have been there with you. I remember how much she loved the Amish. I'm glad you're finding some happiness there. I'm just surprised Hannah invited you to her home."

Trey thought of Barbie and frowned. "Not everyone was happy to see me."

"What do you mean?"

"Hannah's mother-in-law came by to visit this morning and gave me the cold shoulder."

"Did she really give you the cold shoulder or was she just quiet and reserved?"

"Christy, the woman had daggers in her eyes."

"Yikes. I guess I was right about the Amish keeping to themselves. I saw this special on the Amish a few months ago on PBS, and it talked about how tight-knit their community is."

"Yeah, but that's a broad generalization." Trey sipped more Coke and then placed the can on the end table beside him.

"The Amish community is a culture, and they live by certain rules. They stay together. They worship together and they support each other. She could've been violating rules by having you over as a guest alone. You're both single, and maybe it looked like a date or something."

Trey contemplated his sister's words. "A date? I just wanted to see her horses."

"I'm certain it was innocent, but the Amish are very

conservative in the way they act and dress. Having a single man at her farm may have sent the wrong message to her mother-in-law."

"It was broad daylight. We walked to the back of the pasture and back up to the house."

"Trey, you're not listening to me."

"I am listening. I'm just pretending to be ignorant." Trey raked his hand through his hair while staring at the television screen. He was kidding himself if he tried to protest his sister's words. "You're probably right. I hope I didn't cause her any trouble today. She's a really nice lady."

"Uh oh." Christy clicked her tongue. "Tell me you don't have feelings for her, Trey."

"No, no, it's not like that. I just feel like we were meant to be friends. She understands how I feel about losing everything that mattered to me. She can relate to my grief. It feels like God brought us together, like he engineered how we met. And when I was at her farm, I felt a sense of hope for the first time since I lost Corrine and Sammi. I've been going through the motions for months, just living day to day, hoping to feel something other than complete loss. Being with Hannah on her farm made me feel like I was living again—really living and not just breathing and putting one foot in front of the other."

"Wow. That's really deep." She paused and sniffed. "Everything you said makes sense, and it actually makes me want to cry. Just be careful. She's Amish, and you're not."

Trey sipped more Coke. "I know the limitations of

our friendship, but it's nice to have someone to talk to who understands how I feel."

"You know you can always talk to me. I can't relate on the same level as someone who's lost their family like you have, but you know I care."

"Of course I know, and I appreciate you for it. How are things in Charlotte? How are my favorite niece and nephew?"

They made small talk about Christy's family, the weather, and Christy's job until he heard a click on the other end of the line.

"Oh, I better go. Brett is on the other line. I need to find out what time he's heading home tomorrow after the conference ends."

"Tell him I said hello and give Sabrina and Cody a hug and kiss for me." Trey hoped his brother-in-law wasn't making the same mistakes he had, working and traveling too much.

"Yeah, I will. Call me soon, okay? I'd love to come see you when you pick a place for your bed and breakfast. Maybe I can help you set it up."

"That would be great, sis. Thanks. Good night."

"Talk to you soon."

The line went dead, and Trey placed his iPhone on the end table next to the sofa. He drank his Coke and turned up the volume on the television.

While he stared at the screen, he thought about what his sister said about the Amish. He hoped he hadn't created problems for Hannah by visiting her farm today. He also hoped that her mother-in-law wouldn't prevent Hannah from being his friend. He was thankful that he'd finally met someone who truly understood his grief. Hannah's friendship felt like a gift from God, and he didn't want to lose that precious gift.

. . .

Lillian walked beside her sister on their way back toward the house later that evening. They'd helped Andrew put the horses in the stables for the night since their uncle had left before supper. Andrew ran ahead toward the house and Lillian glanced at Amanda. She'd wanted to talk to her all day but hadn't had the opportunity to speak to her alone. "It was nice seeing *Mammi* today, *ya*?"

"*Ya*, it was. I'm surprised she came by to visit. We don't normally see her on a Saturday."

Lillian touched Amanda's arm, causing her to stop walking and face her. "She told me why she came by."

"Oh?" Amanda raised an eyebrow. "What did she say?"

"She was very upset when *Onkel* Josh told her that we'd had an *Englisher* for supper Wednesday night."

Amanda shook her head. "I don't understand. Mr. Peterson is a nice man. Why would she be upset that he came for supper?"

"I got the feeling that *Mammi* thinks it's inappropriate that *Mamm* is spending time with an *Englisher*. She implied that since *Mamm* is a widow the relationship is frowned upon."

"She implied it? What did she say?"

"*Mammi* said that her *mamm* once said widows

shouldn't spend time with men alone, especially with men who aren't Amish. She said she wasn't talking about our *mamm* specifically, but she wouldn't have said it if she wasn't thinking of our *mamm*."

Amanda grimaced. "I love *Mammi*, but I think she's overreacting a bit. It was just supper."

"But he came back today." Lillian gestured toward the house. "And he brought donuts. Don't you think he likes *Mamm*?"

"Of course he likes *Mamm*. They're *freinden*."

Lillian frowned at her twin sister. Why couldn't Amanda see things the way she did? "I don't know, Amanda. I have a bad feeling."

"You worry too much." Amanda smiled. "Have faith in *Mamm*. Maybe God introduced Mr. Peterson into her life so she'd have someone to talk to other than us."

Lillian studied her sister. Amanda always saw blue skies, even when storm clouds were peeking over the horizon. "I don't know if it's that simple. *Mammi* looked really concerned that Mr. Peterson was here."

"He said he came by to see the horses, and I believe him. He's from the city and he missed being on a farm like his grandparents'. *Englishers* love coming here and seeing how we live. I don't think anything inappropriate is going on between *Mamm* and Mr. Peterson."

"Amanda! Lillian!" Their mother's voice bellowed from the porch. "Come inside. It's time for devotions."

"Let's go." Amanda touched Lillian's hand. "Trust God, Lily. Everything will be fine."

They headed for the porch. Cool drops of rain kissed Lillian's cheeks and she glanced up at the dark clouds. A strange feeling of foreboding filled her, and she wished she could be as positive and certain about Mr. Peterson as her sister was.

She followed Amanda up the porch steps and through the back door to the kitchen where her mother and brother sat at the table. Lillian sat next to Amanda and folded her hands.

After a silent prayer, she looked up and found her mother smiling at her. "Lillian, why don't you read and start on 2nd Corinthians tonight?"

"*Ya*. I'll read." Lillian took the book and began to read. She stopped after reading the seventh verse. "'And our hope for you is firm, because we know that just as you share in our sufferings, so also you share in our comfort.'" She looked around the table at her family. "This verse feels very poignant to me. What do you think it means?"

"I think it's comforting," Amanda said with a smile. "No matter what, God is with us."

Andrew nodded. "*Ya*, even when things are hard without our *dat*. Right, *Mamm*?"

Mamm touched Andrew's hand. "That's what it means to me too." She looked over at Lillian. "Why don't you keep reading before it gets too late? We need to head to bed soon. Church comes early in the morning."

Lillian finished reading the chapter and then they closed with a silent prayer. Lillian lingered in the kitchen after her siblings left to get ready for bed. She chewed the side of her lip as her mother stood up from the table. She wanted to talk to her mother about what her grandmother had said, but she didn't want to be disrespectful. The worries and concerns about the *Englisher*, however, were haunting her every thought. She needed to know the truth about her mother and Mr. Peterson.

Mamm stood by the table and tilted her head. "What's on your mind, Lily?"

Lillian cleared her throat. "I want to ask you something, but I don't want to be disrespectful."

Her mother sat in the chair and folded her hands. "You're never disrespectful. What do you want to ask me?"

Lillian ran her fingers over the tabletop while she contemplated the right words. "Did *Mammi* talk to you today while she was here?"

"Not really. Why do you ask?"

"She told me why she came over today. I wanted to ask you if she was right."

"You want to know if she was right about what?" *Mamm*'s eyes narrowed.

Lillian could tell she'd struck a nerve, and she held her breath. Maybe she should've just gone to her room and not said anything at all.

"Lillian?" *Mamm* leaned forward. "What did *Mammi* say to you?"

"She said she was concerned after *Onkel* Josh told her about Mr. Peterson coming to supper Wednesday."

Mamm frowned. "She told me that. Is that all she said?"

Lillian shook her head. "She was very upset when she saw he was here again today. She's concerned you're not a *gut* role model for Amanda and me, and she's worried you're going to get a reputation in the community." Her mother's expression fell, and she was certain she spotted tears in her eyes. Lillian immediately regretted her words. "I'm sorry, *Mamm*. I shouldn't have told you she said that about you."

"It's okay." *Mamm* sniffed. "I'm *froh* you told me. Did *Mammi* say anything else?"

Lillian nodded. "She said she was concerned about your relationship with Mr. Peterson." She hesitated. "I got the impression she's worried that you want to be more than his *freind*."

"You look like you want to ask me something. What do you want to say?"

"Do you like him as more than a *freind*?"

"No, *mei liewe*." She took Lillian's hands in hers. "I like talking to Mr. Peterson. He lost his family tragically, just like we lost your *daed*. He came today only to see the horses and talk about the Lancaster area. That's it. He's *mei freind*, just like you're *freinden* with some of the *buwe* you grew up with."

Lillian nodded as guilt rained down on her. "I'm sorry for doubting you, *Mamm*."

"It's okay." *Mamm's* shoulders drooped. "Your *Mammi* has a way of convincing you to listen and believe whatever she has on her mind." She paused and tapped the table. "Did she also talk to your *schweschder* and *bruder*?"

Lillian shook her head. "She only talked to me when we were cleaning up from lunch. Amanda was outside with Andrew and *Onkel* Josh." She wanted to tell her mother that she'd spoken to Amanda about it earlier, but she felt guilty for talking about her mother behind her back. She couldn't bring herself to admit that she'd done it.

"*Danki* for telling me." *Mamm* stood. "Go get ready for bed. We need to leave early for church."

Lillian hugged her mother and then hurried toward the staircase. As she climbed the stairs, she asked God to forgive her for doubting her mother. The feeling of foreboding that gripped her when she talked to her sister outside, however, continued to haunt her.

EIGHT

During the Sunday service, Hannah sat with the other married women. It was the Ebersol family's turn to host the three-hour service, which was held in the home of one of the church district families every other Sunday.

Hannah thought about how, when she was a child, she was always amazed at how the movable living room and bedroom walls in each member's home could create such a spacious meeting area. Since she was a little girl, she'd become accustomed to sitting on the backless benches that were lined up for the district members and would later be converted to tables for lunch.

Hannah had once walked by an *English* church in town and noticed that the doors were open. She could see that the church's sanctuary décor was much different from the plain houses where the Amish church held its services. Unlike the *English* churches, Hannah's worship area didn't have an altar, a cross, flowers, or instruments.

Now, as the service began with a familiar German hymn from the *Ausbund*, Hannah redirected her thoughts to the present. Hannah joined in as the congregation sang the hymn slowly. The male song leader began the first syllable of each line, and then the rest of the congregation joined in to finish the line.

While the ministers met in another room for thirty minutes to choose who would preach that day, the congregation continued to sing. Hannah saw the ministers return during the last verse of the second hymn. They hung their hats on the pegs on the wall, indicating that the first sermon was about to begin.

The minister droned on like background noise to the thoughts echoing in Hannah's head. Although she tried to concentrate on the preacher's holy words, she couldn't stop looking toward the row in front of her where her mother-in-law was sitting. She'd been awake most of the night thinking about her conversation with Lillian. She'd felt a mixture of betrayal and anger toward Barbie for saying such hurtful things about her. Why would she tell Lillian that Hannah was a bad role model? She knew her mother-in-law was often critical of her, but to say horrible things to her daughter was going too far. Hannah wanted to confront her before the frustration consumed her. She believed in forgiveness, and she would forgive Barbie. She needed, however, to get her feelings off her chest first.

The first sermon ended, and Hannah knelt in silent prayer along with the rest of the congregation. After the prayers, the deacon read from the Scriptures, and then the hour-long main sermon began. Hannah stared at her lap and willed herself to concentrate on the sermon, which was spoken in German.

Her thoughts turned to Trey. She'd enjoyed her visit

with him yesterday, and she'd regretted that Barbie's interference had cut it short. Since Barbie was trying to alienate her children from her because of her friendship with Trey, Hannah knew she should sever the friendship now. She couldn't risk losing her children over a friendship with an *Englisher*, no matter how kind he was.

After the main sermon ended, relief flooded Hannah when the fifteen-minute kneeling prayer was over. The congregation then stood for the benediction and sung the closing hymn.

Hannah moved toward the kitchen with the rest of the women to help serve the noon meal. The men converted the benches into tables and then sat and talked while awaiting their food. She made small talk with them while filling their coffee cups. As she headed back to the kitchen, she smiled and greeted friends and relatives.

Once the men were finished eating, Hannah sat with a group of friends and relatives and filled her plate with food. The women talked about their children and the beautiful weather while they visited together. Hannah spotted her mother-in-law at the next table. When their eyes met, Barbie quickly broke the gaze. Hannah sucked in a deep breath and prayed for guidance. She needed to talk to her mother-in-law and do her best to prevent this chasm between them from widening.

Once lunch was over, Hannah helped clean up the kitchen and then made her way out to the porch. She found Barbie sitting on a rocking chair off in the corner, alone.

Hannah crossed the porch and sat on a bench beside her. "Hi, *Mamm*."

"Hello." Her mother-in-law stared over toward the grassy area where the youth were playing volleyball.

"I'd like to talk to you." Hannah gripped the handrail with one hand. "I spoke to Lillian last night before bed and she told me about the conversation you had with her yesterday."

Barbie turned to her and raised her eyebrows. "What do you mean?"

"She told me that you'd shared with her why you'd visited. You told her about your displeasure about my friendship with Mr. Peterson."

"She said she was surprised to see me on a Saturday, and I told her why I was visiting. I was only telling her the truth."

"You should've only shared your thoughts with me."

Barbie looked surprised. "I believe in being honest, and Lillian is old enough to hear the truth. I'm concerned your friendship with the *Englisher* may be frowned upon in the community. I'm worried about your reputation and our family's reputation as well. I'm only looking out for you."

Hannah shook her head. "Being a *freind* to someone who is new in town isn't wrong. As I told you yesterday, the Bible tells us—"

"You don't need to lecture me, Hannah. I know what the Bible says." She leaned closer to Hannah, causing the chair to creak. "You need to be careful. You're teaching your girls the wrong message about how to behave with men."

Hannah held her breath for a moment to stop angry words from bubbling forth. "Mr. Peterson is a nice person. He lost his *fraa* and *dochder*, just like I lost Gideon. We have a lot in common, and we can share our feelings about our grief."

"There are plenty of people in this community who have experienced loss. You don't need to search for comfort in the *English* world. Looking out there will only get you into trouble." Barbie glanced toward the other end of the porch where a group of women stood talking. "Having an intimate friendship with a man can lead to more than friendship. You may find yourself getting a visit from the deacon and a minister if you aren't careful with your heart."

Hannah shook her head. "*Mamm*, you're really overreacting. He only stayed for supper and then came to take a tour of the farm. We walked back to the pond and then up to the *haus* again. That's it."

"No, I'm not overreacting." She glowered, causing the wrinkles around her blue eyes to bunch up together. "You're disrespecting my son's memory."

Tears filled Hannah's eyes as anger welled up inside her. "I don't think I'm disrespecting his memory. I'm doing the best I can now that he's gone."

Hannah wanted to say more, but she'd been taught to respect her elders, even when she disagreed with them. She felt that no matter what she said or did, Barbie found a way to criticize her. Barbie acted as if she wished Gideon had married someone else.

"You need to calm down or you'll make a scene." Barbie raised her eyebrows and then looked past

Hannah toward another member of the community who walked over to them. "Oh, hello, Miriam. How are you doing? Is Abner feeling better?"

Hannah stood and walked past Miriam. "Excuse me." She made her way down the porch steps toward a group of women who were talking. She wanted to disappear into the group unnoticed despite the hurt and disappointment battling within her. She'd long suspected that Barbie had hoped Gideon would marry someone else. Hannah even asked Gideon about it once, and he laughed it off, telling her all that mattered was their love for each other, not their parents' opinion. But his avoidance of the question also seemed to be a veiled answer, an answer she didn't want to hear.

"Hannah?" Ruth Ebersol sidled up to her. "*Was iss letz?*"

"Hi, Ruth. How are you? It was a nice service, *ya*?" Hannah wiped her eyes. She wished her mother-in-law didn't have the power to upset her with the sting of her words.

Ruth raised her eyebrows. "*Ya*, it always is a nice service."

Hannah pointed toward the house. "Your flowers are so *schee*. You did a beautiful job in your garden this year."

"*Danki* for the compliments, but please stop making small talk about my garden and my flowers." Ruth placed her hand on Hannah's shoulder. "Let's go talk."

Hannah followed Ruth toward the pasture where they stood by the fence. Hannah looked over at the other young people talking and spotted Amanda sitting with her friend Nancy.

Ruth leaned in close. "What's bothering you?"

Hannah shared the stories of Trey's two visits, her conversation with Lillian, and her conversation with Barbie. Ruth listened, nodding occasionally. Her blank expression held no hint of judgment or disappointment, which was a relief to Hannah.

"I can see why you're upset, but I think maybe Barbie is just trying to protect you."

Hannah shook her head. "No, it's not that. She's always criticized me. No matter what I do, it's wrong, whether it's hanging out the laundry or making lunch for my *kinner*. But now she's trying to hurt me by telling *mei kinner* what I do wrong."

Ruth frowned. "I guess you're right. You've mentioned before that she was hard on you. Maybe she's worried about you and the *kinner* since Gideon is gone. She just doesn't know how to express how much she misses her son, so she takes it out on you."

"I don't know. I always thought she wished Gideon had married someone else. I know he dated another *maedel* for a short period of time before we met. Maybe she wanted him to marry her instead of me."

"That's a little odd. She should be *froh* that Gideon had a *wunderbaar* marriage, even for a short time."

Hannah nodded. "I know I can't change how she feels about me, but I wish I could at least smooth things over. We have to get along. We're family."

Ruth smiled. "Let me share one of my favorite Scripture verses with you. It's from Colossians: 'Make the most of every opportunity. Let your conversation be always full of grace, seasoned with salt, so that you may know how to answer everyone.'" She squeezed Hannah's hand. "I think that's *gut* advice, *ya*? Pray for the Lord to soften Barbie's heart and let your conversations always be full of grace. If you do that, you can't go wrong."

Hannah smiled. "You're right. *Danki*, Ruth."

Ruth's smile faded. "You don't have feelings for Mr. Peterson, do you?"

"I see now that being his *freind* may jeopardize my relationship with my *kinner* and possibly even my community." Hannah felt her lips turn down in a frown. "I need to tell him that we can't be *freinden* anymore."

Ruth studied Hannah for a moment and then tilted her head. "Just guard your heart well. I don't want to see you get hurt."

Hannah opened her mouth to insist her heart wasn't in jeopardy but was interrupted by Ruth's son, Solomon, along with his wife and Ruth's four grandchildren as they walked up and began talking. Hannah smiled, but her thoughts were still focused on Ruth's advice. Why was Ruth worried about Hannah's heart? After all, Trey was only her friend. How could anything possibly go wrong when she explained to him that their friendship could cause problems for her in her community? He'd understand, and they would go their separate ways.

She suddenly realized that she had begun to think of Mr. Peterson as "Trey." Although she called him by a formal name when they spoke, her thoughts of him

were less than formal. The realization caused her to
ponder what that meant. Was she developing deep feelings for him?

She turned toward the youth group and found Lillian
standing with Leroy King. She thought back to the time
when she and Gideon had fallen in love. Just like Lillian
and Leroy, they'd known each other for years, but didn't
truly notice each other until they were older.

Hannah looked back toward Ruth and her family
while she contemplated how God worked to provide
love for people. Just like God, love was mysterious and
often appeared when folks least expected it. She wondered if God would provide love for her again in her life
or if she'd already had her opportunity.

Although Hannah didn't know if she'd ever find
another man to love, she knew one thing for certain—
she loved her family and community and didn't want
to risk losing them.

. . .

Later, at the youth gathering, Amanda smoothed her
dress over her knees and then hugged her arms around
her legs while sitting on the grass next to her best friend,
Nancy. The warm afternoon sun kissed her cheeks and
she smiled. Spring was her favorite time of year.

"Do you want to play volleyball?" Nancy gestured
toward the group of teenagers choosing teams by the
net. "We can go join if you want."

"No, *danki*." Amanda tented her hand over her eyes.
"I'd rather sit here in the sun."

Nancy elbowed her in the arm. "There's sun over there too."

"I know." Amanda shrugged. "You can go if you want. I know you just want to get on Manny Kauffman's team."

"No, that's not true. I like playing volleyball. It's good exercise."

Amanda chuckled and rested her chin on her knee. "*Ya*. Exercise."

"Your *schweschder* is getting awfully cozy with Leroy King." Nancy nodded toward the group standing near the volleyball net.

"*Ya*, she is." Amanda watched her sister push her glasses farther up on her nose, the nervous habit she'd had since they were little. "I tease her, but I really think they'd make a cute couple."

"What about you?"

"What about me?"

Nancy angled her body toward Amanda. "You tease me about Manny and you tease Lily about Leroy, but you seem to be the only *maedel* I know who doesn't have a crush."

Amanda shrugged. "I don't know. I guess I haven't met the right *bu* yet." She pulled at a blade of grass and did her best to avoid her friend's probing stare.

"There has to be someone you like."

"No, not really." Amanda shook her head.

"Amanda?" Nancy leaned over. "Are you hiding something from me?"

"Don't be *gegisch*. I don't like anyone in our youth group." She shrugged.

"So you like someone from another youth group?" Nancy's smile was wide, revealing her pearly white, perfectly straight teeth.

"No, I really don't." Amanda rubbed her hands together, sending blades of grass flying through the air like green confetti. "I'm certain I'll find someone. There's no rush, right? We're only sixteen, and we're not even baptized." She hoped that explanation would satisfy her friend.

Nancy nodded, and Amanda felt her shoulders relax.

"Do you still want to play volleyball?" Amanda stood and swiped her hands across her apron. "Let's go."

Amanda followed Nancy over to the group standing by the net. When Lillian caught her eye, Amanda winked at her, and Lillian's eyes widened with embarrassment. Amanda wondered if she'd ever find a boy who made her blush the way Leroy made Lily blush. But the truth was, she wasn't worried about finding a boy to like; she was more interested in following her true dream—going to college and becoming a veterinarian. She just didn't want anyone, including Nancy, to know about that—at least, not yet.

. . .

Later that afternoon, Hannah sat up front in the buggy as Joshua guided the horse up the driveway toward her farm.

"It's a beautiful day." Josh glanced over at her.

"Ya, it is." Hannah looked back toward Andrew. "It

will be quiet in the *haus* since your sisters are gone to their youth gathering."

"*Ya*." Andrew grinned. "Are you going to stay and visit, *Onkel* Josh?"

Josh brought the horse to a stop in front of the barn and then turned to Hannah. "*Ya*, I think I might stay for a while."

"That will be nice." Hannah climbed out of the buggy.

"*Ya!*" Andrew jumped out of the buggy behind her. "I'll go change into my work clothes." He ran toward the house.

Hannah started toward the house. "I'll make us a snack."

"Wait." Josh cleared his throat. "I have something for you."

"Oh?" Hannah watched with curiosity as he retrieved something from the back of the buggy.

"I was going to save this for your birthday, but I couldn't wait to give it to you." He handed her a wooden stand with prongs. "It's for your spools. I heard Amanda tell you once that she had a difficult time finding the thread she needed because they weren't organized. I thought this might help you keep your spools together."

"Oh, Joshua." Hannah took the gift, and her heart warmed at the gesture. "This is wonderful. *Danki*. I can definitely use this. I constantly misplace my spools."

He smiled. "I'm *froh* you can use it."

Hannah ran her fingers over the smooth prongs and wondered how much time it took him to craft the spool holder. "You must have put a lot of effort into this."

Josh shrugged. "I like doing woodworking. I probably would've been a carpenter if Gideon hadn't convinced me to go into business with him."

"I'm so touched that you thought of me." She smiled at him. "You're very thoughtful."

His expression became intense. "I always think of you, Hannah. In fact, I think of you all the time."

Hannah's breath caught as she stared into his eager eyes. For a brief moment she wondered if she truly belonged with someone like Joshua instead of Trey. Joshua was a good, loyal, hardworking, and honest Amish man. Wasn't he the right choice for her? But then Hannah admitted to herself that she had been considering how Trey could give her something she'd always wanted—the ability to live her dream of owning a bed and breakfast. Just as quickly, Hannah thought about her children and the problems her relationship with Trey could cause for them, and she found herself confused again. Where did she belong?

"Hannah?" Joshua tilted his head in question as he studied her. "Are you okay?"

"*Ya*." She forced a smile and then gestured toward the house. "I'm going to put this in the sewing room and organize my spools. *Danki* again for the lovely gift. I will put it to good use." She started toward the house while wondering if she could ever sort through her confused feelings.

NINE

Monday morning, Hannah studied her clipboard and marked off the room she'd just cleaned. She cupped her hand to her mouth to stifle a yawn. She'd spent most of the night staring at the ceiling and contemplating her jumbled feelings for Trey and Joshua. She was surprised and overwhelmed by the thoughtful gift Joshua had given her. He'd spent the rest of the afternoon visiting with Hannah and Andrew, and she found herself marveling at the sight of Andrew and Joshua together. She wondered again if she belonged with Joshua, the man who'd stood by her through her husband's death. If she were with Joshua, she'd be able to stay in a life she knew and loved.

However, Trey's image crept into her thoughts throughout the night. She couldn't forget the intensity of his touch when he'd held her hands while they shared a coffee break on Friday. She also thought about their walk around her farm on Saturday. Her feelings for Trey were palpable and his plans for the bed and breakfast filled her with excitement and longing for a new life, even though they pointed to an uncharted road.

Yet she knew a relationship with Trey would be complicated and would cause many problems for her family. She needed to end the relationship now, even though the idea was breaking her heart.

She looked down the hallway toward Trey's room, and her stomach tightened. She'd considered asking to switch floors with Linda to avoid seeing him, but she knew that was the coward's way out. She had to face him and tell him they could no longer be friends, and one way to see him was to clean the third floor and hope they ran into each other. She'd spent most of the ride to the hotel this morning planning what she'd say to Trey when she saw him. She prayed she could remember everything she wanted to tell him.

Hannah approached another room, knocked, announced herself, and then unlocked it. After propping the door open, she moved into the bathroom and grabbed the used towels slung over the shower door and then headed toward the cart in the hallway to grab new ones. She stepped through the doorway and almost bumped into Trey.

"*Ach!*" She dropped the towels into the bin on the cart. "I'm so sorry. I didn't see you there."

"No, I'm the one who should be sorry." He shook his head. "I didn't mean to startle you. I was hoping you were working up here today. I wanted to see how you're doing. Did you enjoy the rest of your weekend?"

Hannah looked up at him and tried to remember the speech she'd mentally practiced during the ride into work this morning. Yet the sight of his handsome face caused her speech to evaporate from her mind.

"My weekend was fine. How about yours? Did you look at more houses?"

"I did." Trey folded his arms over his chest. "I still like the first one the best. I'm thinking about making an offer on it soon."

"*Gut.*" Hannah fingered her apron while contemplating what to say next. "I'm sorry about Saturday. My mother-in-law has a way of expressing her opinions without considering other people's feelings."

He shrugged. "You don't need to apologize. My grandmother was the same way. We never knew what she'd say. There's no need to feel bad or embarrassed. I know our friendship is unusual, to say the least."

Hannah cleared her throat. She had to tell him the truth, and waiting would only make it more awkward. "Mr. Peterson, I have enjoyed talking with you, and I had a wonderful time when you visited my farm and had supper with my family." He frowned, but she pushed on, ignoring the sadness and regret surging through her. "Unfortunately, I can't spend time with you anymore. Having you over at my house put me in an awkward position with my community. Although I'm permitted to speak with a man who isn't Amish, befriending one could lead to problems. I hope that makes sense." She said the words she'd rehearsed, but her voice sounded weak instead of confident. Why was this so difficult?

"Oh. I see." Trey grimaced and shifted his weight from one foot to the other. "I should've called before I came over on Saturday, but, like I said, I didn't know how to get in touch with you. I thought I'd just take a chance and go out. I never meant to cause you problems. I had a feeling that your mother-in-law was going to give you a hard time about my visit, and I'm really sorry."

"It's not your fault." She paused and tried to find the right words. Nothing felt like the right thing to say as she looked into the eyes of her friend. "My mother-in-law reminded me of how our friendship could be misinterpreted, and I can't risk causing problems for my children."

"That makes sense." He leaned against the wall. "I understand. I talked to my sister the other night, and I mentioned our friendship. She pointed out that she thought I may have gotten you into a sticky situation with your mother-in-law. I'd hoped she was wrong, but she wasn't."

Hannah studied him. "You told your sister about me?"

"Yes, I did." He looked confused. "Why wouldn't I?"

"Oh." She found herself stuck on this detail, trying to figure out what it meant. Why would he tell his sister about their friendship? Did it mean that much to him? The idea filled her with hope and excitement, but she quickly pushed the thought away.

"I better get going." He motioned toward the elevator. "Have a good day. Hopefully I'll run into you again, but I'll be sure to have my shirt on." Humor shone in his eyes.

Hannah gaped for a surprised moment and her senses swam. "Good-bye, Mr. Peterson. I'm certain your bed and breakfast will be a wonderful success."

"You take care of my horses." He waved and disappeared around the corner toward the bank of elevators.

Hannah stared after him and felt her heart breaking with each passing moment. She wondered why it was so painful to say good-bye to someone she barely knew.

. . .

"How are you today?" Amanda stood at the cash register and punched in the prices for the cheese, eggs, and cookies the customer had brought to the counter.

"I'm fine, thank you." The woman pulled out her leather wallet from her fancy-looking purse and motioned toward the package of chocolate chip cookies. "Do you make these cookies? They're fabulous."

"No, I don't." Amanda pointed toward Nancy, who was working at the bakery counter on the other side of the small deli. "My friend Nancy and her mother make them. Aren't they the best?"

"Please tell your friend and her mother that they are amazing bakers. I wish I could bake like that too. I'm better at ordering takeout than making anything in the kitchen." The woman handed her the money, and Amanda gave her change before bagging the items.

"That's funny." Amanda smiled.

"It's the truth. My husband often jokes that he needs to hire a chef." The woman jammed the money into her wallet and then dropped the wallet back into her purse.

"I imagine it would be nice to have a personal chef." Amanda glanced toward the window and noticed that the rain had stopped. The bright sunlight filtered down through the skylights above her and provided the only indoor lighting for the store other than a few gas-powered lamps. "The sun came out. I thought it was going to rain all day."

"Yes, it brightened right up. The temperature is perfect—not too hot, not too cool. I love this time of year. Of course, my kids are counting the days until they get out of school. They can't wait to spend the summer lounging at the pool." She took the bag from Amanda. "Have a great day."

"You too." Amanda grabbed a rag from the shelf under the cash register and began wiping up the counter. She hummed to herself while she worked. She heard footsteps and looked up just as Mike Smithson approached. He held up a package of pumpkin whoopie pies.

"Hi, Amanda." His curly brown hair stuck out from under a blue baseball cap, and he was clad in a green T-shirt and baggy jeans.

"Hi, Mike." Amanda pushed the ribbons from her prayer covering behind her shoulders. "How are you today?"

"Fine." He pointed to the whoopie pies. "You know I can't resist these."

"We always have some ready for you." Amanda rang up the little cakes, and Mike handed her the money. "Where's Julianne?"

Mike turned toward the other side of the store. "There she is. She's talking to Nancy. You know how my sister likes to chat. So, how's the farm?"

"Good." Amanda nodded. "How's school?"

He shrugged. "School is school. I'm counting down the days. Only one more month left. I want to get a summer job instead of just hanging around doing nothing like last summer." He gestured toward the door. "My uncle owns the bookstore just across the street. I'm going to talk to him about a job this weekend."

"I didn't know your uncle owns the Book Café."

"Yeah, he does. I thought it would be the perfect summer job before I leave for college."

"*Ya*, I imagine it would be fun to work in a bookstore."

Julianne appeared next to Mike and bumped his arm. She shared the same brown eyes and brown curly hair, only hers fell in ringlets past her shoulders. "Hi, Amanda."

"Hi, Julianne. How are you?"

"I'm great, thanks." Julianne looked back and forth between them. "What were you two talking about?"

"I was just telling Amanda I'm hoping to get a job at Uncle Rick's bookstore this summer." He bumped her back with his elbow.

"I'm certain Uncle Rick will hire you." Julianne feigned a frown. "Can you believe this will be our last summer together before you pursue your dream of becoming a big-time doctor and then forget the rest of us?"

Mike rolled his eyes. "Yeah, that's exactly what I plan to do."

Julianne handed Amanda a sampler box filled with a variety of desserts. "This is totally going to kill my diet, but how can I come in here and not buy something? It smells so good."

"Nancy's samplers are delicious." Amanda rang up and bagged the desserts, and Julianne paid her.

Julianne glanced at her watch. "We'd better go. We have youth group tonight. We have to be at church by five."

Mike smiled at Amanda. "See you soon."

"Bye!" Amanda waved as her two friends started for the door. She pondered how excited Mike must be to head to college. He dreamt of being a doctor while Amanda had always wanted to be a veterinarian. She wondered what it would be like to be able to have the choice to be more than just a cashier at a deli. If only she had the luxury of choices like her *Englisher* friends had . . .

· · ·

Trey drove through the wet Paradise streets later that afternoon. The rain had cleared and a bright rainbow shimmered in the sky. Yet his mood remained grim. He couldn't wipe the frown off his face that had appeared when Hannah told him they could no longer be friends. He kept telling himself that he and Hannah were from different worlds, and they were never meant to be friends. He knew in his heart, however, that her friendship meant a lot to him—more than he could even express in words.

He steered around a corner and pulled into the parking lot of the Paradise Community Church. He needed to talk to someone and share the confusing feelings that had gripped him since this morning. He pulled his iPhone from his pocket and dialed Christy's number.

After a few rings, her voicemail picked up. "Hi, this is Christy Becker. I can't come to the phone right now. Leave me a message, and I'll call you right back. Thanks!"

Trey waited for the beep before he began to speak. "Hey, Christy. It's me. I just wanted to say hi. Give me a call when you get a moment. Thanks." He ended the call and dropped the phone into the cup holder.

He leaned back in the seat while staring at the church in front of him. He'd longed to visit a church since coming to Lancaster County, but he hadn't made the time. It seemed he was always too busy, putting his goal of finding the perfect bed and breakfast for Corrine ahead of his spiritual needs. He and Corrine had been active members of their church back home in New Jersey.

Trey had gone back to church after he'd lost Corrine and Samantha, but it wasn't the same. He felt the warmth and comfort of his church family when they brought him meals, visited him, and kept him on the prayer list for months. The Scriptures warmed his heart and gave him hope both during the services and also at home at night. But there was something missing when he was in church. He knew what it was—it was the vacant pew beside him. Not having his precious wife and daughter beside him during worship left him feeling empty.

When he moved to Lancaster, he wasn't just trying to bring Corrine's dream to life; he was also trying to escape the loneliness and guilt that had haunted him since he lost his family. When he'd met Hannah, he felt a spark of hope ignite in his soul. But that spark dwindled when Hannah ended their friendship.

Would he ever feel whole again?

Trey blew out a sigh and studied the white church. The tall bell tower and the colorful stained glass cross reminded him of the church back home. He suddenly felt the urge to take a closer look. He climbed from his car and crossed the parking lot to the brick front steps. He pulled open the large door and stepped into the sanctuary. The church had a historic feel with its wooden pews and a matching altar. A wooden board displayed the hymn numbers and total attendance for the previous week.

He walked to the front of the sanctuary and sat in the first pew. Bowing his head, he sent a prayer up to God.

Lord, I'm lost, and I need your help. Please guide my journey toward a new home in Lancaster County. And help me find the peace I need to heal my heart and soul after losing my family. In your holy name, I pray. Amen.

When he finished his silent prayer, warmth filled Trey. He blew out a deep breath and stood.

"May I help you?" A tall man with dark, graying hair and a warm smile approached him. He was dressed in dark clothes with a white minister's collar.

"Hi. I'm Trey Peterson. I was driving by and felt the need to come in and visit." Trey shook his hand.

"It's nice to meet you. I'm Bob Wingate. Welcome to Paradise Community Church. Are you visiting the area?"

Trey shook his head. "I'm in the process of moving here from New Jersey. I'm searching for the perfect location to open a bed and breakfast."

"That sounds wonderful. My wife and I love to stay in bed and breakfasts instead of hotels when we travel."

"My wife did too." Trey gestured around the sanctuary. "You have a lovely church here. I was drawn in by the simplicity of the building and the cross."

"Thank you. I've been the pastor here for about fifteen years, and God has blessed me with a wonderful congregation. You should join us on a Sunday. I think you'll feel very welcome."

"I'd like that. I'm looking for a new church home." Trey looked up at the cross. "This feels like it might be the place."

"I felt the same way when I first visited here. There's something about this sanctuary that feels cozy, like you're sitting in front of the fireplace on a cold winter's night." The minister laughed. "Of course, I told my wife that, and she looked at me as if I were crazy."

"No, you're not crazy at all. I felt that too. I've had a difficult time finding my way lately, but somehow I think I'm finally on the right path."

"That's wonderful. I hope to see you Sunday morning. Service starts at ten."

"I look forward to it." Trey motioned toward the door. "I better get going. It was nice meeting you."

"You too."

Trey started down the aisle toward the door.

"Trey," the minister called after him.

Trey looked back at him. "Yes?"

"If you ever need anything, please let me know." Bob approached him and handed him a business card. "Call anytime."

"Thank you." He put the card in his pocket. "I appreciate that."

Trey walked out to his car, looked up at the rainbow again, and smiled. Suddenly things didn't seem as grim as they had before. *No matter what, God keeps his promises.*

TEN

Later that evening, Josh wiped his mouth and watched the twins carry the dishes to the counter.

Hannah stood at the sink and began washing dishes. Her beautiful face had held a frown that deepened the lines around her mouth during supper. A quiet demeanor replaced her usual talkative personality. She listened as her children discussed their day, but she had very little to say about hers. Something was wrong, and he had to find out what it was.

Josh pushed his chair back from the table and crossed to the sink, where Hannah was scrubbing a dish with such vigor that he thought it might break in half. "Hannah."

She jumped when he spoke. "I'm sorry, Joshua. I didn't hear you come up behind me."

"You seem upset about something."

"I'm fine." She averted her eyes by studying the already clean pot she continued to scrub.

"I'd like to talk to you alone." He looked at the girls, who were busy talking while cleaning the table. "*Maed*, can you take over the kitchen duties while I speak to your *mamm* in private?"

"*Ya.*" Amanda moved to the sink. "I'll wash, and Lily can dry."

Lillian frowned while watching Josh. "*Was iss letz?*"

Josh forced a smile. "I'm certain everything is fine." He motioned toward the door. "Why don't we go talk out on the porch?"

Hannah hesitated. "I'm really fine."

Josh raised an eyebrow and she sighed before following him outside to the porch.

"What's going on?" He leaned against the railing. "You look really upset. Did something happen at work? You know you don't need to work. I think we can manage Daniel's salary just fine."

"Work is fine." Hannah folded her arms over her dress. "I don't want to quit. I just had a long day. It seemed everything I did went wrong."

"You've had long and hard days before, and they didn't end like this. What's going on, Hannah? You can talk to me." He reached for her hand, and she stepped back. He knew he was crossing a line, but he wanted to show her how much he cared for her.

"*Danki*, but I'm fine." She paused, and he wondered if she was choosing her words to avoid sharing too much. "I had to have an uncomfortable conversation today with someone."

"What do you mean?"

She looked past him toward the barns. "You wouldn't understand."

The words stung, causing him to wince. "After all of these years, Hannah, why don't you trust me?"

"How could you say that?" She regarded him with annoyance. "I trust you. I've always trusted you."

"No, Hannah, you don't." He drew himself up straight and tall. "I've always been here, but you continue to ignore me."

"I don't ignore you, Joshua. That's not fair."

"You're right. It *isn't* fair. I don't know what else I can do to show you how much I care about you and the *kinner*." Josh started toward the door. "I'm going to get Andrew, so we can put the horses in for the night." He stopped and faced her. "I forgot to tell you that Daniel King will start working here first thing tomorrow. He checked with his parents and they are fine with our arrangement."

"*Gut*." Hannah nodded but didn't smile. "I know you need the help, and he's a *gut bu*."

"*Ya*, he is." He gripped the doorknob and studied her, wishing he could find out why she was so upset. "I'll finish the chores and then head home."

"That sounds *gut*."

Josh studied her and his thoughts turned to Trey Peterson. "Does this have to do with your *Englisher freind*?"

Hannah hesitated. She didn't respond.

Jealousy and frustration consumed him. He'd thought he and Hannah had reached a deeper friendship after he'd given her the gift last night. He'd believed that maybe, just maybe, she'd see him as a suitor instead of just a friend and business partner. Yet now he found himself right back where he was on

Saturday—fighting a tug of war with that *Englisher* to win her attention. Joshua wished Hannah had never met that man. If their paths hadn't crossed, then the stranger wouldn't have had the chance to toy with her emotions and ruin any chance he may have had with Hannah.

"I had a feeling it had something to do with that man. I don't understand why you've gotten so emotionally involved with someone you met while cleaning at the hotel." He shook his head. "I wish you would quit that job. The business is doing fine. I keep telling you there's no reason why you have to keep working."

"I want to work." She said the words slowly, enunciating them.

"Fine." He leaned in close to her, close enough to inhale the sweet scent of her lilac shampoo. "Just remember that your fancy *Englisher freind* can't give you the life I can. If you choose him, you'll lose everything you have here." He gestured widely. "You'll lose your farm and your place in the community. If you choose him, you'll have to walk away from everything you've ever loved, which will create a mess for your *kinner*. Is that what you really want, Hannah?"

She stared at him wide-eyed, and then blinked her beautiful green eyes.

"I don't think that's what you really want. I can give you love and stability. If you give me a chance, I can give you everything." Josh pushed the door open. "Andrew! Let's go take care of the animals."

Andrew rushed to the mudroom, where he pulled on his boots. He then hurried out the back door to the porch. "I'm ready!" He stomped down the steps toward the barns.

"*Gut nacht.*" Josh followed his nephew down the steps while anger and frustration boiled through his veins. He wondered how he was going to make Hannah forget the *Englisher* from the hotel. What did he need to do to get her attention?

"What's wrong with *Mamm*?" Andrew slowed and fell into step with Josh. "She looked upset."

"She's fine." Josh kept his eyes on the pasture. "She's just upset about something that happened at work, but it's okay. Nothing to worry about."

Andrew climbed up on the split-rail fence and whistled. "Come here, Huckleberry! Come here, *bu*!" The horse trotted over, and Andrew rubbed his blaze and his neck. "You're a *gut bu. Ya*, you are."

Josh smiled. Regret filled him as he thought about his conversation with Hannah. Maybe he was too rough on her. He missed Gideon every day, but he had no idea what kind of grief Hannah had experienced after losing him. He needed to be her uplifter instead of her castigator. He looked up at the clear sky, and silently asked God to guide his relationship with Hannah. Even if he never won her heart, he hoped to keep her friendship close.

Andrew smiled over at Josh while patting the horse. "Isn't he the best horse, *Onkel*? I love him so much."

"*Ya*, he is." Josh started for the gate. "Let's get these horses in the stable so we can feed them."

Andrew trotted behind him. "Okay."

"Daniel King is going to start working with us tomorrow. Is that okay with you?" Josh opened the gate.

"Oh, *ya*." Andrew grinned. "Lillian will be *froh* since she has a crush on his *bruder*."

Josh chuckled. "I guess she will be *froh*."

Andrew started toward Huckleberry and then suddenly stopped and faced Josh. "I love working on the farm with you, *Onkel*. I hope I can work on the farm with you and Daniel when I'm finished with school."

"I love working here with you too, Andrew." Josh smiled. "This is my favorite thing to do."

. . .

Hannah watched Joshua make his way down the porch steps behind Andrew. She wished she could tell him the truth—that she'd been upset ever since she told Trey that they couldn't be friends. But she knew Joshua would only become agitated when he heard she was still thinking about Trey.

She didn't even understand why she was so upset. After all, she'd only known Trey a couple of weeks and had only spoken to him a handful of times, but she still couldn't deny that it hurt. She couldn't deny she missed their talks and the feeling of his hand holding hers. She missed everything about him—his smile, his voice, and the smell of his aftershave. She had fallen for him, and she knew she was doomed to live with a broken heart after telling him that she couldn't be his friend.

She spotted Andrew and Joshua talking near the pasture and she smiled. She loved seeing her children interact with Joshua, and she wished she shared the same romantic feelings he seemed to have for her. Yet she couldn't force those feelings any more than she couldn't stop yearning for a relationship with Trey.

Perhaps I need to pray for God to guide my heart according to his plans.

She walked through the mudroom and entered the kitchen, where Amanda was sweeping and Lillian was wiping the counter.

Lillian met her gaze, and her eyebrows knitted together. "Is everything all right, *Mamm*?"

"*Ya*, everything is fine. I just have a lot on my mind." Hannah sat at the table. "I have news about the farm. Why don't you sit down with me, so we can talk?"

The girls sat across from her. Amanda smiled, and Lillian continued to frown. Her girls often illustrated their stark differences through their expressions. Gideon had summed their differences up by saying Amanda was as positive as the morning sunshine while Lillian was as worrisome as storm clouds brewing in the afternoon.

"Are we losing the farm, *Mamm*?" Lillian placed her hands flat on the table. "Please tell us everything. We can handle it, right, Amanda?"

Amanda nodded, her smile fading. "*Ya*, we're here for you, *Mamm*."

Hannah smiled. "*Maed*, we're not losing the farm. I just wanted to tell you that Daniel King is going to start working here tomorrow. Your *onkel* spoke with him, and he's agreed to take the job."

"Oh." Amanda glanced at Lillian and raised her eyebrows. "Maybe Leroy really *will* wind up working here too."

Lillian's cheeks burned a bright red while she avoided her sister's look. "Was that all you wanted to tell us?"

"*Ya*, that's it." Hannah nodded.

Lillian pushed her glasses up farther on her nose and stood. "May I go read a few more pages before devotions? I'm really enjoying this *gut* mystery."

"*Ya*. Go on and enjoy the quiet." Hannah waved off the question. "I'll call you when your *bruder* comes in."

"*Danki*." Lillian disappeared toward the staircase.

Hannah studied her blond daughter and smiled. "Did you have a *gut* day, Amanda?"

Amanda cupped her hand over her mouth to stifle a yawn. "I did." She tilted her head. "Are you upset that Daniel is going to start working here?"

Hannah shook her head. "No, I'm not upset about Daniel. I'm glad Joshua will finally have some help."

"Are you upset with *Onkel* Josh?"

"No."

"Is there something else bothering you? Are you angry with Lily, Andrew, or me?"

Hannah frowned. She knew her daughter wouldn't stop asking questions until she told her what was burdening her. "I'm not really upset. I'm disappointed, but not with anyone here in this *haus*."

"Oh." Amanda paused and nodded slowly, as if trying to understand her words. "I hope whatever it is that's bothering you gets better."

"I do too, *mei liewe*." Hannah touched Amanda's hands. "I think it will."

Amanda studied her mother. "May I ask you something?"

"Of course. You know you can ask me anything."

Amanda hesitated before continuing. "Do you ever worry you're feeling something you're not supposed to?"

Hannah studied Amanda's questioning eyes. "What do you mean?"

"Sometimes I wonder if there's something wrong with me because I'm not interested in dating any of the *buwe* in our community. Nancy and Lillian are always talking about *buwe* and dating, but I'm not really worried about dating. It's just not important to me right now."

"You mean you haven't found the right *bu* yet?"

Amanda scrunched her nose. "That's sort of what I mean."

"Amanda, you're only sixteen. You'll meet the right *bu* when the time is right, and you don't need to rush dating. You aren't even baptized yet. Don't rush God's plan for you. It will happen when it's meant to happen."

"Right." Amanda forced a smile, which she always seemed to do when something was bothering her—something she was afraid to share.

Hannah leaned forward. "Is something wrong, Amanda? You seem to have something on your mind too."

Amanda shrugged. "No, I'm okay. Nancy was teasing me about not liking anyone on Sunday, and it's been bugging me."

Hannah smiled. "Does Nancy tease you like you tease Lily?"

Amanda smirked. "*Ya*, she does. I don't mean to

upset Lily when I tease her. I'm just joking, but I guess I know how Lily feels now."

"Don't let Nancy bother you. You'll find the right person someday. My *freind* Irma married a *bu* from another district and moved there. Maybe you'll meet someone from another district too."

"*Ya*, maybe I will meet someone from another district. I have time." Amanda pushed her chair back from the table and stood. "I'm going to go see if *Onkel* Josh and Andrew need help. They always tell me I don't need to help them, but I love working with the horses. They don't understand my love of animals. I'll be back in soon."

"Okay. *Danki*." Hannah stood and straightened the canisters on the counter while Amanda disappeared into the mudroom. She looked out the kitchen window above the sink and spotted Amanda crossing to the pasture. While she contemplated her conversation with Amanda, Hannah wondered if her daughter was sharing everything that was going through her mind. Amanda was never the child who worried since Lillian did enough worrying for the both of them.

ELEVEN

Hannah hummed as she put fresh sheets on a king-size bed in a hotel suite. She'd managed to avoid running into Trey during the past couple of weeks, which was both a relief and a disappointment. She was relieved to not have to make conversation after their last uncomfortable meeting, but she felt disappointment at not seeing him to at least say hello. She missed him. He filled her every thought during the day and her dreams at night. She felt as if a piece of her heart were missing since she stopped seeing him. She wished she could erase the heartache, but it lingered in her mind as well as in her heart, like a dull headache.

Hannah knew Trey was still staying in the hotel since his belongings were in the room when she cleaned it a couple of days ago. She longed to ask him how his life had changed during the past two weeks. Was he ready to put in a contract on a home? Was he preparing to move?

After wiping the bathroom counter, Hannah moved to the bedroom area and began dusting. She thought she heard someone calling her name, and she stopped to listen. When she heard it a second time, she rushed to the doorway and found Carolyn running down the hallway toward the room.

"Hannah!" Carolyn paused to catch her breath and then grabbed Hannah's hand. "You need to come downstairs now. There's a phone call for you."

"Who's on the phone?"

"It's Lily." She pointed toward the elevators. "Go now."

Her children never called her at work—except for an emergency. Hannah's heart beat doubletime. "*Ach* no."

"Go on. I'll finish the room." Carolyn nudged Hannah toward the door. "Go now."

Hannah rushed to the elevator. The short ride to the first floor felt like a lifetime while horrible scenarios ran through her head. She wondered if someone was ill or hurt. *Oh no, what if it's worse news?*

She hurried through the lobby to where Stacey Bradley, the young woman who ran the front desk, stood helping a hotel guest.

Stacey nodded at Hannah. "There's a phone call for you on line four." She motioned toward the office behind her. "You may take it in there."

"Thank you." Hannah made her way into the room and picked up the phone. "Hello?"

"*Mamm!*" Lillian's voice wavered on the phone. "Andrew's hurt. He's hurt badly."

"Oh no." Hannah sank into the large leather chair behind the desk. "What happened?"

"He fell while he was playing around in the barn, and he's bleeding badly. There's blood everywhere."

Hannah's heart stopped and her blood ran cold. "What do you mean? Where is there blood, Lillian?"

"On his head and his face. It's all over. I'm not certain where he was cut." A choked sob rang through the phone.

Tears filled Hannah's eyes. "Where is he?"

"*Onkel* Josh carried him into the house, and Daniel ran across the street to get the veterinarian. Then I ran out here to call you." She sniffed, and her voice shook again. "*Mammi* came by to see us and she's sitting with him now."

Hannah's heart pounded against her rib cage. She needed to get home right away. She had to make sure Andrew would be all right. "I'll find a way home. Phyllis told me she had some other rides to give today, so I don't know if she can make it." Her thoughts churned with a way to find a ride to her farm. "I can ask Stacey to check the bus schedule on the computer too. I'll find a way to get home, Lily. You just sit tight. Tell Andrew I'm on my way."

"*Dummle!* Bye, *Mamm*."

Hannah dropped the phone into the cradle and then stepped out to the front desk. "Stacey, can you please help me?" Her voice trembled with worry.

"Sure, Hannah." She pushed a lock of blond hair behind her ear. "What do you need?"

"One of my children is injured, and I need to get home right away." Hannah wrung her hands as she spoke. "Can you possibly see if there's a bus schedule on the Internet? I need to see if there's a bus coming by soon."

"I can give you a ride," a familiar voice said.

Hannah turned and found Trey standing by the

counter. His face was filled with concern. "I can give you a ride, Hannah."

"Mr. Peterson." She hesitated for a brief moment and then thought of Andrew. She needed to get home *now*. Lillian's voice had quaked with fear, which was unlike her brave and confident Lillian. Something was definitely wrong with her youngest child, and she needed to get there as soon as possible. "Let me grab my bag."

She retrieved her bag from the workroom behind the office and then hurried out to where Trey waited at the front door. "Stacey, would you please tell Gregg that my son's hurt and I had to go home?"

Stacey nodded. "Absolutely. Don't worry about a thing. I hope your son is okay."

"Thank you." Hannah hefted her tote bag up on her shoulder and rushed out to the car behind Trey. She buckled the seat belt and then silently prayed.

Lord, please heal Andrew. Let his injury be minor. Please don't take him from me. I know your will is always the best, but please, Lord, spare mei kind. *I can't bear the thought of losing one of my precious* kinner. *Amen.*

The car jolted forward and Hannah opened her eyes. She hugged her tote bag to her chest.

"What happened?" Trey kept his eyes on the road.

"Lillian called me. Andrew fell and it sounds like he's hurt badly. She said there was blood everywhere." She prayed her daughter was exaggerating, but from the sound of Lillian's voice, the situation seemed bleak. Her heart lurched in her chest.

"Oh no." He grimaced and tapped the steering wheel. "Do you want to take him to the hospital?"

Hannah shook her head. "I don't know. I just keep worrying that something awful is going to happen." She sucked in a breath. She didn't want to cry in front of him. She had to be strong.

"I'll get you there as fast as I can." He navigated around a curve.

Hannah gripped her tote bag and continued to pray during the ride to her house. When they arrived, she leapt from the car and rushed into the house with Trey following close behind her.

"Lillian!" Hannah dropped her bag on the kitchen table and hurried toward the stairs. "Lillian?"

"We're in your room." Lillian's voice sounded from down the hall.

"I'll wait here." Trey stood in the doorway and studied her.

"Thank you." Hannah rushed to her bedroom and found Andrew lying on top of several towels in the middle of her bed. Bloody rags covered the floor and blood stained his dark blue shirt. The sight of the blood caused her to shiver.

Cameron Wood, the veterinarian who lived across the street, leaned over Andrew while applying a butterfly bandage. Lillian, Barbie, Josh, and Daniel all looked on.

"Andrew!" Hannah moved to his side, her heart thumping in her chest. "Are you all right?"

Her son shrugged and his lip quivered. "I'm okay, *Mamm*."

"He'll be just fine, Mrs. Glick." Cameron patted Andrew's shoulder. "It looks much worse than it really is. He has a deep cut above his eye, but I don't think he needs stitches. Thank goodness he didn't hit that shovel any lower or he would've hurt his eye."

Hannah touched Andrew's hand. "What happened?"

"I was fooling around with *Onkel* Josh, and I tripped. It was an accident." Tears filled her son's eyes.

Hannah squeezed his hand. "I was so worried."

"I'm sorry I scared you." Andrew's voice was soft and shaky.

"You don't need to apologize. I'm just relieved you're okay." Hannah turned to the veterinarian. "Thank you for coming over to help us."

"You're welcome." Cameron picked up a small bag. "I'm glad I was around to help. I had just returned from an appointment across town. I'm going to head home, but please call me anytime you need help." He nodded at Lillian and Barbie before leaving the bedroom.

"I'm glad you're okay, Andrew," Josh said. "Come on, Daniel, let's get back to work."

As Josh and Daniel left, Barbie frowned at Hannah. "I'm glad you made it home. It was terrible. You wouldn't believe the blood everywhere. Lillian and I cleaned it all up, except for his clothes and these towels."

"I got here as soon as I could." Hannah touched Andrew's arm and studied his face. She spotted a bruise forming near the butterfly bandage. "It looks like you really injured yourself. Does it hurt?"

Andrew grimaced. "*Ya*, my head hurts, *Mamm*."

"We'll give you some Tylenol." Hannah smiled at him despite the worry still coursing through her. *What if the injury had been worse?* She couldn't bear the thought of losing her children.

"I had to call you." Lillian's eyes filled with tears. "I was just so worried something bad would happen. We never expected to lose *Dat* like we did." A single tear trickled down her cheek.

"It's okay." Hannah hugged Lillian while trying to hold back her own tears. "I told you that you can call me if you have an emergency. You did the right thing. You can always call me if you feel uncomfortable. I'll never scold you for worrying about your *bruder*."

"Okay." Lillian nodded and rubbed her fingers under her glasses to wipe her tears.

"She wouldn't have to call you if you were here, which is where you *should* be." Barbie's words were sharp.

Hannah frowned at her mother-in-law as frustration boiled inside of her. "Please don't make this worse. We're all upset Andrew was hurt."

"I'm not making this worse." Barbie raised her eyebrows. "I think you're wrong to leave Lillian in charge of things while you flitter around a fancy hotel like an *Englisher*."

"Lillian is not here alone. Joshua and Daniel King are working on the farm. She can always go to them if she needs help."

"That's not the same as having their *mamm* at home where she belongs."

Hannah sucked in a breath and paused. "We will talk about this later. Not in front of the *kinner*." She looked at Andrew. "Do you need anything? Maybe a glass of water?"

Andrew nodded. "*Ya*. Water please."

Lillian stood. "I'll go get him some water and Tylenol."

"*Danki*." Hannah gestured toward the door. "I need to call Phyllis and tell her I don't need a ride home today. I'll be right back."

"Did you take the bus?" Lillian asked.

"No, I got a ride." Hannah started for the doorway. Lillian followed her out to the kitchen.

Trey stood in the doorway to the mudroom and asked, "How is he?"

Hannah forced a smile. "He's going to be fine. He has a gash above his eye, but it's not serious."

"I'm so glad." Trey returned the smile. "I know you were worried."

Lillian looked at Trey and turned to Hannah with her eyes wide.

Hannah touched Lillian's arm. "Trey gave me a ride." She paused, realizing that she'd said his first name out loud. She was stunned by how natural it sounded to say his first name. It was as if being his close friend felt right. She cleared her throat before speaking. "He walked by while I was at the front desk trying to figure out what to do because Phyllis mentioned she had plans this afternoon." She started for the door. "I'm going to walk Trey out and then call Phyllis. I'll be right back in, okay?"

Lillian nodded. Hannah could tell by her daughter's surprised expression that she was shocked to see Trey again.

Hannah followed Trey outside. It barely registered that Joshua was out in the pasture with Daniel. When they reached Trey's car, they stood together by the driver's side door.

He looked down at her. "I'm glad he's okay."

"I was so worried I was going to lose him like I lost Gideon." Hannah's eyes filled with tears. All of the worry she'd held in since Lillian's phone call poured out of her like a waterfall. She couldn't stop the sobs shaking her body and the tears spilling from her eyes. "There was so much blood, Trey. I couldn't believe it. There was blood all over his clothes and in his hair. And there were towels all over the bed and rags on the floor covered in his blood too."

"Hey. It's okay." Trey wrapped his arms around her and pulled her close.

At first she was shocked by the hug. But then instead of pushing him away, Hannah snuggled into the warmth of his arms. She realized then that forgetting about Trey would be impossible. He was etched in her mind forever. And she needed him like she needed air to breathe.

"Andrew will be fine." His voice was soft and his breath was warm in her ear, like a summer breeze.

Hannah inhaled deeply, and her body relaxed as her sobs dissipated. She breathed in the spicy scent of his aftershave and laid her head on his shoulder. "Thank you," she whispered while enjoying the comfort of his arms. She felt warm and safe, and she wanted the feeling to last forever.

"You don't have to thank me." He rested his cheek on her head.

"*Ya*, I do. I'm so glad you came by today. I can't thank you enough for your help."

"You don't have to thank me," he repeated the words with more emphasis. "I helped you for purely selfish reasons."

She looked up at him. "What do you mean?"

"I missed you." His dark eyes studied her with an intensity that caused her pulse to skip a beat. "I missed you *a lot.*"

She swiped her hand across her tear-soaked cheeks. "I missed you too."

"It's been torture to not be able to talk to you. I have so much I want to tell you." He took her hand in his, and his skin was warm and smooth. "I found a church I really like, and I think I'm going to make an offer on one of the houses I looked at. It reminds me of your place and also of my grandparents' farm."

"That's wonderful, Trey. I'm so happy for you." Holding his hand felt natural, as if she'd known him for years. Why was being with him so easy?

"I better go." Trey squeezed her hand. "Hopefully, I'll see you soon. Hannah, you mean so much to me."

He leaned down and hugged her again, and Hannah didn't want to let go. He was like a magnet, pulling her toward him despite her best intentions of steering clear of him.

Trey opened the car door and climbed in. "Let me know how Andrew is."

"I will. Thank you again."

"And by the way," Trey began, "I'm glad you finally stopped calling me Mr. Peterson and started calling me Trey. I'd like you to think of me as more than an acquaintance."

"You're more than an acquaintance to me. You mean a lot to me too, Trey."

"Good." He smiled before climbing into his car.

Hannah waved as Trey drove out of the driveway.

"Hannah!" a loud voice bellowed from the porch.

Hannah looked back to where Barbie and Lillian stood watching her, and her smile faded. Lillian's mouth gaped while Barbie shook her head and glowered.

Lillian rushed down the porch steps and moved past Hannah.

"Lillian!" Hannah called after her. "Where are you going?"

"I'll call Phyllis for you. I'll tell her you don't need a ride home." Lillian hurried toward the barn.

"*Danki.*" Hannah climbed the porch steps.

"I don't understand you." Barbie glared at Hannah. "How could you let that man touch you?"

"I was upset about Andrew, and he consoled me." Hannah shook her head. "I've told you more than once that he's *mei freind.*"

"You're headed for trouble." Barbie wagged a pudgy finger at her. "You never should've taken that job at the hotel. I knew this would happen."

Hannah folded her arms over her apron as the frustration Barbie had caused earlier seeped through her. "My working at the hotel has nothing to do with this."

Barbie started down the stairs. "I'm leaving. I can't stand here and pretend I agree with your behavior. You're going to cause problems for your *kinner* by behaving like this. I can't watch you ruin their lives."

"I'm not ruining their lives." Hannah rubbed the back

of her neck in an attempt to relieve the tension building there. Would this woman ever stop criticizing her?

"Yes, you are." Barbie faced her. "I've told you that you're going to ruin our family's reputation. You're just like the rest of your family. I didn't want to see this happen again."

"What?" Anger boiled up inside Hannah. "What are you saying?"

"I know about your *onkel* Elam." Barbie jammed her hands on her wide hips. "He divorced his wife and left the community. It took years for your family to get over the pain, and there was quite a ripple of concern that moved through the community back then."

Hannah regarded Barbie with confusion. "What are you talking about? *Mei onkel* Elam died when I was a *boppli*."

"No, he didn't." Barbie shook her head with emphasis. "He left the community and ran off with an *Englisher*. Your *aenti* told everyone he died, but I found out the truth from your *mammi*."

Hannah blanched. Was Barbie telling the truth? If so, why hadn't any of her family members ever told her what had really happened to her *onkel* Elam? She'd heard all her life that he had died.

Confusion mixed with frustration surged through Hannah as she worked to regain composure. "Even if that's true, it has nothing to do with me. I'm not planning on leaving the community."

"I'm going home." Barbie turned toward the pasture where Joshua and Daniel were training a horse. "Joshua! Take me home."

Hannah spotted Lillian scowling while she stood by the barn. She raised her hand to wave to her, but Lillian looked away.

Hannah walked back into the mudroom and leaned against the wall. She wondered how her day could become any more confusing. Not only did she feel intense emotions for Trey radiating inside her, but she just found out her *onkel* had left the community and wasn't dead.

She stepped into the kitchen and looked out the window to where Joshua was hitching his horse to the buggy. Barbie stood near him and gestured wildly while speaking to him. Hannah couldn't even imagine what Barbie was saying about her. She knew the news of her impropriety with Trey would spread through the community. Once word got around, nothing would be the same for Hannah and her children.

Hannah shook her head. In her heart, she knew that one accusation Barbie had made was correct—Hannah was on a road that could lead to trouble. But she couldn't deny how she felt about Trey. When she was with him, she felt comfortable and safe, a feeling she hadn't experienced since Gideon had died. And Trey could offer her a new life enjoying what she loved to do most.

"*Mamm!*" Andrew's voice sounded from the other room. "*Mamm?* Will you sit with me?"

"I'm coming." Hannah hurried toward her bedroom and hoped all of these problems and confusing feelings would evaporate and heal along with Andrew's injury.

• • •

"*Mamm?*" Lillian stood in her mother's bedroom doorway later that evening. "May I talk to you?"

Mamm looked up from the Bible and patted the bed beside her. "Lily. Of course we can talk. Come sit with me."

Lillian sat next to *Mamm* and pushed her glasses up on her nose as she so often did. "I'm glad Andrew's headache is gone. I checked on him, and he's sleeping."

"*Gut.* I'm glad he's okay."

"I wanted to talk to you about what happened earlier." Lillian smoothed her nightgown over her legs while she considered her words. Although her mother had always told her that she could talk to her about anything, bringing up the incident with the *Englisher* made her uncomfortable. "*Mammi* was really upset when she saw you outside with Mr. Peterson."

Mamm frowned. "I know. She told me she was upset." She leaned over. "Are you upset with me, Lily? You can tell me the truth."

Lillian shrugged. "I don't know if I'm upset, but I'm confused."

"Why are you confused?"

"I've never seen you hugging anyone else the way you hugged Mr. Peterson." She paused. "Except for *Dat.*"

Mamm nodded slowly. "Trey was there when I needed him, and I was really upset today. I was afraid I might lose your *bruder* like I lost your *dat.*"

"You call him by his first name now?" Lillian struggled to understand her mother's sudden attitude change toward this man.

"*Ya,*" she said slowly. "Trey is *mei freind*, and we

call our friends by their first names. But he's only *mei freind*, no matter what *Mammi* says."

Lillian understood her mother's words, but she wasn't convinced the hug was merely innocent or without repercussions. "*Mammi* says people may make assumptions about you because of what you did. I don't want you to be shunned."

Mamm took Lillian's hands in hers. "Lily, I don't want you to worry about this. I haven't done anything to be ashamed of. Your *mammi* is entitled to her opinion, but I disagree with her. We need to respect our elders, but that doesn't mean we have to agree with everything they say. We can silently and respectfully disagree." She glanced at the clock on her nightstand. "It's late. You really should go to bed so you're ready to teach in the morning."

"Okay." Lillian stood. "Who was your *onkel* Elam? I don't remember hearing about him."

"*Mei onkel* Elam was married to *mei aenti* Sarah. I was told he died before I was born, but your *mammi* says that isn't true. She said he divorced *Aenti* Sarah and married an *Englisher*." She shook her head. "I have no idea if that's true, but I'll ask my cousin Susan at church on Sunday. Since she's older than I am, I imagine she'd know the truth."

"*Ach*." Lillian fingered her nightgown. "Why would *Mammi* bring that up today?"

Her mother frowned. "I'm certain *Mammi* is concerned I'm going to wind up like *Onkel* Elam."

"What do you mean?"

"She thinks I'm going to run away with Trey."

Alarm gripped Lillian as her eyes widened. "Do you want to run away with him?"

"No." *Mamm* spoke with emphasis. "Do me a favor, Lily. Don't believe everything your *mammi* says about me. Please always give me the benefit of the doubt." She tapped the comforter. "I want to stay right here on this farm with you and your siblings. This is my home. Do you understand me?"

"*Ya.* I understand."

"*Gut nacht.*" Her mother yawned. "You better get to bed."

"I will. *Gut nacht.*"

Lillian climbed the stairs to her room while thinking about everything that had occurred today. She'd gone from worrying about Andrew to confusion about her mother's public display of what seemed like affection for Mr. Peterson, even though her mother said he was only a *freind*. She needed someone to talk to so she could sort through all of the confusing feelings coursing through her. She hadn't gotten a chance to talk to Amanda and tell her everything that had happened.

She quickened her pace as she reached the top step and hurried to their room at the end of the hall. She pushed the door open and looked over at the bed.

Lillian frowned when she found Amanda snoring and lying on her side facing the door. She considered waking her up, but she knew it was best to just let her twin sleep. She'd once awoken Amanda to tell her about a strange dream. Instead of being interested in the contents of the dream, Amanda fussed at her, saying it had taken her more than an hour to fall asleep.

Lillian crawled into bed and snuggled down under the quilt. She said her prayers and then stared at the ceiling while listening to the rhythmic sound of her twin's snoring. She wished she too could fall asleep and forget everything that had happened today. She wanted to believe that everything would be okay. Yet she knew deep in her heart that nothing would be okay. This was only the beginning.

TWELVE

Lillian waved as each of the children filed out of the schoolhouse on Friday afternoon.

Mattie Smucker, the full-time teacher, walked from the doorway toward her desk. "It was a *gut* day, *ya*?" At the age of nineteen, she stood at five-foot-six, just an inch taller than Lillian, with light brown hair and brown eyes.

"*Ya.*" Lillian gathered up the stack of books from the desks and placed them in the bookshelf. "The scholars are so bright. I love watching them figure out a math problem. There's nothing more rewarding than helping a *kind* learn something new. And they never give up. They soak up new ideas like little sponges."

"*Ya*, they do." Mattie smiled. "I have a secret."

"*Ach!* Tell me!" Lillian moved to the front of the classroom and sat on one of the desks in the first row. She folded her hands over her apron.

Mattie ran her finger over the desk. "Can you keep my secret?"

"*Ya!* I can! I'm bursting at the seams. Please tell me."

Mattie bit her lower lip. "Stephen asked me to marry him last week. I've been dying to tell you."

"*Ach!*" Lillian hopped down from the desk and rushed over to Mattie. "That's *wunderbaar*! I'm so *froh* for you." She hugged Mattie. "You must be so excited."

"*Ya*, I am." Mattie sighed. "Stephen is so sweet and kind. And handsome." Her ivory cheeks flushed bright pink. "I met with the school board members last night, and I told them I won't be returning to teach in the fall." She paused. "What do you think about becoming the full-time teacher?"

Lillian's eye widened. "Do you think they might consider me?"

"Absolutely!" Mattie gestured toward the desks. "The scholars love you! You've seen how they ask you to join their baseball games outside, and they bicker about who gets to sit next to you when we eat our lunch on the playground. You'd be a *wunderbaar* teacher."

"But you know most teacher's assistants go to work full-time at a school in another district. Do you think they'd consider letting me teach here?"

"Oh, *ya*, I do think they would consider you." Mattie nodded. "You've been the assistant here for a year, and you know teachers are hard to find. We can talk to them together and explain that you want to stay here. I'll put in a *gut* word for you, and you know the scholars will too. You're the best teacher's assistant I've had since I started teaching here three years ago. You're patient with the *kinner*, but you're also firm when necessary. I think you'll do an excellent job."

"*Danki*. I would love to do it." Lillian couldn't prevent the smile from spreading across her face. It had been her dream to become a teacher ever since she was a little girl. She couldn't wait to run her own classroom.

"We better get going. Chores await us at home." Mattie started for the door. "I'll see you Sunday at church."

"Okay. Bye." Lillian grabbed her bag and headed out the door. As she walked up the street toward her farm, she grinned. Maybe her dream of becoming a teacher would come true after all. She couldn't wait to tell her mother and Amanda the news! Amanda worked until the late afternoon at the deli today, but her mother would be home.

Lillian rushed toward the farm and into the house, where her brother sat at the table eating a snack and her mother stood at the sink washing baking dishes.

"Hi, Lily." *Mamm* looked up from washing a pan. "How was your day?"

"*Wunderbaar!*" Lillian dropped her bag on a kitchen chair.

"Here." Andrew pushed a plate of oatmeal raisin cookies toward her. "Have some *kichlin*. They're my favorite. *Mamm* made them fresh for us."

"*Danki.*" Lillian picked up a cookie and bit into it. "They're *appeditlich*. They're still warm, which is just how I like them."

Mamm smiled. "I'm *froh* you like them. Now tell us why your day was so *wunderbaar*."

Lillian sat in a chair next to Andrew while she finished the cookie. "I'm going to tell *Mamm* something, and you need to keep it to yourself. Understand, Andrew?"

"It's a secret?" He grinned. "I like secrets."

Lillian leaned over toward him and leveled her eyes with his. "The question is—do you like *keeping* secrets?"

He nodded and then gestured as if to lock his mouth with a key.

"*Gut bu.*" She patted his shoulder and then looked at her mother. "Mattie told me she won't be returning as teacher next year."

Her mother raised her eyebrows.

"Is she getting married?" Andrew's words were distorted by a mouthful of cookie.

"Andrew!" *Mamm* raised her eyebrows. "Take smaller bites, and don't talk with your mouth full."

"Well?" Andrew wiped his mouth on a napkin. "Is she getting married? Our last teacher, Lydia, left to get married."

Lillian smiled. "*Ya*, she's getting married."

"How exciting!" Her mother clapped her hands. "I bet she was bubbling over when she told you."

"Oh *ya*. She was." Lillian picked up another cookie from the plate. "I was thinking of talking to the board about becoming the teacher."

"I'm not surprised to hear you say that. When you were six, you told me you wanted to be a teacher."

Lillian gasped. "I remember that! That was the second day of school. I came running home and told you I knew what I wanted to be when I grew up—a teacher and a *mamm*."

"That's right. And I told you that you had to be a teacher first since mothers can't teach because they have too much to do at home."

Lillian laughed.

"That's very true." Andrew held up a cookie and gestured with it. "If you were a teacher, *Mamm*, there wouldn't be anyone here to make my snack on the days Lily is working."

Mamm sat across from them at the table and nodded. "You'll be a magnificent teacher, Lillian. That is a fabulous idea-—for you to try to get the job."

"Will my teaching work with your schedule, since you work three days a week?"

"Of course it will. Andrew will be older, and he will have *Onkel* Josh and Daniel at the *haus*. He'll be just fine." *Mamm* turned to Andrew. "You can handle walking home to Joshua if Lillian has to stay later, right?"

Andrew nodded. "*Ya*, I can handle it."

"*Wunderbaar.*" Lillian looked at her brother. "You can't tell anyone about this discussion. I don't think Mattie wants her engagement blurted around the community yet."

He glowered at her. "I said I won't tell anyone. You don't have to keep reminding me."

"I agree you should talk to a member of the school board about it." *Mamm* took a cookie.

"But should I wait until a formal school board meeting to ask them?" Lillian tapped the table. "I don't know if I should do it before the end of the school year."

"You should tell them soon. They have to plan for next year since Mattie already gave notice. You could approach one of the board members at church and show your interest. Tell one of them you'd like to look for a full-time teaching position and see if they have any thoughts on it. Be sure to tell them you love teaching and would like to be considered for a position in the future."

"Okay. I'll do that." Lillian's stomach tightened at the thought of becoming a teacher. Her goal might be within reach soon.

. . .

That same afternoon, Amanda sat on the bench outside the back of the deli and bowed her head in silent prayer. She then placed her lunchbox on her lap and pulled out her turkey sandwich. The warm sunlight kissed her cheeks, and she smiled as a bird sang in a tree nearby. *It's the perfect spring day.*

"Beautiful day, huh?" a voice asked.

Amanda turned and found Mike standing behind the bench. "Hi, Mike. I didn't hear you come out. How did you find me?"

He pointed toward the back door leading into the deli. "Nancy told me you were out here." He placed his hand on the back of the bench. "Is it okay if I sit with you for a couple of minutes?"

"Of course." Amanda moved to the far end of the bench and then smoothed her apron and dress. She hoped her prayer covering and hair were straight. "How are you?"

"I'm fine." Mike smiled. "How are you?"

"Fine. I haven't seen you for almost a week. Have you been busy?"

"Yeah, I have." He frowned. "I'm struggling in one

of my science classes, which isn't good for a hopeful med student."

"Oh." Amanda wished she could talk in depth with him about school, but she had no knowledge or experience when it came to high school science classes. "I hope it works out for you."

"Thanks." He crossed his ankles and she stared down at his fancy-looking sneakers. "I'm working with a tutor, and he's really good. I have a big test coming up next week. I'm hoping I do well on the test and I can pull off a B in the class, which is much better than a D. I can't have a D on my high school record. It'll hurt my chances at a decent scholarship."

Amanda nodded slowly while holding the sandwich in her hand. She didn't know anything about grades or scholarships, and she hoped he didn't think she was stupid.

He pointed toward the sandwich. "Please, go ahead and eat. I don't want to interrupt your lunchtime."

"It's okay." She took a small bite and then sipped her cup of water. "Have you eaten?"

He shook his head. "I'm going to pick up something on my way home."

"You got out of school early today?"

"Yeah. It was a half day."

"Oh." She wondered what his day at school was like. He'd once mentioned he had different teachers throughout the day, which was a foreign concept to Amanda. It sounded like a lot of running from room to room. How did the scholars keep up with such a busy schedule? And then they graduated and went to college, which sounded even more busy and stressful. She pulled herself from her thoughts and found him watching her. "Are you excited about college?"

"Yes, I am." He gazed off toward the trees. "I can't wait to be on my own. I mean, I love my family, but it will be nice to be independent. Sometimes I get tired of my parents telling me what to do, where to go, and what time to be home. I'm ready to figure things out for myself, you know?"

Amanda shrugged. "I guess so."

"I guess life is different for you."

"It is. We normally stay close to our families and help them out. Most young people don't move out of their parents' house until they're married. Some married couples live with one set of parents until they can build a house of their own. And then they build on their parents' property."

He chuckled. "That's a lot of togetherness."

"It is." She paused for a moment while considering the differences between their lives. "I often wonder what it would be like to be in your shoes and go to college."

"You do?" He raised his eyebrows.

"*Ya*, I do. I've always wondered what it would be like to be a veterinarian. We have one who lives across from our farm. He comes over whenever one of the animals is sick. I've watched him work, and I'm fascinated. I would love to work with animals all day. I could help the ones that are sick. It would be so rewarding." She chewed the side of her lip when she realized it was the first time she'd admitted out loud that she wanted to experience life beyond what her community permitted. Both relief and guilt soaked through her.

"Wow. That would be amazing if you could become a vet." Mike shook his head. "But you can't, can you?"

She sighed. "It's a dream, but I know I can't do it for real. I'm not allowed to go to college."

"Because it's against your community's rules."

She nodded slowly. "*Ya*, but you're the first person I've told." She leaned in closer to him and lowered her voice. "What would I have to do if I wanted to go to college? Hypothetically, of course."

"Hypothetically?" He tapped the back of the bench behind her. "Well, that sort of depends on a few things. Do you have a high school diploma?"

She shook her head. "Not really. The Amish only go to school through the eighth grade."

"Oh, then you don't have a high school diploma. You'd have to get your GED before you could apply to college."

"GED?" She tilted her head. "What's that?"

"A GED is like a high school diploma. I can't remember what the acronym stands for, but it's considered a high school equivalency. It's like you went to high school without suffering through the four horrible years of torture."

She looked up at him and wished her face would stop burning. "High school is torture?"

"I'm kidding, but some of it was pretty awful. Like the endless nights of homework."

Amanda pulled a Ziploc bag of chocolate chip cookies from her lunchbox and handed him one.

"Thanks," he said.

"You're welcome. My sister made these yesterday." She thought about the GED and more questions filled her mind. "What would I need to do if I wanted to earn a GED? Again, I'm only asking hypothetically."

"You'd have to get this huge catalog-size book, study a lot, and take a test." He finished the cookie and wiped his hands together. "My older brother's friend got his GED last year. He said he had to study pretty hard, but he was really excited when he did it. Because he got his GED, he was able to get a better job with a bigger salary."

Amanda handed him another cookie. "Thanks. These cookies are fantastic. How is this—hypothetically, of course—going to be possible when the Amish aren't allowed to go to school beyond eighth grade?" he asked.

"It's okay if I go before I'm baptized, but if I do something like that after I'm baptized, I'll be shunned."

"Shunned? Wow. That's harsh." He shook his head. "I guess it's not something you really want to do then. You wouldn't want to risk being shunned, right?"

Amanda shook her head, but she wasn't really certain if she wanted to be baptized. She didn't want to lose her family, but she also wasn't sure the Amish life was right for her. She finished her sandwich and then started to eat a cookie. "Did you talk to your uncle about the job at his bookstore?"

"Yeah." He faced her. "I haven't had a chance to tell you I got the job. He hired me full-time for the summer." He nodded toward the cookies. "Would it be okay if I had another one?"

"*Ya*, of course." She handed him the bag. "My sister is a really good baker and cook."

"I bet you are too." He palmed another cookie.

Amanda shrugged. "I'm not as good at my mom and sister. So tell me about the test you have to study for."

While Mike explained his science class, Amanda considered what he'd told her about getting her GED. She wondered if she was smart enough to do it and what her *mamm* would say.

THIRTEEN

Trey bowed his head for a prayer and then flipped to the appropriate page in the songbook for the service's closing hymn. He glanced around the sanctuary and found it nearly jam-packed. He was so glad he'd decided to come to the service at Paradise Community Church.

He'd been greeted with smiles and hellos when he entered the sanctuary before the service, and he'd shaken many hands during the sharing of the peace, when members of the congregation greet each other with a handshake during the service. The congregation appeared to be warm and welcoming, which was just what he craved. And he'd enjoyed the service too. It reminded him of the services at his church back home.

Throughout the service, Trey had thought of Hannah and wondered what she was doing today. He knew that the Amish worshiped formally together every other week. Was she also at a church service today?

Hannah had haunted his thoughts, both day and night, ever since Wednesday. He couldn't forget the fear in her eyes when they'd rushed to her house to check on Andrew. He felt her worry while they sat together in the car, and he'd wished he could take the burden off her shoulders. He'd longed to help her. He'd prayed for Andrew while Hannah was in the bedroom with him. He'd hoped it was just a minor injury and nothing more.

Trey had sensed her relief when she'd returned from her bedroom, and he was stunned by the way she'd opened up to him, cried, and let him hold her. Their embrace was overwhelming. He'd pulled her close and drank in the sweet smell of her lilac shampoo. Having her next to his heart felt natural, familiar—as if he'd held her before. He didn't want to let go, but he also knew that getting attached to her would put him on a road to heartbreak.

As much as Trey wanted to have Hannah in his life, he knew he couldn't. They were from different worlds. Yet, he found himself wishing and praying they could be together. He'd love to see her sitting next to him in church. He would enjoy having her help as he planned the bed and breakfast. He couldn't give up the dream of being her friend—and possibly even more.

The congregation finished singing the last stanza of the hymn, and the minister closed with announcements and then the benediction prayer. As Trey placed the hymnal back into the pocket shelf in front of him, he wondered again what Hannah was doing. He hoped he'd see her soon.

· · ·

After service on Sunday, Hannah searched the sea of faces in the kitchen for her cousin Susan. She had to find out the truth about their uncle Elam, and she knew Susan would hold the key. As she walked past a group of women, her mother-in-law frowned and then turned her back. Hannah kept walking, hoping to see Susan.

She found her cousin standing with another group of women. She smiled and nodded at a few friends as she approached, and they each hesitated before returning the greeting. Hannah wondered why they didn't return the gesture immediately, but she pushed the thought away as she reached Susan.

"Susan." Hannah smiled at her cousin. "*Wie geht's?*"

"Oh, hi, Hannah." Susan cleared her throat. "I'm fine. How are you?" She was standing with two other women, who each stared at Hannah before walking away.

Hannah shook her head. "I feel as if my prayer *kapp* is missing or my cape is on backward today. It's as if everyone I talk to stares at me like there's something wrong with me. I don't understand it. What could I have possibly done for everyone in the entire district to stare at me?" Hannah hoped it had nothing to do with Trey.

Susan grimaced. "You really don't know why?"

"No, I don't." Hannah studied her face. "You *do* know why?"

Susan touched her arm. "Let's find somewhere to talk."

Hannah followed her outside where they walked down the porch steps. They made their way toward the line of buggies parked by the pasture and then stopped. "What's all this about, Susan?"

Her cousin frowned. "A rumor has been flying through the community about you. I don't know who started it, but people are saying you were seen embracing an *Englisher* man the other day." She glowered. "I refuse to believe a word of it. We've been close since we were kids, Hannah. I know you would never behave that way."

Hannah shook her head. She knew it was inevitable, but she didn't think it would happen so quickly. "I wouldn't be surprised if Barbie started that rumor."

"What do you mean?"

"I've become *freinden* with a man who's staying at the hotel. Andrew fell and hurt himself on Wednesday. Lillian called me to tell me that it looked really bad. He had a gash above his eye, and there was blood everywhere. It was so bad Lillian couldn't tell where he was cut. I had to get home immediately, and *mei freind* gave me a ride home. I had no other means of transportation, and I was desperate. I was really upset and worried about Andrew."

"He only gave you a ride?" Susan clicked her tongue. "I see no harm in that. I wonder why people would spread such nasty rumors. If she's lying about you, then you should go to the bishop."

"It's not that simple." Hannah paused. "We hugged before he left my farm."

"What?" Susan raised her eyebrows. "Why would you hug him?"

"I was really emotional. Every injury and illness

worries me after losing Gideon. I was thankful Andrew's injury was minor. I was so scared after seeing all of that blood on his clothes, on the rags, and in his hair. It looked much worse than it was. After I released all of that worry and stress, I needed a hug."

"Why would you hug an *Englisher* you barely know, Hannah? That doesn't make sense to me."

"I don't know. It just felt right at the time, and I don't regret it." Hannah shrugged. "Honestly, it doesn't make much sense to me either."

Susan eyed Hannah. "Do you think you need to talk to someone? Maybe you should meet with the bishop and tell him you're having feelings you don't understand. He can counsel you on how to turn your heart back to God so you don't have feelings like this again."

"It's not like that. My friend understands me better than other people do. He's lost his *fraa* and his *dochder*, and we can each relate to the grief and loss the other has faced."

"There are other people in this district who have had to cope with loss and grief. You don't need to go to an *Englisher* about things like that."

"Now you sound like Barbie."

"I know you've had problems with Barbie in the past, but I think she's right about this." Susan's frown softened. "You need to be careful. If Barbie started these rumors about you, you know where that will lead. Rumors like this led to Irma Yoder's shunning a couple of years ago. She had to confess her transgressions in front of the whole church. You don't want to do that, do you? Her *kinner* were mortified."

"I know." Hannah nodded. "I actually wanted to talk to you about something else. Barbie told me something about *Onkel* Elam, and I wanted to ask you if it was true. You were closer to *Aenti* Sarah than I was."

"What do you want to know?"

"Did he really divorce *Aenti* Sarah, leave the community, and marry someone else?"

Susan nodded. "*Ya*, it's true."

Hannah gasped as if the wind had been knocked out of her. "Why didn't my parents ever tell me the truth?" She pointed at Susan. "Why didn't you tell me?"

"I thought you knew. Actually, I thought everyone knew. No one ever talked about it publicly."

"Who told you?"

"*Mei mamm* did." She leaned against the buggy behind her. "I think I was about sixteen or so. I asked her why *Aenti* Sarah didn't remarry after *Onkel* Elam died because she was so *bedauerlich*. I told her I knew another widow who had remarried and that I felt bad *Aenti* Sarah was so alone. *Mei mamm* told me *Aenti* Sarah didn't remarry because *Onkel* Elam was alive, and she felt it would be wrong. She explained he'd left *Aenti* Sarah and married an *Englisher* woman who had visited his shoe shop. She was so heartbroken she couldn't get out of bed for nearly two months after he left."

Hannah shook her head. "I don't understand why *mei mamm* never told me."

"Why are you asking about this now?"

"Barbie told me Wednesday that *Onkel* Elam's situation caused a lot of pain in the community. She said the family went through a lot, and she never wanted that for her family. She implied I'm going to leave the community and cause pain and rumors too."

Susan shook her head. "What *Onkel* Elam did has nothing to do with any of us." She frowned. "But you need to be careful, Hannah. Everyone will be watching you now."

"I know."

Susan touched Hannah's arm. "I need to get back inside, but I'll be thinking of you. Let me know if you need someone to talk to. You can always come to me instead of your *Englisher freind*."

"I appreciate the offer. *Danki* for telling me the truth." As Hannah watched Susan march back toward the house, loneliness stole into her. She knew Susan would listen if Hannah needed her to, but deep in her heart she believed that only Trey would truly understand her. She wanted to talk to Trey more than anyone in her community.

. . .

Lillian's hands shook as she approached Elizabeth Beiler, who was married to a member of the school board. Elizabeth was sitting with her sister. Lillian folded her hands in front of her apron. "Hi, Elizabeth. May I please speak to you for a moment?"

"Lillian." She patted the place on the bench beside her. "Have a seat."

Lillian sat and heaved a deep breath. *Please, Lord, guide my words.* "I wanted to talk to you about the school."

"Oh." Elizabeth glanced over at her sister. "Would you mind getting me another cup of water?"

"I'd be happy to. I'll be right back." She stood up from the bench and walked to the kitchen.

"What would you like to discuss?" Elizabeth turned toward Lillian. "Are things going well in the school?"

"Oh, *ya*. Things are going wonderfully." Lillian nodded. "In fact, I'd like to be considered for full-time teacher. Mattie shared that she won't be returning next year. It's always been my dream to be a full-time teacher. I love the scholars, and I think they like me too."

"Oh." Elizabeth's smile faded. "That's very sweet, Lillian."

"I'll work hard. I'll put my heart and soul into the job." She couldn't understand why Elizabeth was frowning. Was Lillian not saying the right words, or had they already hired someone else? "Did you already hire another teacher to replace Mattie?"

Elizabeth shook her head. "No, the board hasn't chosen another teacher yet."

Lillian folded her hands as if she were praying. "Please give me a chance to talk to the board and tell them how much this means to me. I'll do my very best."

"I'm sorry, but I don't know if it would be a *gut* idea for you to talk to the board."

"Oh." Lillian cleared her throat, hoping to stop the lump forming there from swelling. "Do they have someone else in mind?"

Elizabeth shook her head, and Lillian stared at her.

"Have I done something wrong?" Lillian's voice quavered.

"No, Lillian, you haven't done anything wrong." Elizabeth shook her head. "From what Mattie has told us, you're a wonderful teacher, and the scholars love you. But I think there may be some board members who are concerned about an issue with your family."

"I don't understand. What has my family done?"

"There has been some concern about your *mamm's* behavior lately." Elizabeth's smile didn't seem genuine. "I will mention your interest to my husband, but I'm not certain he will want to consider you. I think they may have to look for another full-time teacher." She patted Lillian's hand. "But *danki* for expressing your interest." Her sister approached and handed Elizabeth a cup of water.

Lillian stood and studied Elizabeth. She hadn't expected to get the job on the spot, but she'd never expected to be rejected so quickly, either. "*Danki* for your time."

"*Gern gschehne*. Have a *gut* day." Elizabeth turned to her sister and began discussing her children.

Lillian walked out the back door and moved toward the group of young people playing volleyball. In a matter of minutes, she'd watched her dream shatter in front of her eyes, and she was left reeling. She needed to find a way to change the school board's opinion of her. What was the community saying about her *mamm*, and what could Lillian do to remedy it?

FOURTEEN

Amanda sat on the backless bench between Nancy and Lillian during the hymn singing later that evening. The benches were set up in Nancy's family's barn with the young men on one side of the room and the young women on the other. Amanda glanced across the barn and spotted Leroy King staring at them. She elbowed her sister in the ribs.

"Ouch!" Lillian leaned closer to Amanda. "What was that for?"

"Guess who's watching you?" Amanda waggled her eyebrows. "I think someone likes you."

"Who?"

"Leroy King." Amanda nodded in the direction of the young men. "He's been staring at you."

Lillian looked toward the young men and then buried her face in the hymnal. "I can't believe he's watching me."

"Looks like your feelings are mutual, *ya*?" Amanda smiled.

"You think so?" Lillian's eyes were round, making her seem younger.

"*Ya*, I do." Amanda was used to her sister appearing to be determined and certain of herself. *She must really like him!*

Nancy leaned over and raised her eyebrows. "What are you two whispering about?"

"Leroy King is watching Lillian." Amanda nodded toward the young men. "I think he likes her."

Nancy looked toward the other side of the barn. "Interesting. He's watching her now."

Lillian glowered. "Will you two stop being so obvious?"

"Shh!" Someone hissed a few rows in front of them.

Amanda scanned the rows of young men across the barn and found Manny Kauffman looking in the direction of Nancy. "Manny is watching you too. I think you and *mei schweschder* both have admirers."

"*Ach*, I see him. I think you may be right. I was hoping the smile he gave me earlier was special." Nancy continued to lean into Amanda. "We need to find someone for you now."

"Don't be *gegisch*." Amanda shrugged. "I'm fine by myself."

"You're the one being *gegisch*. There's someone here for you. You're just not looking." Nancy smiled.

Amanda had been contemplating the conversation she shared with Mike and wondering what it would be like to get her GED. Was she intelligent enough to pass the test? And if she passed, could she get into college? She doubted she could afford to go to college, but she could find out what it took to obtain a scholarship. And what would she study if she went to college, besides what would be necessary to become a vet? The possibilities seemed endless!

She longed to borrow a study guide from the library just to look at it, but she thought her *mamm* would never understand her curiosity. And she knew Lily wouldn't since she already seemed set in her ways and satisfied with the Amish lifestyle. Amanda, however, couldn't stop the questions from swirling in her mind.

Amanda looked toward the opposite side of the barn and spotted Leroy as he got up and headed toward the exit. He turned back toward them before he left.

Lillian stood. "I'm going to go to the bathroom." She quickly weaved through the row of young women and then slipped out the door.

"Where's she going?" Nancy asked.

"I think she's going to meet Leroy. I saw him leave just before she did."

Nancy grinned. "*Gut* for her."

"*Ya.*" Amanda stared down at the hymnal.

. . .

Lillian's heart pounded in her chest as she made her way through the barn door to where Leroy stood waiting for her. She touched her prayer covering and pushed the ribbons past her shoulders. "Hi, Leroy."

"Hi." He nodded toward a grassy area located past a second barn. "Want to go for a walk?"

"*Ya.*" Lillian gripped her sleeves as she fell into step with Leroy. "It's a nice evening, *ya*?"

"It is." When they reached the grassy area, he stopped and motioned toward the ground. "Want to sit?"

"*Ya*." Lillian sank onto the cool grass and smoothed her dress over her legs. The sky above her was streaked with orange, yellow, and red. "Look at that sunset. Isn't it *schee*?"

"*Ya*, it is." He smiled at her.

She silently admired his brown eyes and hair. She lost herself in the moment, and the confusion about her conversation with Elizabeth Beiler disappeared. She turned her eyes toward the pond and studied the dark water while she wondered how she'd handle the situation with the school. She wanted the teaching job more than anything, but she didn't know how to talk to her *mamm* about the community's perception of her. How could she bring herself to tell her *mamm* what Elizabeth had said without upsetting her?

"You seem distracted tonight. Is something wrong?" Leroy's question broke through her thoughts.

She picked up a smooth stone and rolled it between her fingers while she contemplated telling him what was on her mind. She longed to share with him what Elizabeth Beiler had said, but she worried he'd look down on her and not want to be her friend anymore.

"You don't have to tell me, Lily. I'll understand if it's too personal."

"No, I'll tell you." Lillian cleared her throat. "I talked to Elizabeth Beiler earlier after the church service. She's married to a member of the school board."

He nodded. "I know."

She picked up another stone. "I wanted to find out

how I can put my name in the running for a full-time teaching position."

He raised his eyebrows. "Did Stephen finally ask Mattie to marry him?"

"*Ya*, he did. But please don't tell anyone. I'm not supposed to tell. Mattie told me a few days ago." She tossed the stones and then wiped her palms together. "It's always been my dream to be the full-time teacher."

"That's great."

She frowned. "I don't think it's going to happen."

"Why not? Have they already found another teacher?"

"No. I wish it were that simple."

"I'm sorry, Lily, but I'm not following you. What happened?" He bent his knees and folded his arms over them.

"Elizabeth said that although I'm a *gut* teacher's assistant, I probably won't be considered for the full-time job because the community is concerned about *mei mamm's* behavior." She sniffed as her eyes filled with tears. "I'm so upset, and I'm also confused. I don't understand why the community is concerned about *mei mamm*. What could she possibly have done? She's doing her best to take care of my siblings and me."

Leroy grimaced, which caused Lillian to become suspicious.

She angled her body toward him. "Leroy, do you know something about it?"

He shrugged and looked toward the meadow. "I don't know."

"Leroy." She faced him. "If you know something, you have to tell me. I can't fix the problem if I don't know what it is."

He looked down at his lap. "All I know is what I've heard, but I don't know if it's true."

"What is it?" She folded her hands as if to plead with him. "Please tell me. You don't have to tell me who said it, but I need to know what it is so I can clear *mei mamm's* name and clean up this mess before it gets worse."

He frowned at her. "A rumor is going around that your *mamm* is having a relationship with an *Englisher*."

Lillian's mouth fell open in shock. How had the community found out about what happened on Wednesday? She then gasped when she realized her *mammi* had witnessed the scene. *Is* Mammi *spreading the rumor about* Mamm? "Do you know who's spreading the rumor?" She wanted to know after all.

"I don't know." He paused and then shook his head. "*Mei bruder* Daniel said he saw your *mamm* hugging the *Englisher*, but I'm the only person he told."

"Are you certain he didn't tell anyone else?"

Leroy nodded. "He's afraid he'll lose his job at your place if the word gets around. He likes the job and the salary, so he's worried my parents will make him quit. He told me last night after he found out the rumor was spreading through the community."

Lillian ran her hand over her face while the severity of the situation gripped her. "It must've been *mei mammi* who told everyone."

"What do you mean?"

"She was there beside me when it happened."

Leroy's eyes widened. "You witnessed it too?"

"*Ya.*" Lillian explained what had happened. She told him that Andrew was injured, Mr. Peterson had brought her mother home, and they hugged before he left. She also shared the conversation she'd had with her mother later that evening.

He shook his head. "I know Daniel didn't tell anyone what he saw because he doesn't want to lose his job, but the word has spread quickly. I don't mean to be disrespectful, but people are frowning on your *mamm's* behavior."

"I think it was *mei mammi* who started the rumors." Lillian wished she could stop the tears from streaming down her hot cheeks, but she couldn't. "I'm so upset and confused. *Mei mamm* says Mr. Peterson is only her *freind*, but she looks at him as if she feels more than friendship for him. Now that rumors are spreading, I don't know what to do. I don't want to upset *mei mamm*, but if I don't say anything, it will only get worse."

"I'm sorry you're going through this." Leroy scowled. "I wish I could help you, but it seems like this is something only your *mamm* can fix."

Lillian sniffed and wiped her eyes. "You're right. *Mei mamm* has to fix it."

"I think your *mamm* would want to know what people are saying about her. Then she'll have to decide what to do. Maybe she needs to talk to the bishop and ask for his help clearing her name."

They both were silent for a moment.

He turned his gaze toward the sunset in the west. "Look at those colors. Aren't they spectacular?"

She looked up at the sky, which was a mosaic of bright colors that seemed to mock her glum mood. "*Ya*, they are."

She glanced over at him and swallowed a frown. If the rumors continued and the members of the community turned their backs on her *mamm*, she might lose a chance at being Leroy's girlfriend. She had to find a way to make things right. Her job and her relationship with Leroy depended on it.

FIFTEEN

Later that evening, Amanda climbed out of the buggy behind Lillian. They stood at the bottom of the rock driveway leading to their house.

Amanda waved at Nancy and her brother, Joe, in the driver's seat. "*Danki* for the ride! See you tomorrow, Nancy."

"*Danki*," Lillian called before they started up the long driveway.

Amanda grinned at her. She'd wanted to find out about Lillian's private conversation with Leroy, but she didn't want to ask in front of Nancy and Joe during the ride home and embarrass her.

"Is there a reason you insisted on having Joe drop us off here?" She bumped Lillian with her hip. "Did you want to talk to me in private and tell me about your conversation with Leroy?"

"I do want to talk to you in private, but it isn't really about Leroy."

When her twin frowned, Amanda stopped and faced her. "Is something wrong, Lily?"

Lillian nodded. "*Ya.*"

Amanda's eyes widened as Lillian shared the painful

conversation she'd had with Elizabeth Beiler. "Why did she say there are concerns about *Mamm*?"

"Leroy told me why." Lillian took a deep breath. "*Mamm* hugged Mr. Peterson Wednesday after he brought her home when Andrew was injured. The rumor is now going around the community that *Mamm* is having an inappropriate relationship with an *Englisher*."

"You're joking, right?" Amanda tried to laugh, but her sister's bleak expression told her it was no laughing matter. "I can't believe it. This is outrageous, Lily." She shook her head. "I had no idea *Mamm* had hugged Mr. Peterson. Why didn't you tell me?"

"I should've told you, but I just couldn't bring myself to say anything. It was too confusing and painful. I talked to *Mamm* about it, and I hoped Mr. Peterson would just go away. I wanted to forget the whole scene and everything *Mammi* had said to me about him."

"Are you certain *Mammi* is the one spreading the rumors? I don't understand why she would do that. We're all family."

Lillian grimaced. "I don't think *Mammi* ever thought *Mamm* was *gut* enough for *Dat*, and I guess she wants to hurt her."

"But that goes against everything we've been taught since we were little. We're supposed to love and support each other, and she's hurting *Mamm* and us." Amanda gestured widely with her arms. "You're watching your dreams disappear because of what *Mammi* is saying about our *mamm*." She kicked a stone with the toe of her black sneaker. The irony of the situation caused frustration to surge through her. If her *mammi* was spreading rumors about her *mamm*, she was committing a sin. Her *mamm* wasn't sinning by being friends with someone outside of their community, but people were acting as if it were a sin. How was this fair?

Lillian began to walk toward the house with her expression full of determination. "I'm so upset. I have to tell *Mamm* about the rumors. This has to stop."

Amanda fell into step beside her, their feet crunching their way up the rock driveway. "Maybe she can talk to the school board and help you get the job or something." She felt like she was clutching at vague possibilities. She knew her *mamm* would probably have to apologize to the church body to stop the rumor mill, but she didn't want to see her humiliated for having a friend.

"That's a *gut* idea. I'll ask her to help me get the job." Lillian stopped at the bottom porch step and her expression was full of anger. "I don't understand why *Mamm* hugged Mr. Peterson. She had to have known there would be consequences. If she hadn't hugged him, I would have a chance at getting the teaching job, and everything would be just fine. I don't understand why she did this to us."

Amanda studied her sister's smoldering green eyes. "I'm certain *Mamm* didn't mean to cause all of this. I believe the hug was innocent. She was probably upset about Andrew, and she needed a hug."

Lillian shook her head. "I don't know, Amanda. I'm starting to wonder if *Mammi* was right. Maybe *Mamm* loves Mr. Peterson and she wants to be with him."

Amanda shook her head and touched her sister's arm. "You know you don't mean that. Give *Mamm* the benefit of the doubt. Mr. Peterson is her friend."

Lillian shook her head. "I'm trying my best to give her the benefit of the doubt, but I'm really upset right now. I was humiliated after I talked to Elizabeth Beiler."

"I'm sure you were, but just calm down a minute." Amanda paused and wondered if her sister ever dreamed of having more opportunities beyond their community. "Lily, I need to ask you something before we go inside."

"What?"

"Everyone is so critical of *Mamm* having an *English freind*, but don't you ever wonder what it's like to be *English*? I mean, do you ever even have a little, tiny fleeting thought about it?"

Lillian blinked and then scrunched her nose as if she were disgusted. "No. Why would I?"

"You want to be the teacher, right?"

Lillian studied Amanda. "You already know the answer to that."

"Wouldn't you love to be even more educated than you are before you start teaching the scholars? Don't you ever wonder what it would be like to go to college?"

Lillian's eyes widened. "You're scaring me."

"I'm talking hypothetically." Amanda wished she could take back everything she'd said. She'd hoped her sister might understand her curiosity, but Lillian's shocked expression said something different. "Never mind. Forget I said anything at all." She started up the steps.

"Wait." Lillian grabbed Amanda's arm. "Are you thinking of leaving the community and going to college?"

"No. I'm only curious, and I was wondering if you were too. There's a whole big world out there, and sometimes I wonder about it."

Lillian's eyes remained wide. "I've never considered leaving. I know what I want. I want to be the full-time teacher. I want to be baptized, and I want to marry an Amish man." She pointed toward the ground. "I want to raise a family right here in Paradise. I hope to stay in this church district with the people I've known my whole life."

Amanda nodded. *I wish I could say the same.*

Lillian raised her eyebrows and opened her mouth to speak, but the back door opening interrupted her.

Amanda swallowed the breath she was holding. She was thankful Lillian didn't have the opportunity to ask her what she wanted out of life because she knew Lillian would never comprehend her desire to go to college and become a veterinarian.

"*Maed?*" Mamm stepped out onto the porch. "Why are you standing out here? Come in."

Amanda followed her sister into the house and prayed the Lord would guide their words as they spoke to their *mamm.*

. . .

Lillian stepped into the kitchen and took a deep breath. "*Mamm*, we need to talk."

"*Ach.*" *Mamm* frowned. "From the look on your face, it must be serious."

"It is." Lillian motioned toward the table. "Would it be okay if we sat for a few minutes?"

"Of course." *Mamm* sat in a chair on one side of the table, and the twins sat across from her. "Did something happen tonight?"

Lillian glanced at Amanda and wished her sister would start the conversation. She didn't know where to begin.

"Do you want me to start?" Amanda offered.

"No." Lillian sat up straighter. "I can do this." She cleared her throat. "I took your advice and spoke to Elizabeth Beiler after the service."

Her mother smiled. "How did it go?"

"Not well at all. She told me I most likely wouldn't be considered for the position, even though I'm a *gut* assistant." Lillian shook her head. "She said there were concerns about you."

Her mother looked back and forth between the sisters. "What concerns do people have about me?"

"Leroy King and I talked tonight at the singing, and he said he knew why Elizabeth said that." Lillian's lip began to tremble with a mixture of disappointment and anger. "There are rumors spreading about you and Mr. Peterson. Apparently someone has told folks about how you hugged him on Wednesday when Andrew was injured."

"Oh, dear." *Mamm* shook her head. "I'm sorry." She paused. "I don't know why anyone would do this."

Lillian felt her expression harden. "Leroy said

Daniel saw you hug Mr. Peterson, but he didn't tell any-one since he's afraid of losing his job here. I can only imagine it was *Mammi* who told people about it. I don't know if *Onkel* Josh saw it."

"I'm so sorry, Lily." *Mamm* leaned over to touch Lillian's hand, but she pulled it out of reach. Her mother looked hurt, but she continued speaking. "I never meant to hurt you or your siblings."

"Why did you hug him?" Amanda asked.

She touched Amanda's hand. "I was upset and wor-ried about Andrew. I never thought I would lose your *dat*, but now I find myself worrying I will lose the rest of you too. I needed a friend, and Trey was there. But I never intended to hurt any of you. You know that, right?"

Lillian shook her head. "If you never meant to hurt us, then why did you hug him in public, *Mamm*? This has really made a mess for me, and I don't know what to do. What if I can't work in the school anymore because of what people are saying? That's my dream, and I may have lost it now."

Mamm blew out a deep breath. "I said I'm sorry, Lily. I would never deliberately hurt you or the rest of the family." She paused and then shook her head. "I'll make it right for you. I'll talk to the bishop. I'll tell him I made a mistake, and I'll confess in front of the con-gregation if I have to."

"No." Amanda's word was strong and loud, causing Hannah to blanch. "I'm sorry. I didn't mean to say it with such force, but I think this is ridiculous."

"What do you mean?" Lillian studied her sister. *Why is Amanda acting so* narrisch *tonight?*

"I don't think *Mamm* has done anything wrong. She was upset, and she hugged Mr. Peterson. That's all she did." Amanda tapped the table as she spoke. "But if *Mammi* is the one who is spreading rumors, she's committing a sin. Yet *Mammi* isn't in any trouble while the whole community is picking *Mamm* apart and Lillian isn't allowed to be a teacher. Why doesn't anyone see the irony here?"

Lillian glared at her sister. "We've already discussed this, Amanda. These are the rules we live by."

"Sometimes I think the rules are wrong." Amanda slumped in the chair and folded her arms.

Lillian stared at her. "What's going on with you? You've never been this outspoken before, and you've never questioned our beliefs."

Amanda studied the tabletop.

Lillian looked at her mother, who shrugged in response.

"Lily," *Mamm* began, "I'll talk to the bishop and get this all cleared up."

"Don't do it." Amanda looked up, her eyes full of determination. "Everyone will forget about it eventually. There's no reason for you to talk to the bishop and draw more attention to yourself."

Their mother looked back and forth between her daughters. "I'll do whatever Lillian wants me to do."

Lillian considered her sister's words. "Fine. Don't talk to the bishop yet. Let's wait a few weeks and see what happens. I can always apply for a teaching job in another community too. It's only May."

"That sounds *gut*." *Mamm* stood. "We'd better head to bed. Work comes early in the morning."

They said good night, and then Lillian followed her sister up to their room, where they changed and then climbed into bed. Lillian couldn't stop thinking about how different Amanda seemed. She'd never before heard her sister talking about leaving the Amish community or getting more schooling. What had happened to her twin?

"Amanda?" she whispered through the dark. "Are you still awake?"

"*Ya*."

"Is everything all right?"

"I'm fine. Why?"

Lillian rolled over and faced her sister. "You just seem different."

"I do?"

"You never used to question our rules before. Did something happen to you?"

"No, nothing has happened. I guess I'm just seeing the world differently lately. I don't think the way we live is wrong, but I also don't think it's the only right way to live."

Lillian contemplated Amanda's words for a moment. Although they made sense, they seemed unusual for Amanda.

"Lily, I'm not going anywhere. I'm just doing a lot of thinking." She paused, and her voice softened. "I don't think I'm ready to be baptized."

"It's okay." Lillian touched her sister's arm. "You don't have to rush into it. *Mamm* always said we shouldn't be baptized until we're certain."

"I hope you're not disappointed in me, but I need more time." Amanda yawned through the dark. "Get some sleep. Everything will be okay. I promise."

"*Gut nacht*." Lillian stared up toward the dark ceiling and watched the shadows transform into strange shapes.

Amanda's breathing altered to a slow and steady pattern, and soon she was snoring quietly from her side of the bed. Lillian listened to her breathing and wondered how life could change so quickly. It seemed as if only last month she was happy working as the assistant teacher and admiring Leroy King from afar. Now her mother was the subject of community rumors, her sister was wondering about college, and Leroy King was spending time talking to her alone. How could everything be so wonderful and so confusing all at the same time?

Lillian rolled onto her side facing away from her sister and closed her eyes. She sent a silent prayer up to God, asking him to guide her confusing feelings and lead her family toward the right path.

· · ·

After her daughters had disappeared up the stairs, Hannah stepped onto the back porch. She stared up at the clear, dark sky and wondered how she'd wound up in this predicament.

She'd never doubted her place in the community before, but now she found herself just a few steps away from being ostracized. Not only had friends and family stared at her and treated her differently after the church service, but now her daughter was the victim of the vicious rumors that were circling about Hannah.

And, to make matters more complicated, she was still daydreaming about Trey Peterson. Her heart warmed every time she thought of the embrace they'd shared, and she was excited about any chance to continue helping him plan the bed and breakfast. She was falling in love with him, and she was both excited and terrified to follow her strong feelings for him. How could she love a man when that love was causing problems for her precious children?

Hannah closed her eyes and sent up a silent prayer.

Lord, please help me sort through these confusing feelings. I loved Gideon with all my heart, and I was content in our life together. Now that he's gone, I'm not certain where I belong. Trey's friendship feels like a gift from you, and all that comes from you is gut. However, my relationship with him is causing problems for both me and my children. What does all of this mean? Where do you want me to belong? Please give me a sign so that I can do your will. In Jesus' holy name, amen.

She opened her eyes and heaved a deep breath. Opening up to God always gave her comfort, but tonight she was still confused. She hoped a sign would come to her soon. She couldn't deny that her feelings for Trey were growing, despite the community's negativity.

Hannah made her way back into the house and locked the door. She changed into her bedclothes and then climbed into bed. As she fell asleep, she wondered what the future would hold for her and her family.

SIXTEEN

The following Wednesday afternoon, Hannah sat with her coworkers during lunch. She smiled while Carolyn shared a story about her nephews playing in the mud before they were supposed to leave for church. She wished she could share a funny story as well. Yet her thoughts had been tied up with confusion about her feelings for Trey and her heartbreak over Lillian's problems getting the teaching job. She prayed about it every night, but the solution didn't seem obvious to her. She wondered if she was concentrating on it too much or if she was missing the answer that was right before her eyes.

After lunch, she cleaned up the table while Linda and Carolyn left to complete their chores for the afternoon.

"Hannah?" Ruth lingered in the doorway to the break room. "Are you all right?"

Hannah looked back toward Ruth. "Honestly? No, I'm not."

Ruth closed the door and gestured toward the table. "Sit. We still have a few minutes before our hour is up." They sat across from each other. "Tell me what's wrong."

"I'm confused about some things." Hannah bent her arm and rested her chin on her hand. "I've been praying about it, but the confusion hasn't gotten any better."

Ruth nodded slowly. "Is this about the *Englisher*?"

Hannah frowned. "You've heard what they're saying about me?"

"I wish I could deny it, but that would be lying." Ruth shook her head. "I heard it Sunday, and I wanted to say something to you."

"What do you think of me now?"

Ruth smiled. "You're *mei freind*, and you'll always be *mei freind*, Hannah, no matter what people say."

"Do you really feel that way?" Hannah leveled her eyes at Ruth. "You know that's not what we're taught. We're supposed to be faithful to our beliefs, and we need to rein in those who sin."

"*Ya*, that's true, but I think sometimes people forget the Scripture verse from Ephesians: 'Be kind and compassionate to one another, forgiving each other, just as in Christ God forgave you.'"

"What I did wasn't immoral, but I feel as if I'm being treated like I did something immoral."

"Did you hug the *Englisher*?"

Hannah nodded. "I did. His name is Trey, and we've become *gut freinden*. He helped me last Wednesday when my son was injured. Andrew fell and got a bad gash above his eye."

"Linda told me that you had to rush home."

Hannah explained what had happened that day, and Ruth listened. "I didn't really think it through. I hugged him because I needed someone to comfort me, and being with him feels natural. It's as if I've known him my whole life."

"The Lord puts special people in our lives when we least expect it." Ruth's smile faded. "But you know what happened will have implications in the community. Someone witnessed it and told another person. And you know how news spreads in our district."

"I know, and it's already affecting my family, especially *mei dochder* Lillian." Hannah glowered. "Lillian wants to be a teacher and has learned about a teaching opportunity. She spoke to Elizabeth Beiler about it on Sunday, and Elizabeth said the board may not consider her because of concerns about me." She studied Ruth's caring eyes, hoping to find an answer there. "I just don't know what to do. The other night I talked to *mei dochdern* about it, and I offered to go to the bishop. Amanda told me not to do it. She doesn't want to see me humiliated in front of the whole community. But Lillian is suffering over this."

"You could just talk to the bishop and promise to never see the man again."

Hannah hesitated. "I don't know if I can promise that."

Ruth's eyebrows careened toward her graying hairline. "How do you feel about this man?"

"I can't deny I care for him."

"Hannah. . ." Ruth leaned forward and lowered her voice. "You're treading on dangerous ground. I understand you're lonely, but you're looking for company in the wrong places. I'm certain there's someone in our community who has experienced a similar loss. You just haven't given it enough time."

"I wasn't looking for this, Ruth. That's what I'm trying to tell you. This has shocked me as much as it has shocked you. I always wanted to be Amish. I never doubted my future when I was *mei dochdern's* age. I was baptized with *mei freinden*, and I pledged my life to the community." Hannah paused and thought of Gideon. "When I met Gideon, I felt my life was complete. I loved him with my whole heart, and our *kinner* were our greatest blessing. I never imagined I'd feel confused about my life and about where I belong."

"You have doubts about being Amish?" Ruth grimaced.

Hannah couldn't speak for a moment. "My community is my home, and it's all I've ever known. My family and my friends are here. But I doubt I can walk away from my friendship with Trey."

"What if you're shunned? What will you do then?"

"I don't know. That's why I've been praying with my heart and soul, begging God to show me the right path."

"But where does that leave your *kinner*? They're a part of this community." Ruth tapped the table for emphasis. "Everything they know is in our church district. Are you willing to take them away from that?"

Hannah shook her head as her eyes filled with tears. "No, I'm not."

"I think you need to pray about this some more. You need to figure out what you want and what you want for your *kinner*. I don't want to see you upset anymore, but I also don't want to see your *kinner* suffer. They went through a lot when Gideon died." Ruth's expression softened. "You'll find the answer. Just be certain you're listening."

Hannah sniffed and wiped her eyes. "I never imagined I'd feel unwelcome in the community I've known my whole life. I wish *mei mamm* were still alive. I'd love to talk to her about all of this."

Ruth touched her hand. "I understand. Sometimes it seems as if only a *mamm* can fix things for us, but you can do this. Your *kinner* will look to you for guidance, and you need to be strong for them, no matter what decision you make. You know I don't want to see you leave the community. It would break my heart to see you shunned, but God will lead you toward the right path."

Hannah wiped her eyes and stood. "We better get back to work." She started for the door, and then turned back toward Ruth. "*Danki* for listening. And you know this stays between us, *ya*?"

"Of course, Hannah. Your secrets are safe with me." Ruth hugged her. "Let me know if you need to talk again."

"I will." Hannah moved to the elevator while contemplating what Ruth had said. She knew her actions affected her children, and she never wanted to hurt them. Seeing the disappointment in Lillian's eyes was too much to bear. She had to stay away from Trey to give her children the lives they deserved. Yet, she kept wondering, how could she walk away from the man who had begun to heal her broken heart?

She thought about the bishop as she stepped into the elevator. Elmer Smucker was a kind and fair man. She believed he would listen to her when she explained the incident and why she'd embraced Trey. Hopefully he'd give her the benefit of the doubt and understand she meant no harm; she'd only reacted to the stress of the incident. Surely Elmer had sinned by accident? After all, they were only human.

Hannah smiled. This seemed to be the correct solution. She could stop by to see him at his farm on her way home tonight. She would tell him she'd made a mistake, and she wanted to repent for her sins. Hannah would agree to make things right with the community and ask the bishop to talk to the school board. Then Lillian would be happy and could apply for the teaching position.

Hannah's eyes moved toward Trey's room as she stepped off the elevator on the third floor, and her heart skipped a beat. She wanted to make things right for Lillian, but it seemed an impossible task when her heart was drawn to Trey Peterson. How could she promise to deny her relationship with Trey when the relationship meant so much to her?

. . .

"You can take your lunch now, Amanda," Nancy's mother called from the other side of the deli.

Amanda smiled and waved from behind the cash register. "Okay. I'm going to walk to the Book Café."

"Can I come too?" Nancy sidled up to Amanda.

"Oh. Sure." Amanda tried to hide her disappointment with a shrug. She'd hoped to sneak over to the bookstore alone and take a look at a GED book. Her curiosity about the GED had been haunting her ever since she'd talked to Mike about it.

Nancy raised her eyebrows. "*Was iss letz?* You don't want me to come?"

"No, no. Don't be *gegisch*." Amanda waved off the comment while wondering how her best friend came to be as perceptive as her twin sister. "I'd love for you to come."

"*Mamm!*" Nancy hollered to her mother, who stood by the baked goods counter. "Amanda and I are running to the Book Café. We'll be back soon."

Her mother smiled. "Okay, but don't linger, and don't spend any money."

Amanda followed Nancy out the front door of the store, and the bright sunshine blinded her for a moment.

"What do you need at the bookstore?" Nancy squinted and turned to Amanda.

"Lily asked me to look for a certain book for her." It wasn't really a lie. Lillian had mentioned she wanted to get a Christian novel she'd seen listed in the back of the novel she was reading. "I thought I'd look today at lunch and surprise her. They have some *gut* deals on used books."

"That's nice." Nancy smiled. "I'm going to browse too. I love looking at books."

They crossed the street and walked past two other stores before reaching the bookstore. A bell above the door rang to announce their arrival. As they stepped into the store, the smell of coffee permeated Amanda's nose. She glanced toward a small café area with tables, chairs, and a food counter. The remainder of the store was crammed with shelves of books.

"Good afternoon!" Rick, the owner, called from behind the counter. "Welcome to the Book Café."

Amanda waved and then headed with Nancy over to the Christian fiction section.

Nancy began perusing the shelves. "What book is Lily looking for?"

Amanda told her the title and author.

"I love that author." Nancy pointed toward the end of the aisle. "I'll find it for you."

Amanda followed her. "I'm going to look over there, okay?"

Nancy studied the shelves in front of her, not looking up to see if Amanda had motioned where. "Take your time." She lifted a book off the shelf. "Oh, this looks *gut*. I wonder if Lily would like this too."

Amanda moved to the other end of the aisle and turned toward the front of the store. She spotted Rick standing behind the cash register alone while looking through a book. She longed to ask him about a GED preparation book, but she didn't want anyone else to know about it. She looked back at Nancy and found her flipping through a novel. Amanda had to act now, or she'd risk getting caught by Nancy.

Amanda made her way across the store and approached the counter. "Excuse me. I was wondering if I could ask you something."

Rick looked up at her and smiled. "How can I help you?"

"Do you have GED books?" Amanda tried to keep her voice just above a whisper.

"GED books?" He tilted his head. "You mean like the GED prep book you study before taking the test?"

Amanda nodded while wishing he'd keep his voice down. "*Ya*, that's it."

"I think I do have them. Let me check." He pushed some buttons on the computer. "Yes, I do. I should have three GED prep books in stock. Do you want me to get one of them for you?" He pointed toward the other side of the store. "The GED prep books are over there by the SAT books, in the reference section." He smiled at someone behind Amanda. "Hi. Can I help you?"

"No, I'm with her."

Amanda grimaced when she heard Nancy's voice. *Oh no. I've been caught.* She forced a smile. "Thank you for your help."

Rick raised his eyebrows. "Do you want me to get the book for you?"

"No, thank you." Amanda turned to Nancy, who smiled. Relief flooded her. *Oh, gut! Maybe she didn't hear Rick say, GED book" nearly a dozen times!* She looked down at the book in Nancy's hand. "Did you find Lily's book?"

"*Ya.*" Nancy handed the book to her.

"*Danki.* Are you going to get anything?"

"Not today. *Mei mamm* told me not to spend any money. She says I buy too many frivolous things. I don't think books are frivolous, but she'll tell me to go to the library instead." Nancy jerked her thumb toward the door. "We'd better get back to the deli."

Rick looked between them. "Oh, do you girls work at Fisher's Deli?"

"We do." Amanda handed him the book.

"I thought I recognized you. I love going there. You have the best baked goods and cold cuts in town." Rick grinned.

"Thank you." Nancy smiled. "I'll tell my parents you said that."

"I'm a loyal customer." Rick told Amanda the total cost for the book.

Amanda handed him the money. "Thank you." She took the bag he gave her and slipped the change into her apron pocket. She followed Nancy out to the sidewalk while thinking about the GED book and wondering if Nancy had overheard the conversation.

"What's a GED book?" Nancy's question confirmed Amanda's worries.

"It's nothing." Amanda quickened her pace. "We'd better hurry back so we have time to eat lunch."

"Wait." Nancy grabbed Amanda's sleeve and stopped her. "What are you hiding from me?" She eyed Amanda with suspicion.

"I'm not hiding anything from you."

"Then why can't you tell me what a GED prep book is?" Nancy jammed her hands on her small hips. "If you're not hiding anything, then you'll tell me."

Amanda swung the shopping bag containing the book. "It's a book you use as a study guide for the GED test."

"What's a GED test?"

"It's a test you take to get your high school equivalency."

Nancy scrunched her nose. "I don't understand."

"You take the GED in place of going to high school and getting a diploma."

"A GED is like a high school diploma?"

"*Ya*. It's like a high school diploma without going through four years of high school." Amanda remembered how Mike called it torture, and she smiled.

"What?" Nancy's eyes flew open. "Why are you smiling?"

"I was just remembering something Mike told me." Amanda bit her lip to stop her smile.

"What's going on with you, Amanda? Are you going to try to get your high school diploma?"

Amanda shrugged. "No, I'm just curious."

"You're more than just curious." Nancy's frown deepened. "You want to go to college, don't you?"

"No." Amanda slipped her hand into her apron pocket. "Well, maybe. I've been wondering what it would be like to go to college. Like I said, I'm curious."

"So you want to leave the community?"

Amanda shook her head. "I never said that."

Nancy's eyes narrowed. "I didn't want to believe what people were saying about your *mamm*, but now I'm starting to wonder if it runs in the family."

"What did you say?" Amanda glared at Nancy.

"You heard me. Everyone is talking about how your *mamm* was seen hugging an *Englisher*. I guess you'll be the next one in the family to break the rules."

Angry tears stung Amanda's eyes. "I can't believe you would say that about *mei mamm* or me. I thought you were *mei* best *freind*."

"And I thought you were mine, but *mei* best *freind* wouldn't consider going to college." Nancy spun on her heel and started back toward the deli.

Amanda wiped her eyes while watching Nancy cross the street. She stood by the crosswalk and silently debated what to do. She couldn't risk losing her job, but she also didn't want to work with Nancy if she had such low opinions of her and her mother.

Nancy turned and faced her from the other side of the street. "We need to get back to work."

Amanda crossed the street and approached her. "Are you going to tell your parents about the book?"

Nancy shook her head. "No, but I don't agree with it. And if anyone finds out, I won't be a part of it at all." Her frown softened. "I don't like what you're doing, but I know what your family has been through since you lost your *dat*. I know you need this job." She wagged a finger at her. "But if *mei mamm* finds out you want to get a high school diploma, I'm not going to lie to her if she asks me about it."

"That's fine." Amanda walked back to the store while hoping Nancy would keep her word.

. . .

Trey smiled as he made his way from his car to the hotel's front entrance. He looked up at the bright sunshine and couldn't help but think it was appropriate for his mood. Today had been a wonderful day. He'd finally made an offer on a farm, and he felt satisfied that he'd made the best choice. It was the first farm he'd looked at, the one that reminded him of his grandparents' and Hannah's places. He'd followed his realtor's advice and offered a fair but lower price than what the owners asked, and now he just had to wait and see if they would accept it. He had a strong feeling they would, and he'd be closing on his new home and future bed and breakfast at the end of the month.

He spotted Hannah exiting the hotel as he approached, and his smile widened. "Hannah!" He quickened his pace. "How are you?"

"Trey." Hannah's smile seemed more like a grimace. "I'm well. How are you?"

"I'm doing great." He tilted his head while studying her troubled eyes. She seemed sad and possibly even uncomfortable. "Is something wrong? You don't seem like yourself."

"No, no." She adjusted the large tote bag on her shoulder. "I'm just in a hurry. My ride should be here soon."

"Oh. I have some great news to share. I made an offer on a place today."

"I'm so happy for you."

He was unconvinced she was happy, but he didn't want to question her when she was in a hurry. "I also found a really nice church. I went to a service on Sunday, and the congregation was very warm and friendly."

"That's wonderful, Trey. I'm glad you're making Paradise your home."

"How's Andrew doing?" He moved closer to her, and she took a step back. Could she be the same woman who'd put her arms around him last week? What had happened to her?

"He's fine. Thank you for asking. The gash is healing well. He has some bruising around the bandage, but his headache is much better."

"Good." He wished he could take away the uneasiness in her eyes. "Hannah, what's going on? You're not yourself."

"It's complicated. I can't explain it now." She shook her head, and he was certain he spotted tears glistening in her beautiful eyes.

"So, let's talk. I can come by your place tonight."

"No." She said the word with such emphasis that he flinched. "You can't come by. I can't see you at all. In fact, if I'm seen speaking to you, it will only make things worse for my family and me."

"Make things worse?" Confusion surged through him. "What do you mean? What happened?"

She stepped closer to him, and he drank in the sweet scent of her shampoo. "Word got around that you and I hugged, and it's caused problems for my daughter and also for me. I'm going to visit the bishop on the way home and try to clear things up."

"You've got to be kidding me." He shook his head. "Nothing happened."

"In the eyes of my church, something did." She looked past him and took a step away from him. "My ride is here. I have to go. Take care, Trey. I wish you well with your new home."

A blue van pulled up to the curb and stopped. Hannah moved toward the van and opened the door.

"Wait." Trey pulled a business card from his pocket and handed it to Hannah. "Take this. My cell phone number is on it. Call me if you ever need me. Any time, day or night."

She looked at the card, and he hoped she wouldn't refuse it. He had to leave the door open to their friendship. He couldn't say good-bye and walk away from her forever.

Hannah slipped the card into her apron pocket, and he breathed a sigh of relief. "Good-bye, Trey." She climbed into the van and slammed the door.

"Good-bye," Trey whispered as the van drove off. He couldn't bring himself to accept that this was the end of their friendship. She meant too much to him, and from the pain in her eyes, he believed she cared for him too. Loneliness rushed in, drowning him.

Trey sent up a prayer begging God not to take Hannah away from him. Somehow, there had to be a way for them to continue their friendship. Only God could figure out the way for it to happen.

SEVENTEEN

Phyllis turned from the driver's seat and faced Hannah beside her. "Are you certain you don't want me to wait while you talk to the bishop?"

"There's no need for you to wait, but thank you for offering." Hannah gathered up her bag from the floor.

"Hannah." Phyllis touched Hannah's arm. "You seem upset about something. Is everything okay?"

The concern in her driver's face caused Hannah to pause. "I'm fine, but thank you. I'll see you Friday."

"All right then. Have a good evening."

"You too." Hannah climbed from the van and began her trek up the long rock path to the bishop's two-story white home. A line of red barns that served as his dairy farm stood behind the house.

She couldn't erase the memory of Trey's hurt expression from her thoughts as she made her way toward the porch steps. She could feel his concern and disappointment as she'd climbed into Phyllis's van, and her heart twisted with sharp pain.

She knew she shouldn't have accepted Trey's business card, but she wanted to keep something, a token, from their friendship. If she couldn't be his friend, at least she could remember the special times they'd shared during the past month.

Hannah climbed the steps, and her stomach tightened. She wished she'd prepared a speech before this meeting. She had no idea how to apologize for something she didn't regret. She hoped the Lord would provide the correct words so she could remove the stigma against her family, despite her own breaking heart.

After knocking on the door, Hannah cleared her throat and touched her prayer covering. She hoped she looked presentable. She'd known the bishop all of her life. In fact, he'd been the bishop since before she was born. She hoped he'd be as understanding and fair as she'd witnessed him being with other members of the district.

The door opened with a loud creak, and Elmer Smucker smiled at her. In his late seventies, Elmer was short and stocky with a long, graying beard. "Hannah. *Wie geht's?*"

"Hi, Elmer." She adjusted her bag on her shoulder. "I'm fine. How are you today?"

"Fine." He cleared his throat. "How can I help you?"

She made a sweeping gesture toward the line of rocking chairs on his wraparound porch. "I was wondering if you had a moment to talk. I promise I won't take up much of your time."

"Of course I have time. Please have a seat."

Hannah lowered herself into a rocking chair, and placed her bag on the porch beside her.

He sat in a chair next to her. "What's on your mind?"

"I've heard some rumors about me are making their way through our community. I would like the rumors to stop, and it seems I need to start with you to make things right."

"What are the rumors you're referring to?"

"People are saying I'm having an inappropriate relationship with an *Englisher.*" Hannah placed her hands in her lap and fingered her apron. "And these rumors are affecting my family. Lillian has requested to become the full-time teacher next year, and she was told she wasn't allowed to have the job because there are concerns in the community about my behavior."

He fingered his beard. "Are these rumors true?"

Hannah shook her head. "The *Englisher* is an acquaintance. I met him while working at the hotel. He and I have spoken a few times, and he drove me home last Wednesday when Andrew was injured."

"Is Andrew okay?"

"*Ya.*" Hannah nodded. "He fell and got a terrible gash above his eye. We thought it was much worse because of how much it bled. But he's fine, *danki.*"

"*Gut.*" Elmer frowned. "I try not to listen to rumors, and I don't like to spread gossip. I was surprised, however, when I heard you were seen hugging this man. Is it true, Hannah?"

"*Ya,* it is true." She absently ran her hands over the arms of the wooden chair. "I gave him a hug after I found out Andrew was going to be okay. I was worried something bad would happen to Andrew." She paused, thinking of Elmer's daughter, who'd drowned many years ago. "Do you remember when you lost Rachel?"

The bishop sat up straight. "Of course I do. Why would you ask that?"

"After experiencing that kind of pain, do you ever worry about losing your other *kinner* or your *fraa*?"

He nodded. "Sometimes I worry about my *grandkinner* when they swim in the creek, but then I remember that if I worry, that means I don't trust God."

"I understand, and I know we should always trust God. I never expected Gideon to leave me, however, just as you didn't expect to lose your Rachel. I know it was God's plan, but it still hurts. I don't think I'll ever get over that worry or hurt. I carry it in my heart." She paused. "On that Wednesday, I was concerned about Andrew, and I was trying to keep myself together and be strong. Once I knew he was going to be okay, I let all of the emotion come out of me. I hugged Mr. Peterson and he gave me comfort. It felt like a natural reaction."

Elmer continued to finger his beard while he listened.

"What I did may be considered a sin, but it was an honest mistake. We all sin and fall short of God's glory. I want to know how I can be forgiven so my family doesn't have to suffer for my actions any further." She gripped the arms of the chair and hoped her voice sounded confident instead of revealing her jumbled emotions. "I'll do anything to make things right with the community for my family. I love this community, and I never meant to jeopardize my place in it. If I need to confess in front of the congregation, I will."

The elderly man leaned back in the chair and crossed his legs at the ankles. "I don't think that's necessary. You didn't do anything immoral."

Hannah felt the tension ease in her shoulders.

The elderly man studied her expression. "It sounds like you're *gut freinden* with this man."

"*Ya*, I am." Hannah ran her hand over the pocket where the business card was hidden. "We've spoken a few times. He lost his *fraa* and *dochder*, and I lost Gideon. We have a lot in common."

"It seems to me that your friendship with him has gotten very deep. Do you feel an attachment starting with him?"

Hannah nodded. She couldn't lie to him.

"I can tell this man means a lot to you, Hannah, but I feel you should stop all contact with him immediately. If you don't, then things could get complicated again for your family. He is *English*, and you are Amish."

Hannah frowned. "*Ya*, I know I should avoid him."

"As long as you concentrate on what kind of role model you want to be for your *kinner*, everything will be fine. I'll take care of the school board. I planned to take a walk in the morning since the doctor ordered more exercise for my diabetes. I always go past Elizabeth Beiler's *haus*, and I'll stop in and speak to her then." He stood and smiled. "Everything will be just fine."

"*Danki* for taking the time to talk with me." Hannah stood and shook his hand.

"*Gern gschehne*."

"Have a *gut* evening." Hannah started down the porch steps and hefted her bag onto her shoulder. She headed toward the main road with a mixture of happiness and disappointment. Although she'd made things right for Lillian without having to go before the entire

church district, she also agreed with the bishop when
he said she should avoid the one person who held the
key to healing her broken heart.

· · ·

Later that afternoon, Amanda packed up her bag. She'd
never been so happy to see closing time. After eating
lunch by herself on the bench outside, she'd spent the
afternoon avoiding Nancy. Whenever they looked at
each other, Nancy frowned. They were cordial and
polite when they were forced to speak to each other,
but the distance between them felt like a chasm the size
of the Grand Canyon. And that distance was breaking
Amanda's heart.

Amanda and Nancy had been best friends since first
grade. Amanda recalled having only one disagreement
with her. It had happened in third grade, and they'd
argued over who should be picked first when they were
playing baseball. The disagreement lasted ten minutes
and ended with both of them laughing. Why couldn't
this argument be just as simple to resolve?

Yet this was more than simply a disagreement; Nancy
had hurt Amanda's feelings by comparing the horrible
rumors about her *mamm* to Amanda's curiosity about
going to college. Amanda had never seen Nancy be so
hateful. Had she lost her best friend forever?

"Do you need a ride home?" Nancy's *dat's* question
broke through Amanda's thoughts.

"No, *danki*." Amanda motioned toward the front
door. "It's a *schee* day, so I'll walk."

Nancy's *mamm* tilted her head. "Are you certain?"

"*Ya*. I'll see you tomorrow." Amanda focused her eyes on Nancy. "*Gut nacht*."

Nancy nodded and then quickly looked away.

Amanda lifted her bag onto her shoulder and stepped out the front door. She walked down the path and started for the crosswalk.

"Amanda! Wait up!" Turning, she found Mike jogging from the bookstore toward her. "I was hoping to catch you before you left."

"Hi, Mike." She smiled up at him. "What are you doing here?"

"I have news." His grin was wide. "I not only passed that test, but I got an A!"

"That's wonderful news!" Amanda clapped her hands. "You must be so excited."

"Yeah." He raked his hand through his hair. "To be honest, I'm stunned. I was praying for a B and I got an A."

"The power of prayer." Amanda laughed. "I'm so happy for you."

"Thanks." He nodded toward the bookstore. "My uncle Rick told me you stopped in today."

"Oh." She fingered the strap on her tote bag. "I needed to get a book for my sister."

"He said you asked about a GED prep book." He leaned closer to her. "Are you thinking about taking the test?"

She hesitated, debating if she should be honest with him. How could she tell him she was confused about everything, including her feelings about taking the test? She didn't want him to think she was silly.

"It's okay." He looked down toward the toe of his sneaker. "I don't mean to pry. I won't keep you. I just wanted to tell you about my grade." He started to walk backward while gesturing behind him. "I better get going. I'll see you later."

"Wait." She held her hand up to stop him. "Do you want to walk me home?"

"Yeah." His smiled returned. "That would be awesome."

"Great. It's only a few blocks." Amanda fell into step with him as she pointed toward the direction of her farm.

"Let me carry your bag for you." He reached over and lifted the bag off her shoulder and placed it on his.

"Thank you."

"So, about the GED," Mike began while walking with his hands in his pockets. "I wasn't trying to pry. I was just going to tell you I'd be happy to help you study if you need a tutor."

"Thank you for offering, but I don't know if I want to take the test or not."

"Oh. Can I help you decide?"

She looked up at him. "I don't know if you can."

"Try me." He shrugged.

Amanda frowned. "My family is sort of having a hard time."

"What's going on?"

While they walked, Amanda told Mike what was going on with the rumors about her *mamm* and how they affected Lillian's plan to get the teaching job.

"It sounds like your community is really critical

of what everyone does." He shook his head. "That's rough."

"*Ya*, it can be. It's not always like that. We just have certain rules we're supposed to follow. My mother always says it's our culture."

"I see that, but what about Jesus' command to love one another? Isn't spreading rumors the opposite of that?"

"*Ya*, I agree. I feel bad for my mom, and, honestly, I'm angry too. It's unfair that everyone is treating her this way. She's friends with a man who isn't Amish, but she didn't do anything wrong."

Mike stopped walking. "Wait a minute." He pointed back and forth between them. "Are you saying you and I can't be friends?"

She paused. "*Ya*, that's true. We shouldn't be friends. At least, not friends who spend time alone."

"Does that mean I could get you in trouble just by walking you home?"

She nodded.

"I don't want to get you in trouble. I only wanted to be your friend." He held out her bag. "I should go, then."

"I don't want you to go. I don't care about getting in trouble."

He raised his eyebrows. "You really don't care?"

She pursed her lips. "I care about getting in trouble, but I don't want to lose your friendship. I told you, I'm confused. I don't know where I belong. I'm curious about getting my GED and going to college, and I really want to be your friend. That means I have no idea who I am or where I belong."

"How old are you?" He slipped her bag back onto his shoulder.

She studied him. "I'm sixteen. Why are you asking me that?"

"My dad says no one knows who they are until they're thirty."

"Thirty?" Amanda laughed. "We have a long way to go then, *ya*?"

He nodded. "I think he's being facetious. But his point is that we're not supposed to figure out who we are until we're much older."

Her smile faded. "I don't think it's supposed to work that way in my community."

"Why?"

"We're expected to join the church when we're around eighteen and then live in the community for the rest of our lives. My sister is already talking about getting baptized, but I'm not sure."

"You're not your sister." He pointed toward her. "You're Amanda. Don't be so hard on yourself. And you're not eighteen yet, are you?"

"No, I'm not."

"There you have it." He smiled. "You have time to figure out what you want in life. I'm not even sure what I want, but I do know I want to go to college. I think I want to go to medical school, but I may not be cut out for it. I'll figure it out when I get there."

She gestured toward the driveway leading to her house. "My farm is right there. I wish I could invite you up to see it, but it would be better if you and Julianne came together sometime."

"I understand." He handed her the tote bag.

"Thank you for walking me home."

"You're welcome." He touched her arm. "I'll see you soon."

"Okay."

He started down the street, turning around once to wave. She returned the wave and then walked up the long rock driveway toward her house. She was relieved to have had the opportunity to share her discombobulated feelings with someone, and she was thankful for her special friendship with Mike.

. . .

After supper that evening, Hannah stood at the sink and dried the last dish. She'd spent the meal thinking about her conversation with the bishop and wondering how she was going to avoid Trey. She wanted to tell the girls that she'd done her best to make things right, but she didn't want Andrew to overhear the conversation. She was afraid he'd misinterpret something and be upset.

She looked over at her son while he swept the floor. "Andrew. Go on and get your bath. We'll have devotions when you're finished."

"*Ya, Mamm.*" He disappeared through the family room toward the stairs.

"I wanted to talk to you both alone," Hannah said to her daughters as she gestured toward the table. "Have a seat."

Lillian's eyes were wide as she sank into the seat across from her sister. "*Was iss letz?*"

"Nothing is wrong." Hannah sat next to Amanda. "I wanted to tell you I met with the bishop on my way home from work today."

"What?" Amanda shook her head. "I thought you weren't going to stir things up even more, *Mamm*. Why did you do that?"

"It's okay, *mei liewe*." Hannah touched Amanda's hand. "I only did it to make things right for Lillian. I explained to him that Trey was only *mei freind*, and I never meant to hug him. I told him all about how Andrew was injured, and I was emotional. He said he understood, and I don't have to confess in front of the congregation because I didn't do anything immoral."

Amanda blew out a breath and looked relieved. "*Gut*. I didn't want to see you humiliated like that."

"Did you mention the school board?" Lillian wrung her hands while studying Hannah.

"*Ya*, I did." Hannah smiled. "He's going to talk to Elizabeth Beiler for you tomorrow."

Lillian squealed, came around the table, and hugged Hannah. "*Danki!* Oh, *danki, Mamm*. I'm so very *froh*."

"I know you are, Lily." Hannah nodded. "I'm hoping it works out for you. I just want you to be *froh*."

"I will be. *Danki* again!" Lillian headed for the stairs. "Andrew! Why are you spying? Go get your pajamas and get your bath. Go on."

Hannah turned to Amanda and found her frowning. "Amanda? Is something wrong? You've been quiet all evening." Her normally happy and easygoing daughter was unusually pensive tonight.

"I've had a lot on my mind." Amanda ran her finger

over the wood grain on the table. "I think it's wrong that you had to talk to the bishop to make things right."

"That's just how things are." Hannah studied Amanda. "Amanda, is there something you're not telling me? What's really bothering you?"

Amanda looked up at Hannah and her lips quivered. "Sometimes I feel like I don't belong here."

"What do you mean?" Hannah rubbed Amanda's arm. "We're your family, and we love you. Of course you belong here. Why would you say something so *gegisch*?"

"No, that's not what I mean. I don't mean here, like in this *haus*." She pointed around the kitchen. "I mean in this community. I don't agree with all of the rules we have to live by. I don't agree with how you were treated. I know I'm not supposed to feel that way, but it's the truth."

Hannah nodded slowly. Although she wanted to tell Amanda that she understood, she knew she had to be the role model Gideon would expect her to be. Gideon was a loving man, but he was also a conservative father. He believed in teaching the children the rules and always being an example to them. In this moment, she felt she had to honor his memory despite her own feelings. "You know we have to follow the rules. It's how we've chosen to live, and it's our culture. It's what God intended for us."

To Hannah's great surprise, Amanda's frown transformed into a wry smile.

Hannah gaped.

"Is that what you really believe, *Mamm*?"

Hannah was speechless for a moment, and Amanda stood.

"I'm going to go upstairs. Call me when it's time for devotions." Amanda pushed her chair in. "*Mamm*, I understand how you really feel, even if you aren't saying it out loud to me."

Hannah watched Amanda leave the kitchen, and she wondered just how deeply her daughter understood her.

EIGHTEEN

The following afternoon, Lillian swept while Mattie organized the books at the front of the classroom.

A knock sounded at the door, and Lillian looked up as Elizabeth Beiler stepped into the schoolhouse. Lillian sucked in a breath and hoped the visit was connected to the bishop's plan to speak with Elizabeth today.

"*Wie geht's?*" Mattie crossed the room and shook Elizabeth's hand.

"I'm doing well." Elizabeth smiled. "How was your day?"

"*Gut!*" Mattie clapped her hands together. "The scholars are doing so well with their multiplication tables."

"That's *wunderbaar*." Elizabeth looked at Lillian. "I was hoping to speak with you."

"Of course." Lillian's stomach tightened as she stowed the broom. She walked over to Elizabeth and gestured toward the row of desks. "Would you like to sit?"

"No, no." Elizabeth waved off the question. "We can talk right here." She turned toward Mattie, who was gathering up her bag and heading for the door. "There's no need for you to leave. You can stay if you'd like."

"What would you like to talk about?" Lillian smoothed her hands over her apron and pasted a smile on her face. She prayed it was good news and assumed it was since Elizabeth said Mattie could stay. Certainly she wouldn't have invited Mattie to stay if it was bad news.

"I spoke with the bishop this morning." Elizabeth folded her hands. "He told me I should recommend you to the school board for the teaching position next year. He and I spoke about a few things at length, and I agreed with him."

Mattie clapped her hands again. "That's *wunderbaar gut!*"

Lillian smiled. "*Danki.* I'm so excited. I'll work hard and be the best teacher I can be."

Elizabeth held up her finger. "Now, don't get your hopes up too high. The board will have to interview you at the end of the school year. I just wanted to let you know I'm going to give my recommendation to the board. I'll let you know when the members want to meet with you."

"*Danki* again." Lillian shook her hand. "I truly appreciate your help with this."

Elizabeth nodded and then headed for the door. "Have a *gut* evening."

"You too." Once Elizabeth was gone, Mattie hugged Lillian. "You'll be the best teacher."

"I hope so. It feels too *gut* to be true."

"No, it's not too *gut* to be true. The Lord has led you

to this job, and he'll guide your path. Just put your faith in him."

Lillian nodded. "I will."

. . .

Lillian rushed through the back door and into the kitchen, where Andrew was eating cookies. Her mother pulled an apple pie from the oven, and the smell filled the room.

"I'm so excited!" Lillian dropped her bag on a chair. "Elizabeth Beiler came to see me today."

Her mother raised her eyebrows. "What did she want?"

"She's going to recommend me to the school board as the teacher next year." Lillian danced over to her mother and hugged her. "*Danki* so much."

"You're really going to be my teacher?" Andrew grimaced. "Why don't you apply in another district instead?"

Mamm wagged a finger at him, despite a smile forming on her lips. "That's not nice, Andrew."

Andrew shrugged and stood. "I'm going to go help *Onkel* Josh and Daniel." He took his empty plate to the counter before disappearing through the mudroom.

"I'm so *froh, Mamm. Danki* for talking to the bishop. That had to be difficult for you."

Mamm nodded. "It was difficult, but I did it for you. I just want you and your siblings to be *froh*." She touched Lillian's face. "It's so *gut* to see you smile again."

"I can't wait to tell Amanda." Lillian leaned over

and inhaled the sweet scent of the pie, which caused her stomach to growl. "I can't wait until this is cooled. I want to cut it now."

"No, no." *Mamm* wagged a finger at her. "We have to let it cool."

Lillian started for the stairs. "I'm going to get changed and then start weeding the garden."

As she climbed to the second floor, she grinned. Things were starting to look up. She couldn't wait to tell Leroy she might be the teacher next year. Maybe they would both be baptized in a couple of years and could start dating. The possibility caused her heart to thump in her chest.

. . .

Josh wiped his brow with a handkerchief and smiled as Andrew approached him. "Hi, Andrew. How was school?"

"*Gut*." He shrugged. "You know, the usual. Boring."

Josh chuckled and touched his nephew's arm. "You know you have to go to school so you can be smart enough to help me run this farm."

"I'm already smart enough." Andrew flexed his arms. "And I'm strong enough. I was the only *bu* strong enough to lift a giant rock on the playground today. See? Look at my muscles."

"You do have big muscles." While Andrew chattered on about the large rock on the playground, Josh glanced toward the house and thought of Hannah. He'd been thinking of her and wanted to talk to her, but didn't know what to say ever since he saw her in Trey Peterson's arms that day. He felt as if he'd been punched in his chest when she allowed that man to touch her. The feeling was so intense he thought he might be physically ill. Why couldn't Hannah see that she didn't belong with a man like Trey? Instead, she belonged with someone like him, a good, faithful man who was true to the Amish way of life.

Hannah invited him to stay for supper a few times, but he came up with excuses. She'd stopped asking him after the third time he turned her down. Although he was hurt and angry by the sight of her touching that *Englisher*, he still cared about her.

"You should try to pick up that rock sometime, *Onkel* Josh. It's huge!" Andrew gestured widely. "It was bigger than a cat!"

"That's pretty big." Josh leaned against the fence. "How's your *mamm* doing?"

"She's fine." His expression became quizzical. "Last night I listened in on a conversation that confused me. I was supposed to go upstairs and get my bath, but I stood by the stairs and listened while *Mamm* talked to my *schweschdere*."

"What were they talking about?"

"*Mei mamm* went to see the bishop yesterday. She said something about people talking about her. Why would people say bad things about *mei mamm*?"

Intrigued, Josh rubbed his chin and wondered if it had to do with her and that *Englisher*. "Well, I'm not certain, Andrew. Did she give you any idea what they've been saying?"

"No, but she told the bishop she was sorry for what she did, and she was going to stay away from Mr. Peterson." He squinted as if trying to figure out a puzzle. "Why would talking to Mr. Peterson be a bad thing?"

Josh paused, wondering how to explain the situation in terms Andrew might understand. "It's sort of complicated, Andrew. People think your *mamm* shouldn't talk to him because he's *English*."

"So, we're only allowed to talk to Amish people? But I've seen you talk to *Englishers* when they come to look at horses."

"It's a little more than just talking to someone when they want to buy a horse. When people see your *mamm* talk to Mr. Peterson, they might think she likes him as more than a *freind*. Do you understand what I'm saying?"

"Oh." Andrew nodded. "People might think she wants Mr. Peterson to be her boyfriend." His eyes widened. "She doesn't want him to, does she?"

Josh frowned. "I hope not."

"Oh." Andrew paused as if to consider this. "I guess that makes sense. *Mamm* also said she asked the bishop to talk to the school board and tell them to give Lillian a chance to be the teacher next year." He grimaced. "Mrs. Beiler came to see Lillian today and told her she may get the job. Why does *mei schweschder* have to be my teacher? I see her enough at the *haus*."

Josh grinned at his nephew's bleak expression. "Your *schweschder* will be a great teacher. You'll do just fine."

"Josh!" Daniel called from the other side of the barn. "Are you going to come help me shoe these horses or what? I have the stock all set up."

Josh stood up straight. "Since you have these big muscles, you're ready for some real work. Do you want to help Daniel and me shoe a couple of horses?"

"*Ya!*" Andrew's eyes were wide. "I'd love to help."

"Great." Josh placed his hand on Andrew's shoulder as they walked toward the shoeing stock on the other side of the large barn. He frowned as he thought of what Andrew had shared about Hannah. He'd felt guilty for telling a few of his friends about seeing her in an embrace with the *Englisher*. Maybe he was the one who'd started the rumor.

Yet he wondered if the rumor was what had inspired her to make things right. After all, she promised not to see the *Englisher* anymore because people were talking about her. Perhaps if Hannah was sorry for her actions, she was ready to see what was right before her eyes: the love Josh wanted to give to her and her family. He wasn't ready to give up on her. He was going to find a way to win her heart.

. . .

After supper was over, Hannah brought the apple pie to the table. "I baked this earlier."

Lillian smiled as she grabbed the vanilla ice cream from the propane freezer. "*Ya*, she wouldn't let us sample any. Believe me, I tried to convince her."

Hannah shook her head, marveling at the change in Lillian's temperament ever since she'd gotten the news that Elizabeth Beiler was going to recommend her for the teaching job. Although she was relieved to see her daughter so happy, she wished she could squelch the empty feeling inside her. She missed Trey terribly and wondered how she'd ever mend the hole in her heart.

"It smells *appeditlich*." Josh smiled up at Hannah as she served him a piece.

The eagerness in his eyes caused her to nervously finger her apron. She wondered why Joshua was so determined to stay for supper tonight after turning her down the last few times she'd invited him. Something had changed in him, and it made her uneasy.

"*Mei mamm* makes the best pies." Amanda dropped a large piece onto her plate.

Lillian studied her sister. "How do you stay so thin when you eat such large pieces of pie?"

Amanda shrugged while cutting her piece. "I stay on my feet all day at the store. I guess that's my exercise."

"It's so unfair." Lillian scowled. "No matter how much I cut down my portions, I still can't get as thin as you."

"You're perfect the way you are, Lily." Hannah sliced through the air with her fork for emphasis. "Don't worry about your weight. It's not *gut* to obsess over your appearance. Pride is a sin, you know."

"How are things at school, Lily?" Josh wiped his mouth. "Are you staying busy?"

"Oh, *ya*." Lillian launched into a long discussion about the students and their antics on the playground.

Hannah watched Joshua's reactions while he listened to Lillian's story. He smiled when she said something funny and frowned when she was serious. It was apparent he truly cared about her children.

She knew he cared about her too, but she couldn't reciprocate the love he had for her. She knew if she'd fallen in love with someone like Joshua, her life wouldn't be as complicated. Yet the love in her heart was intended for someone she couldn't have. She felt herself caught between her love for the community she'd known all her life and her blossoming feelings for a man she couldn't consider dating unless she left her beloved community.

Once the pie was gone, Hannah stood and began taking the dirty dishes to the counter.

"Dinner and dessert were outstanding." Josh stood and rubbed his abdomen. "I'm stuffed."

"*Gut.*" Hannah turned on the faucet and waited for the water to warm. "You'll have plenty of energy to work on the farm again tomorrow."

"*Ya.* I will." He touched Andrew's back. "You get a *gut* night's sleep so you can help Daniel and me tomorrow. You were a *wunderbaar* assistant today while we shoed the horses."

Andrew grinned. "You got it, *Onkel* Josh."

Hannah added dishwashing liquid to the water. A hand on her back caused her to jump. Turning, she found Josh looking down at her.

"I'm walking out." He leaned in close to her. "Would you like to come out with me?"

Hannah hesitated.

"You can go, *Mamm*." Lillian brought the utensils to the sink. "Amanda and I will take care of this."

"*Danki.*" Hannah wiped her hands on a dish towel and then followed Joshua out the door and down the porch steps toward his buggy. "I'm glad you stayed for supper tonight."

"I am too." He stopped at his buggy and faced her. "I've missed you."

Hannah studied his eyes, wondering why he was suddenly so pleasant after he'd berated her over her friendship with Trey. She forced a smiled and then gestured toward the house. "It's getting late, so I better get back inside. See you tomorrow."

"Wait." He reached for her hand and then pulled back before making contact. "I wanted to talk to you alone. That's why I asked you to come out here with me."

Hannah folded her arms over her chest as alarm surged through her. She wondered what Joshua wanted. Was he going to lecture her again about Trey?

"Andrew told me that he overheard a conversation last night."

Hannah stood up straight. "What did he hear?"

"He said you spoke to the bishop about what happened with that *Englisher.*"

"His name is Trey." She nearly spat out the words.

"Right. Trey." He smiled. "I was *froh* to hear you're reconsidering your friendship with him and you're sorry for what you did."

Hannah blinked. *Am I dreaming or is Joshua truly patronizing me?* "My discussion with the bishop was private. I only wanted *mei dochdern* to know about it."

"I know." Joshua touched his chest. "I'm sorry. Andrew asked me what it all meant. I think he just needed someone to talk to because he was confused. It wasn't like I was listening to gossip."

Hannah snorted. "I think our whole community needs to stop listening to gossip. Have you heard what's been said about me? Have you seen how folks have turned their backs on me? Even the school board has formed opinions about me. I had to go apologize to the bishop so Lillian could be considered as a candidate for teacher next year."

Joshua nodded. "I know what they've been saying. And I know you just had a momentary lapse of reason. You didn't mean to put your arms around the *Englisher.* You really want to be with someone in the community, not him."

"A momentary lapse of reason?" Hannah pursed her lips as anger boiled inside her. "Joshua, I've known you since we were *kinner,* and I'd hoped you were more perceptive than that. Apparently I was wrong." She started for the porch. "*Gut nacht.*"

"Wait!" Joshua ran after her. "I've said something wrong. I'm sorry."

She spun and faced him. "No, you're not sorry. I'm the one who's sorry. I'm sorry you and the rest of the community can't be a little more open-minded about the *Englishers.* Trey is someone I can talk to, and he understands me. He knows what it feels like to wake up in the middle of the night and, for a moment, forget he's alone because he still can't believe his spouse is gone."

Josh's eyes widened. "I lost Gideon too. No, he wasn't my spouse, but he was *mei bruder.* We were close. I know what you're going through, Hannah. I can help you too."

"No, you can't. It's not the same thing."

He opened his mouth to protest, and she interrupted him.

"I'm not done." She wiped away a tear and wished her voice wouldn't quaver. "I promised I would stop seeing him for my family's sake, not because I wanted to. I'm tired of getting dirty looks at church services. I'm tired of watching *mei dochder* mope around the *haus* because a rumor about me is preventing her from being a teacher. I swallowed what little self-respect I had left and went to see the bishop yesterday even though I don't think I have anything to apologize for."

"Hannah, I just want—"

"Stop." She held up her hand. "You think you know what's best for me, but, honestly, you don't. I think I know what's best for me." She raised her chin. "*Gut nacht.*"

"That's not it." His frown deepened. "I wasn't going to tell you what's best for you. I was going to tell you that I love you. I've always loved you."

She blanched. "What did you say?"

"You heard me." He frowned and shook his head. "I've loved you since we were teenagers, but I was invisible next to Gideon. You're the reason I never married. No one could ever compare to you."

Hannah grimaced. "Joshua, that's ridiculous."

"Is it?" He clicked his tongue. "You have no idea how much you mean to me, and every time I've tried to tell you, you've rebuffed me. I've been trying to get your attention ever since Gideon passed away. I never resented him for marrying you, but now that he's gone,

I want to try to make a life with you." He pointed
toward the stables. "We can run this farm together and
be a family, a real family. You know I adore those *kinner* like they're my own."

Hannah wiped another tear as regret and guilt filled
her. She should never have been so nasty to Joshua. "I
know you do, and they love you too."

"But you don't love me." His scowl was deep, causing
her heart to ache. She'd never intended to hurt him.

"Joshua, you know I care about you."

His expression softened. "That's a start. All mar-
riages are based on a caring relationship, Hannah.
We've been family a long time, and we both want
what's best for your *kinner*." His eyes were full of hope.
"You may not be in love with me now, but give yourself
time. My parents started out as friends and fell in love
later. You could eventually fall in love with me too."

Hannah sighed. "Joshua, it's not that simple."

"*Ya*, it can be." He reached for her hand and cradled
it in his. "I truly believe God wants us to be together.
Why else would he have given us this successful business? It makes sense, Hannah. Just think about it." He
nodded toward the pasture. "We have this beautiful
farm. Let's build a life together. Please, Hannah." His
eyes pleaded with her. "Please give me a chance to
prove to you just how much I love you and the *kinner*. I
think this is what Gideon would want."

She studied his hopeful expression and couldn't
bring herself to break his heart. His eyes were full of
love for her and what could be. Was he right? Was this
what Gideon would want? She couldn't imagine that

Gideon would want her to leave the community for an *Englisher*. After all, the community was where they'd grown up and where they'd planned to raise their children. Maybe Joshua was right. Maybe she did belong with him.

"Will you just think about it, Hannah?" His words filled the uncomfortable silence between them.

She gave him a slight nod.

"*Gut*." He gestured toward the buggy. "It's getting late. I should go."

Hannah wrung her hands as she followed him. His proposal echoed through her mind.

He smiled as he stood by the buggy. "We'll talk again soon. *Gut nacht*."

Hannah watched the buggy roll down the driveway, and she wondered how her life had suddenly become so complicated. Confusion swarmed within her as she considered her quandary—Joshua's offer of a life in a community she loved as opposed to the possibility of exploring a relationship and a new life with Trey.

NINETEEN

Sunday morning, Hannah sat at the table surrounded by her children. "Who would like to read for devotions?"

"I would." Amanda took the Bible from the center of the table. "I'd like to read from Romans today."

"That sounds *gut*." Hannah smiled at her daughter.

Amanda cleared her throat. "I'm going to start with Romans chapter eight, since we read chapter seven the other night. 'There is now no condemnation for those who are in Christ Jesus, because through Christ Jesus the law of the Spirit who gives life has set you free from the law of sin and death.'"

"Wait." Hannah held up her hand. "Amanda, would you please read that again?"

"*Ya.*" Amanda repeated the first two verses.

"I like that." Andrew tapped his fingers on the table. "To me, it means we're free because of Jesus."

"Exactly." Lillian touched Andrew's nose. "You're a smart *bu*."

Andrew glared at her. "Don't talk to me like I'm a *boppli*."

"No bickering during devotions." Hannah looked at Amanda. "Those are two beautiful verses. Continue, Amanda."

She finished reading the chapter, and then they bowed their heads in silent prayer.

Amanda closed up the Bible. "Who are we going to go visit today?"

"*Onkel* Josh says we can go to *Mammi's* today." Lillian stood and pointed toward the door. "We can ride with him."

"Let's go!" Andrew started for the door. "I think he was finishing up when I came in for devotions."

Amanda followed him with Lillian in tow.

Hannah's stomach lurched. She couldn't imagine a day spent with Barbie. She knew she needed to forgive her for all she had said, but she couldn't stand the idea of trying to make small talk knowing about the rumor she had started. She also wasn't ready to face Joshua after he'd nearly proposed to her the other night. Although she appreciated his desire to marry her, she wasn't comfortable with the idea of marrying a man she didn't truly love. Yet she also didn't want to break his heart.

"*Mamm?*" Lillian turned to her. "Are you coming?"

"I think I'm going to stay home today. My stomach is a little upset." She pointed in the direction of her bedroom. "I'm going to lie down."

Lillian's eyes rounded. "You're *grank*?"

"Do you want me to stay home with you?" Amanda stepped toward her. "I can make you some tea."

"No, no." Hannah waved off the offer. "I'll be just

fine. You all go and enjoy your time with your *mammi*. I'll be fine here. Just go on without me."

"I hope you feel better." Andrew smiled and then rushed through the mudroom toward the porch.

Lillian frowned. "If you need us, just leave a message on *Mammi's* answering machine. I'll check it periodically."

Hannah nodded. "I will. *Danki, mei liewe.*"

Lillian exited through the mudroom, but Amanda hesitated.

"I'm fine, Amanda." Hannah gestured toward the door. "You can go."

"Are you certain?" Amanda raised her eyebrows. "Is there something you're not telling us?"

Hannah considered telling her daughter the truth, but she didn't want to upset Amanda or drag her into something that had nothing to do with her. Why burden a child with adult problems? "I just would like some time alone."

Amanda nodded. "I understand that. I'll explain to *Onkel* Josh. Enjoy the quiet."

"I will. *Danki.*" Hannah smiled. "I'll see you around supper time."

"See you later." Amanda made her way out the door.

Hannah watched out the kitchen window as her children climbed into Joshua's buggy. The horse came to life and soon the buggy was rattling down the driveway and out of sight. She was grateful Joshua hadn't come in to check on her.

Hannah scanned the kitchen and listened. The walls blanketed her in deafening silence. Loneliness filled her like a suffocating fog. She'd hoped being alone would give her a sense of peace, but instead she felt hollow.

Hannah sat at the kitchen table and opened the Bible. She flipped to Romans chapter eight and scanned the verses Amanda had read aloud. She concentrated on verses 1 and 2, which had spoken so loudly to her earlier: ". . . because through Christ Jesus the law of the Spirit who gives life has set you free from the law of sin and death."

The Scripture spoke to her heart and erased the loneliness that had filled her when her family left. The Scripture told her she was forgiven. If she was forgiven, then why did she have to ignore her feelings for Trey?

Hannah closed the Bible and padded to her room, where she opened her top bureau drawer and dug through her clothing to find the business card Trey had given her the last time they'd spoken. She stared at his cellular phone number and considered calling him. What damage could a phone call do? She just wanted to hear his voice and see how he was. It would be an innocent phone call between two friends and nothing more.

She clutched the business card in her hand while she headed out to the barn. She stood in front of the phone and her stomach tightened. She'd never called Trey on the phone before. What would she say to him? Hannah shook her head and quietly laughed at herself. She was acting like a silly teenager who had a crush on a boy.

She lifted the receiver and dialed the number. After three rings, the call connected.

"Hello?" Trey's voice came through the phone. It sounded warm and smooth, just as she'd remembered.

"Hi, Trey. This is Hannah." She coiled the cord around her finger as she spoke. "How are you?"

"Hannah!" The excitement in his voice caused her to forget her worries and smile. "I'm great. How are you doing?"

"I'm fine." She lowered herself onto the stool by the desk that held the phone.

"I'm surprised to hear from you. I thought you couldn't see me."

"I needed to know how you are." She glanced toward the barn door and looked up at the blue sky. "It's a beautiful day."

"Yes, it is. I was just heading out to church." He paused. "Don't you have church?"

"Not today. It's an off Sunday." She ran her fingers over the desk, which Gideon had built many years ago when they first moved out to the farm. "We have church every other Sunday. Today's a day for visiting. My children went to visit their grandparents, but I decided to stay home."

"Oh." His tone was inquisitive. "Would you like to go to church with me?"

Hannah hesitated. Although she was permitted to visit other churches, she knew that being spotted with Trey again might be a risk. Yet she felt drawn to both Trey and the possibility of experiencing his way of worshiping the Lord.

"Yes." Her voice was more confident than she'd expected. "I would like that very much."

"Great! I can be there to pick you up in about ten minutes."

"Wonderful. I'll see you soon." Hannah hung up the phone and her heart skipped a beat.

She rushed into the house to get ready. By the time Trey's car pulled into the driveway, she had freshened up and changed into her best dress.

She hurried down the porch steps and met him at the car. He seemed more handsome than she'd remembered, and she found herself captivated by him. He was clad in a gray suit with a blue tie. His hair and goatee were perfectly manicured, and his eyes were warm and kind. She smiled up at him, and her heart turned over in her chest.

Was this love?

Confusion gripped her and she felt lightheaded for a moment. How had she managed to fall in love with an *Englisher*? The question hit her like a thousand bales of hay falling from the loft in the barn.

All her life Hannah had wanted to be Amish. She'd been baptized when she turned eighteen, and she cherished the members of her community. She coveted the plain life and raising her children on the horse farm Gideon and Joshua had built together. She'd never longed for the opulent *English* life. Never once had she longed for fancy clothes, or jewelry, or the convenience of cars and cellular phones. Working at the hotel had only helped to secure her Amish faith.

Yet now she found herself standing at a crossroads, and her heart was stuck in her throat. She felt as if she didn't know herself anymore. She'd never expected her love for the only life she'd ever known to be threatened. She felt excitement mixed with fear bubble up inside her, and she needed God to guide her through this confusion.

Lord, what does this all mean? Is this the path you've chosen for me? Do you want me to leave the community I love and be shunned?

Trey's smile cut through her thoughts. "Good morning."

"Good morning." She hoped her voice didn't reveal the confusion rioting within her.

"You look lovely."

"Thank you." She smiled while marveling at how he made her feel alive for the first time in years. Her heart pounded for him after not having felt the excitement of falling in love since she was a young woman.

Trey opened the passenger side door and made a sweeping gesture. "Please get in and make yourself comfortable. We have to get on the road if we're going to make it for the opening hymn."

Hannah settled herself into the seat and breathed in the leather while fastening her seat belt.

Trey steered out of the driveway and the car bounced onto the paved road. "I was really shocked but happy to get your call this morning. What made you change your mind about seeing me again?"

Hannah turned toward him. "I've been doing a lot of thinking, and it seems like every road leads me to you."

He gave her a sideways glance while raising an eyebrow. "What do you mean?"

"I've tried to keep myself from thinking of you.

When my children left this morning, I thought I would enjoy the peace and quiet and instead I felt lonely. The house was too quiet. I found myself longing to call you to fill the void."

"I'm honored that you called me."

"I also have a story I want to share with you. There was a reason I was so distant when we talked the other day." She watched the farms pass by out the window while she told him about her meeting with the bishop.

"You had to go apologize for hugging me to get Lillian a chance to be the teacher?" Trey asked after she'd finished her story.

Hannah nodded. "We live by rules, and the rules are very important to us. The community perceived our relationship as immoral, even though we didn't do anything wrong."

"And you're breaking another rule by being with me again. Couldn't the rumors be worse this time?"

"*Ya*, they could be. People may assume I want to leave the community or they may continue to accuse me of having an immoral relationship."

"What would happen then?"

"If I don't confess in front of the congregation, I could be shunned."

Trey slowed to a stop at a red light and looked at her with his eyes wide. "Do you want to be shunned, Hannah?"

"All I know is that I need to be with you. And there is nothing wrong with that. If everything comes from God, then that means this relationship does too. How can our friendship be wrong if it came from God?"

He shook his head. "But you just said you apologized for hugging me so that you could help Lillian. What will happen to your children if you're shunned?"

"I don't know," she whispered.

"Hannah." He touched her hand, and his skin was warm. "I don't want you to do anything to hurt your children. Nothing is worth hurting them."

"I know, but it's more complicated than that. I'm not trying to hurt them. I'm trying to do what I believe is right." She shook her head. "Amanda read Romans chapter eight this morning during devotions and two verses spoke to my heart." She recited the verses. "I don't believe I need to let my community prevent me from doing something that in my heart I believe isn't a sin. Does that make sense?"

The light turned green, and a horn tooted behind them.

Hannah smiled. "You'd better go. The people behind us are in a hurry too."

Trey negotiated a turn and then pulled into the parking lot of Paradise Community Church.

Hannah looked up at the white church and admired the bell tower and stained glass window. It seemed like any other church she'd ridden by in her life. Her stomach tightened at the idea of walking inside it. She'd never stepped foot in a church before, and the possibility of worshiping in a different way was exciting.

"Are you ready?" Trey's smile was hesitant. "If you're uncomfortable, I can take you home. I don't want you to feel like I'm forcing you to go to church with me."

"I agreed to this, Trey. Don't feel as if you're forcing

me to do anything." She pushed the door open. "I'm ready."

They walked across the parking lot, and Trey waved and smiled at members of the congregation who greeted him by name. Hannah nodded in response to their curious smiles and waves to her.

A man in a suit held open the large wooden door as Hannah and Trey entered the church. Another well-dressed man standing at the entrance to the sanctuary handed Hannah a folded booklet with a beautiful image of a waterfall and a Scripture verse under it.

"Thank you." Hannah took the booklet and glanced up at Trey as they moved toward the pews.

"It's called a bulletin." His words were soft in her ear. "It has information in it, such as the order of the service, hymn numbers, and church meetings and events."

Hannah followed him to a row near the back and sat beside him by the aisle. She glanced through the bulletin. It felt strange to have the service printed out in her hand. She'd never been in a sanctuary or sat in a pew. She was used to sitting on a backless bench in the home or barn of a community member every other week.

She looked up toward the front of the room and found an altar with two large vases filled with a spray of purple and white hyacinths and orchids. Although they were beautiful flowers, they seemed out of place to her since there was neither an altar nor flowers in the Amish church tradition. Hannah turned her gaze up toward the large stained glass cross hanging over the pulpit and wondered what her children would think of the beautiful display. The cross gave the large room a warm feeling. She could almost feel God's presence above her, and the thought gave her a chill.

"Good morning." A man leaned down and shook Trey's hand. "It's good to see you back here." He looked at Hannah and smiled.

"Hi, Tony." Trey gestured toward Hannah. "This is my friend, Hannah. She wanted to come to worship with me today. Hannah, this is Tony."

"It's nice to meet you." Tony shook her hand. "Welcome to Paradise Community Church. We're happy to see you here."

"Thank you." Hannah pushed the ribbons from her prayer covering behind her shoulders. She smiled at a few members of the congregation who made their way past Tony and nodded a greeting to her.

Tony and Trey chatted about the weather for a moment, and Hannah turned her attention back to the bulletin. She read a lengthy prayer list that warmed her heart. It was wonderful to see members of the congregation praying for their family and friends. She perused a list of the weekly events, taking in the different church committees and organizations that were active there.

Suddenly the organ sounded, and Hannah jumped. The music was another foreign element to Hannah. No instruments were ever played during Amish services. The voices swirling around Hannah faded to a murmur as if on cue. The knot of people loitering in the aisle filed into pews.

Trey leaned over to her and Hannah enjoyed the familiar scent of his aftershave. "Are you okay?"

"*Ya.*" She nodded. "I was startled by the organ, but

it's beautiful. I'm enjoying the music. It's different from what I'm used to, but I like it."

When the music stopped, the minister took his place in the pulpit. He was a tall man with a warm voice and pleasant smile. He looked to be in his early fifties. Although Hannah was used to hearing Pennsylvania *Dietsch* and German during her community's services, she felt at ease listening to his greeting in English.

She glanced around and found the other members of the congregation nodding and smiling while the minister spoke. Hannah marveled at how comfortable she felt.

The organ began playing again, and the congregation stood. Trey handed Hannah a hymnal and she flipped through it to find the appropriate hymn listed in the bulletin and on the board at the front of the sanctuary. The congregation began to sing, and Hannah listened for a few moments, enjoying the warm rich sound of Trey's voice beside her. She smiled up at him and he winked, causing her heart to flutter. She joined in with the hymn singing, enjoying the opportunity to worship the Lord with a new song. Happiness filled her heart.

Once the hymn was over, the congregation sat and a woman approached the pulpit and read aloud the lessons for the day. Hannah folded her hands and concentrated on taking in God's Word. The verse in Psalm 62 struck a chord in her: "Trust in him at all times, O people; pour out your hearts to him, for God is our refuge."

The verse echoed through her mind while the reader

finished the lesson and continued to float through her thoughts during the minister's sermon. The minister's message of hope and trust through adversity spoke to her heart, just as the psalm had. It seemed as if God was blessing her through this small church. Although the building and the service were foreign to Hannah, she felt at home.

Once the sermon was over, Hannah followed along with the remainder of the service, singing the hymns and reciting the prayers. When the members of the church lined up to go to the front of the sanctuary for communion, Hannah touched Trey's arm. "I'd like to stay here. I'm not comfortable taking communion."

"That's fine." Trey smiled. "Only do the things that feel right to you, okay?"

"Okay." She nodded.

After one last hymn, the service ended, and Hannah followed Trey into the aisle, where they stood in line to meet the minister. A few people walked over to greet Trey, and he introduced Hannah to them. Each person welcomed her to the church and invited her to come back. She smiled and thanked them for their kindness.

They reached the front of the line, and Trey shook the minister's hand. "Pastor Bob. This is my friend Hannah Glick. She wanted to come to church with me today. Hannah, this is Pastor Bob."

"Hello." Hannah shook his hand. "I enjoyed your service today."

"It's very nice to meet you, Hannah." The minister's smile was genuine and his handshake was firm.

"Welcome to our church. I imagine this was a very different service than what you're used to."

"*Ya.*" Hannah nodded. "But I truly enjoyed it. Your church has a very warm and homey feeling. I can see why Trey enjoys coming here."

"That's very true," Trey said.

"We hope to see you again, Hannah." The minister smiled. "May God bless you."

"Thank you." Hannah followed Trey toward the exit. "This was very nice. I really enjoyed the service."

"I did too, and I enjoyed having you beside me in the pew." His smile was full of tenderness and caused her heart rate to surge. "May I take you to lunch?"

"That would be lovely." Hannah looked up at him and wished that the day would never end.

TWENTY

Trey sat across from Hannah at a small sandwich shop and watched her while she studied the menu. He was captivated once again by her bright red hair and deep emerald eyes, which were complemented by her green dress. She looked so beautiful that she seemed to glow. He'd been stunned ever since she called this morning. It was as if she could read his mind since he was thinking of her when the phone rang. He'd worried about her ever since their conversation last week. And today, she'd fallen right back into his life as if they'd never parted ways.

"I think the Reuben sounds good." She glanced up and her expression became curious. "Why are you staring at me?"

"I'm sorry." He lifted his glass of water. "I was lost in my thoughts."

"Have you decided what you're going to have?" She placed her menu on the table.

"I think I'll have a BLT." He sipped the water and then put it back by the napkin dispenser. "So you liked the service?"

Hannah nodded. "I loved the music, and the sermon

really touched me. I think that your minister is wonderful."

"Do non-Amish ever attend your services?"

"It's rare to see them at a regular Sunday service, but
I've seen *Englishers* at weddings." She swirled the straw
in her glass of water while she spoke. "But I assume
they don't enjoy it much since they can't understand
what the ministers are saying."

Trey studied her ivory complexion and wondered
how she felt about him. He wanted to ask her if the
same intense feelings haunted her that haunted him.

"May I take your order?" A young woman appeared
at the table with a notepad. "What would you like
today?"

Hannah ordered a Reuben sandwich with chips,
and Trey ordered a BLT with chips and a Coke.

"How are things at the farm?" Trey sipped his water
again.

"They're good. We hired a young man to help
Joshua." Hannah folded her hands on the table while
she talked about the farm.

Trey enjoyed studying her while she spoke. He
wanted to commit to memory every detail of her beautiful face just in case this wound up being their one and
only date. He was afraid that after today she would be
forbidden from seeing him and the community would
find a way to prevent their friendship permanently. The
thought caused his stomach to twist. At that moment,
he knew he was falling in love with her and couldn't
bear the idea of never seeing her again.

The waitress arrived with their food. After she placed

the plates in front of them, Hannah bowed her head in silent prayer. Trey followed suit and thanked God for the opportunity to enjoy a meal with her.

Once the prayers were over, Hannah grabbed a chip from her plate. "You haven't told me the latest about the house you want to buy. Did the owner accept your offer?"

Trey nodded while eating a chip. "Yes, the owner accepted it. I'm hoping the inspection can be done quickly. If it goes well, we should be closing soon since I'm preapproved for the loan."

"That's wonderful." Hannah ate another chip. "I hope it works out for you. Have you thought about what you'll name the bed and breakfast?"

Trey shook his head. "I haven't come up with any good names yet. I was thinking about doing something with my last name."

"Is the house in Paradise?" She lifted her sandwich and took a small bite.

"Yes, it is. It's not far from the church."

"Peterson's Paradise." She laughed, and the sound was a sweet melody to his ear. "I guess that's a bit silly."

"No, not really. I kind of like it." He lifted his sandwich and bit into it.

"I'd like to see it. Maybe we can take a quick ride past it on the way home."

He finished chewing and then wiped his mouth. "I'd like that."

They talked about the weather and the best places to eat in Lancaster County while they finished their meals. Trey felt as if he'd known Hannah for years instead of only a little over a month. She shared stories about her life growing up on a dairy farm, and he told her more of his memories from his grandparents' horse farm.

Soon they were finished eating, and Trey paid the bill before following Hannah out to the car.

He looked at the clock on the dashboard as he started the engine. "It's a little after one. Do you still have time to see the house?"

"*Ya*, if we make it quick. I want to be certain I'm home before my children." She shook her head and grinned. "I feel like a teenager who's sneaking around and worried about getting caught by her parents."

He raised his eyebrows with feigned concerned. "Did you sneak around a lot as a young lady, Hannah?"

She swatted at him. "No, I didn't. I never defied my parents. Did you?"

"Would you still like me if I admitted I did?" He slipped the car into gear and steered toward the parking lot exit.

"*Ya*, of course I would. How could I not like you?"

Her warm smile caused his pulse to skip. Could she possibly love him the way he loved her? A relationship like theirs was almost a modern day Romeo and Juliet story. Yet her words from earlier rang through his mind. She'd said she believed their friendship was from God. If that were true, would their relationship be doomed to fail?

Trey pulled up to the house and parked in the driveway. "This is it."

Hannah climbed from the car. "This is beautiful,

Trey." She tented her hand over her eyes as she looked up at the three-story clapboard house. "How many bedrooms does it have?"

He walked around the car and stood beside her. "There are six on the second level, but there are also a couple of rooms in the finished attic. I'm not certain if I'll use those for the business, but it will be great for storage." He pointed toward the far side of the house. "It also has this little apartment with another four rooms and a separate kitchen. It's huge on the inside."

"Does it have electricity?"

"Yes, it does." He nodded toward the row of barns. "It even has electricity in that big barn over there."

"It must've been Amish at some point. It has the apartment for the grandparents." She gestured toward the house. "I love that porch."

"It reminds me of yours." He watched her study the property and thought about their conversation the day they shared a cup of coffee. He wondered if she would ever consider running the bed and breakfast with him. She had so many wonderful ideas about the business. She could cook Amish meals and tell the guests about the culture. He knew it was a far-fetched idea, but he couldn't let it go. It would be a dream come true for both of them, and he longed to share this new life with Hannah.

She stepped over toward the fence by the pasture. "It's breathtaking. I can see why you fell in love with this place first."

"It feels like home." He crossed his arms over his chest. "I wish I could show you the inside, but it's locked up. The rooms have a primitive charm. They are simple, but elegant."

Hannah smiled. "You mean they look Amish?"

He laughed. "From what I know about the Amish, yes, they do."

"Sounds like home to me." She gestured toward the car. "I better get back to the house. My children may be home soon."

They continued discussing the house on the way back to her farm.

He parked in her driveway and cut off the engine. He then faced her while wishing that they had at least a few more hours together. "I had a great time today."

"I did too." Her smiled faded. "The day flew by too quickly. It seems as if you only just picked me up."

"I was just thinking the same thing." He tapped the steering wheel. "Hannah, I really care about you. Where do we go from here?"

"I don't know," she whispered.

He waited for her to continue, but she was silent. He wished she would open up more. Did she care about him too?

"May I see you again?" he asked.

"I care about you too, but I don't know what to do. I need to figure out some things." She gripped the door handle. "You'll be at the hotel for a little while longer, right?"

He nodded. "Yes, I'll be there until I close on the house. That's if the sale works out, of course."

"*Gut*." She pushed the door open. "Thank you again, Trey. I look forward to seeing you soon."

"I look forward to seeing you too."

Hannah exited the car and then walked swiftly up to the porch. She turned and waved before disappearing into the house. And at that very moment, he knew he was deeply in love with Hannah Glick, and his heart would break if he was forbidden from seeing her again.

• • •

Later that afternoon, Hannah sat in the family room and tried to concentrate on a Christian novel while she awaited her children's arrival. She'd scanned the same page more than a dozen times, but she couldn't seem to absorb the words. Her thoughts were focused only on Trey and his church. She couldn't stop the confusing thoughts spinning in her mind. She'd enjoyed her time with him more than she'd ever imagined, and she wanted to see him again soon. But how could she continue to sneak around like an out-of-control teenager?

"*Mamm?*" Amanda's voice sounded from the kitchen.

"I'm in the *schtupp.*" Hannah closed the book and placed it on the end table beside her.

Amanda stood in the doorway. "How are you?"

"Fine." Hannah stifled a yawn with her hand. "Excuse me. I'm a little tired."

Amanda frowned. "Maybe you need to lie down for a while. Lily and I can serve supper."

"Don't be *gegisch*. I'll take care of supper." Hannah patted the chair beside her. "Tell me about your visit."

"It was *gut*." Amanda sat on the chair. "*Mammi*

and *Onkel* Josh said they were disappointed you didn't come, and they hope you feel better." She studied her fingernails. "I really didn't want to go without you. I'm still upset about everyone talking about you."

Hannah touched Amanda's arm. "*Danki*, but you have to forgive everyone, including your *mammi*. She thinks she knows what's best for our family. She means well even if what she does is sometimes misguided."

Amanda looked up at her. "Is *Mammi* the real reason you stayed home? You can tell me the truth. I won't share it with anyone."

Hannah couldn't lie to her daughter. "*Mammi* was part of the reason."

"What was the other part?"

"I had an uncomfortable conversation with your *onkel* Joshua Thursday night, and I'd like to let things settle between us for a couple of days."

"Oh." Amanda wrinkled her nose as if she were trying to figure out a difficult puzzle. "Does it have to do with how he feels about you?"

Hannah tried to hide her surprise. "How did you know that?"

"I've noticed things." Amanda shrugged. "It's kind of obvious. If you watch someone's body language, you can figure out what they're feeling."

"How did you learn that?"

"Nancy read a book about it." Amanda suddenly frowned. "I'm not going to go to the youth gathering tonight for a similar reason."

"*Was iss letz?*"

Amanda ran her finger over the arm of the wing

chair, which had been Gideon's favorite. "I sort of had an argument with Nancy."

"You did?" Hannah sat up straighter. "What did you argue about?"

"Hannah!" a voice called from the kitchen.

Amanda popped up from the chair and moved to the door. "Hi, Ruth. My *mamm* is in here."

Hannah stood as her friend entered the family room. "Ruth. What a nice surprise. I wasn't expecting to see you here today."

Ruth smiled. "I've been thinking about you ever since we talked on Wednesday."

"Please, have a seat." She gestured toward the sofa, and Ruth sat down. Hannah then turned to Amanda. "Would you please go check on your siblings?"

"Of course." Amanda hurried off to the kitchen.

Ruth folded her hands on her lap. "How are things going?"

Hannah hesitated. Although she'd always enjoyed talking with Ruth, she was worried Ruth might criticize her for not visiting her family today and instead spending time with Trey.

"I'm not here to chastise you." She touched Hannah's hand. "I'm here to offer support. No matter what other people may say, I support you. You're *mei freind*, Hannah, and I treasure *mei freinden*, especially dear ones like you."

"*Danki*. I treasure you too, Ruth. You seem to always listen without judgment and I need that right now."

"And I promise you I always will." She tilted her head. "Did you see the bishop Wednesday after work?"

"*Ya*, I did." Hannah explained her visit with the bishop.

Ruth nodded her head while she listened. "You did the right thing, Hannah. I'm *froh* you spoke up about the rumors and explained yourself. I'm certain he kept his word and spoke to Elizabeth Beiler about giving Lillian a chance for the teaching position."

"He did. Elizabeth went to see Lillian at work and told her that she'd recommend her to the board for the teaching position."

"That's *wunderbaar!*" Ruth clapped her hands together. "Everything worked out the way it should."

Hannah shook her head while she thought about the day she'd spent with Trey. "I'm not certain about that."

Ruth frowned. "This sounds serious."

"It is." Hannah looked toward the doorway and then moved her chair closer to Ruth. "What I'm going to tell you must stay between us and only us."

"Of course it will remain between us."

"I stayed home today while the *kinner* went to see Barbie. I couldn't imagine spending the day trying to make small talk with her after knowing how she feels about me." Hannah shook her head while guilt rained down on her. "I had planned to stay home, but once the *kinner* were gone, the house was too quiet." She paused, wondering how she could admit what she'd done.

"Go on. I'm listening and I'm not judging you, Hannah. Remember, I'm your *freind* no matter what."

"I called Trey, and I spent the day with him."

Ruth's eyebrows careened toward her hairline. "You called Mr. Peterson and spent the day with him?"

Hannah nodded.

"What did you do with him?"

"We went to his church service. We then went to lunch and visited a property he's buying." Hannah gnawed her lower lip and hoped that Ruth wouldn't be disappointed in her.

"Hannah, do you realize what might happen if word gets around to the bishop?"

"I thought you were listening without judging me." Hannah frowned. "I know I can be shunned, but I also realized something else today."

"What did you realize?"

"I'm in love with him."

Ruth gasped. "You can't be serious. You hardly know him. How can you possibly make a relationship work? The only way it would work would be if he joined the Amish church or you left it."

"I know." Hannah rubbed her temple where a migraine was brewing. "I've mulled this over again and again. It doesn't make sense at all. I don't understand why God would bring our paths together if there's no way for it to work."

"Do you think he wants to be Amish?"

Hannah shook her head. "I can't see him converting."

Ruth's eyes were wide once again. "Are you thinking of leaving the faith?"

"No, I don't think so." Her voice was tentative.

"You don't think so?" Ruth's eyes narrowed. "That sounds to me like you're not certain."

Hannah's shoulders drooped. "I know. I've been thinking about this all day, and my stomach is in knots.

I can't imagine leaving this community. This is my home, and it's the only life I thought I'd ever want. My heart is here."

"Your decision to leave won't only affect you. Hannah, if you left the faith, what would happen to your *kinner*? What if they don't want to leave the faith?"

"I know. The decision to leave would mean I would force my *kinner* to also leave, possibly against their will. But this is about more than just leaving the only community I've ever known. I wouldn't be able to do business with anyone who is Amish. That means I also would have to move out of *mei haus* because I can't rent a home or buy a home from anyone who is Amish. And I'd have to sell my part of the horse farm since Joshua wouldn't be allowed to do business with me anymore. I know I can't support myself well with only the salary from the hotel." She rubbed her temple again. "It's all so overwhelming, but I can't deny how I feel about Trey. I just don't know what to do. I feel like I'm standing at a great crossroads. The decision I make now will affect my life and *mei kinner's* lives forever."

Ruth nodded slowly. "You're right. That means you need to choose wisely and not make your decision in haste."

"I know." Hannah wanted to ask Ruth what she should do, but she knew this had to be her decision. Only she could decide what was best for her and her children, and she prayed that God would make the right decision obvious to her.

. . .

Trey answered his phone on the second ring while driving back to the hotel after supper that evening. "Hello?"

"Trey!" Christy's voice sang through the phone. "You left me a message last week, and I've been meaning to call you back. It's been crazy here. How are you?"

"I'm doing fine, thanks. I was actually going to give you one more day and then call you again."

"I'm so sorry. What's new? How's your Amish friend?"

"Funny you should ask." Trey motored through an intersection while he spoke. "I spent today with her."

"You spent the day with her?" Christy's voice raised an octave. "How did you manage that? As I said before, I always thought the Amish kept to themselves."

"You're right. They normally do keep to themselves, but she called me this morning. I picked her up and we went to my church and then we had lunch together." He smiled while he thought of her beautiful smile as she sat across from him at the sandwich shop.

"Did you say she went to your church?"

"Yes, I did. It's a nice little community church located in Paradise. You'd love it. Hannah said she liked the service too. I was really surprised." He contemplated how nice it had been to have her next to him in the pew. He'd like to enjoy that feeling every Sunday if he could. He stopped at a stoplight and rested his free hand on the steering wheel. "We had a really nice time."

"Wait a minute. From the sound of your voice, you seem to really like her. I mean *really* like her."

"Yes, I do really like her. I more than like her. I think I'm in love with her."

"Trey." Christy clicked her tongue. "Have you lost your mind?"

"Yes, that's definitely a possibility."

"I hope you realize you can't have a relationship with her unless you become Amish or she stops being Amish."

"I know." The light turned green and he gripped the wheel as he accelerated. "I'm playing with fire. I feel like I'm living out the story of Romeo and Juliet."

"That's exactly what I was thinking. What are you going to do?"

He shrugged as if his sister could see him through the phone. "I have no idea. I guess I'll just enjoy what time I have with her. What else can I do?"

"You can put a stop to this before you find yourself with a broken heart." She sighed. "I know you suffered after losing Corinne and Sammi, but I hate to see you torture yourself this way. You're very vulnerable."

Trey glowered. "I'm not as vulnerable as you think, Christy. These feelings are real, and I think she feels the same way about me. Remember, I told you she called me. I didn't call her."

"I understand, but I'm worried about you."

"Thanks for worrying about me, but I'm a big boy. I can handle myself." He didn't want to be treated like a child. "You need to hear about the place I found. I put an offer on it." He told her about the farm, describing the house and the property in great detail.

"That sounds perfect. I'd love to come see it."

"That would be great." He asked about her children, and she shared how busy they were with school and extracurricular activities.

"I better let you go. I have to get the kids ready for bed. It was nice talking to you." She paused for a moment. "I know you don't want to hear it, but I think you're going to wind up hurt if you get involved with this Amish woman. She's bound by rules we don't live by. I wish you'd stop seeing her. You're going to get hurt, and I don't think you need more heartache right now."

"I think it's my decision if I want to face more heartache." Trey steered through another intersection. "I'm tired of being alone, and I enjoy Hannah's company."

"You can find another woman to spend your time with. What about joining one of those online dating services? One of my divorced friends found a really nice man through one of those sites. Or maybe you'll meet someone through your church. There are plenty of nice women out there who don't have the complications Hannah has."

Trey shook his head. Christy just didn't understand, but he knew he'd never convince her to look at the situation from his point of view. Once his sister made up her mind, there was no use trying to change it. "Fine. I'll try to meet someone at church."

"You're humoring me, aren't you?"

"Not at all." He couldn't help his smile.

"Look, I'm just worried about you." A flurry of activity sounded behind her. "Oh, I need to go. Sabrina needs me to help her study for a math test. We'll talk soon, okay?"

"That would be great. Tell Sabrina I hope she does well on her test tomorrow. Good night." He hung up and then steered into the hotel parking lot.

He nosed his car into a space near the back. He strode toward the front door while thinking about Christy's warning. He knew in his heart that she was right; the relationship was too complicated to work out. His gut tightened with sorrow and dread.

Yet he also knew he loved Hannah too much to just give up. He would keep the door open for Hannah and let her guide their future.

Trey would also keep praying and asking God for a chance to build a relationship with her. If he could just have a chance, he'd do his best to make her happy and possibly even build a life with her.

TWENTY-ONE

Monday evening, Josh wiped his brow and glanced up at the ominous storm clouds gathering in the sky while he stood in the pasture. He'd hoped to finish repairing the fence in his parents' pasture before the storm hit, but he was quickly running out of time as thunder rumbled in the distance.

He picked up another nail and then retrieved the hammer from the post. While he drove another nail into the loose plank, his thoughts returned to Hannah. He'd been contemplating their last conversation when he'd opened his heart to her and told her he wanted to marry her. He'd all but thrown any caution to the wind and asked for her hand in marriage, and he thought he'd possibly convinced her since she said she'd think about it. Yet when she didn't come along to his parents' house with her children on Sunday, he realized he hadn't gotten any closer to having her as his wife.

He worried that she was actually going to leave the church for that *Englisher*. He had to convince her to stay. He couldn't bear the thought of her leaving. He didn't want to lose her or the children. He wanted them to be a family.

Josh shared his worries with the church district's deacon, Jonas Chupp, and one of the district's ministers, Melvin Bender, when they came to visit his parents yesterday, and now he worried that he shouldn't have told them. They probably went straight to the bishop. He knew he couldn't bully her into staying in the community and marrying him. He had to prove his love to her. He thought that giving her the spool holder was a way to show his love, but that hadn't worked either. He was at a loss as to how to get her to marry him.

He drove another nail into the post, hoping to relieve some of the tension and frustration gripping his shoulders and neck. He didn't know how to get through to Hannah. How could he convince her that he'd be a good husband and father? Why didn't she want them to be a family?

"Joshua?" His father approached him from behind. "Do you hear that thunder? You should come in before the storm hits. Don't forget that *bu* who was hit by lightning while working in the field last year."

"*Ya*, I know." Josh hammered one more nail and wiped his brow again. "I was hoping to finish this."

"You can finish it later." His father eyed him. "You've been awfully tense for the past couple of days. *Was iss letz?*"

Josh leaned against the post as another clap of thunder sounded. "I've been wondering what I'm doing wrong with Hannah."

"What do you mean?"

"I've been trying to convince her that I want to take care of her and the *kinner*." He folded his arms over his chest. "I love them all, and I feel like it's my duty to be there for them since Gideon's gone. We already handle the farm together, so it just makes sense that we're a family."

Eli studied him a moment. "Are you saying you love her?"

"Oh *ya*." Josh nodded. "I'm crazy about her, *Dat*."

"Do you think she loves you too?"

Josh shrugged. "I don't know. We're close *freinden*, and we get along well. I've told her I care deeply about her. In fact, I finally came out and told her I love her, and I'm certain our relationship could develop into a loving marriage."

"Have you asked her to marry you?"

Josh shrugged. "I've mentioned it."

"But have you asked her the direct question?"

"Well, I haven't officially asked her. I've talked about how I think we should get married." Another clap of thunder sounded, and Josh picked up the nails and hammer.

"So you haven't really asked her." *Dat* gestured with his hands. "You haven't asked the direct question."

Josh shook his head. "No, I haven't officially said, 'Will you marry me?'"

Dat smiled. "She needs to hear the question, Joshua. You can talk about marriage until you run out of words, but it won't become reality until you ask her. You have to say, 'Hannah, will you marry me?' You can't dance around a subject as serious as that one."

The thunder boomed, and Josh nodded. "I'll ask her." His stomach tightened at the thought of saying the question out loud and having Hannah finally say the magical word—*yes*.

"We'd better get inside." *Dat* gestured toward the barn, and Josh followed him while he contemplated when he would ask Hannah the question. He couldn't wait. He'd go see her today, and then they could finally choose a wedding date.

. . .

A rumble of thunder sounded in the distance while Hannah worked to patch the holes in the knees of a pair of Andrew's work trousers. She looked at the spool holder on the desk and wondered if Joshua was working outside. He'd told her he planned to fix the fence in his parents' pasture before it got dark. She hoped he came in before the storm hit.

Hannah glanced out the window of the sewing room to observe the approaching storm, and she spotted a horse and buggy moving up the rock driveway.

"I wonder who that could be." Hannah peered out the window and saw Jonas Chupp and Melvin Bender climbing from the buggy. She grimaced, knowing the only reason they would visit would be if there was a concern with her family. She imagined it had to do with the rumors circling about her relationship with Trey.

Hannah checked her reflection in the mirror hanging above the mountain of material teetering on the desk next to her sewing machine. She smoothed her hands over her apron and touched her prayer covering before hurrying down the stairs to the kitchen. She opened the back door just as Jonas and Melvin reached the porch.

"*Wie geht's?*" Hannah forced a smile as lightning streaked across the dark sky above her. "Please come in."

"*Danki.*" Melvin removed his hat as he stepped into the mudroom.

"Good to see you, Hannah." Jonas followed the minister into the kitchen.

She fiddled with her apron as she stood in front of them. "May I offer you a glass of meadow tea and some *kichlin*?"

"Oh no, *danki*." Jonas touched his beard.

Melvin folded his arms over his wide chest. "We won't be here long."

She pointed toward the table. "Let's all have a seat." She sat across from them and folded her hands. "What brings you out here this evening?" She thought she heard a squeaking sound from the stairs leading to the second floor, and she wondered if one of her children was eavesdropping.

Jonas fingered his beard as thunder rumbled around them. His expression was soft and devoid of accusation. "The bishop has expressed some concern regarding your relationship with an *Englisher*." He motioned toward the minister. "We talked about it earlier and thought it would be best to come speak with you instead of waiting for you to come to us about it."

Hannah's stomach dropped. The deacon and minister were often sent when a member was suspected of immoral behavior or if a member was planning to leave the church. She opened her mouth to speak, but hesitated. She wasn't certain what to say to these men. Her mind raced with questions and worries. Did she need to confess her love for Trey? She wasn't certain if she wanted to leave the church or what she should share with the two men watching her from across the table.

"There's no reason for you to be *naerfich*, Hannah." Melvin's smile was tentative, and his words didn't ease her worry. "We want to know if you're planning to leave the community."

"I don't know where you got the idea that I plan to leave the church. I didn't tell Elmer I was planning on leaving." Hannah folded her clammy hands on the table. "I only told him I agreed I should discontinue my relationship with *mei English freind*, Mr. Peterson, because I want *mei dochder* to have a chance to be teacher. I was tired of the rumors that were floating around about me, and I want my family to be treated fairly."

Melvin held up his hands as if to calm her. "We're not here to chide you, and we don't plan to feed any rumors. Some discussions have been brought to our attention, however, and, after also hearing from the bishop about his concern, we felt we should be proactive and talk to you."

Frustration coursed through Hannah. Who was talking about her behind her back? "What discussions are you referring to? I haven't had any other discussions about my friendship with Mr. Peterson. I visited Elmer on Wednesday, and Elizabeth Beiler spoke with Lillian on Thursday about applying for the teaching position."

The two men shared a glance.

Jonas shifted in the chair. "There has been talk that the *Englisher* is very special to you and may be more than your *freind*."

She looked between the men and wondered what they were hiding. "Who told you that?"

"I don't think I'm at liberty to share my source's name." Melvin's smile was apologetic.

"I think I have a right to know who's been talking about me. I'd like to set that person straight." Hannah hoped she sounded more confident than she felt.

Jonas sat up straighter in the chair as if he were taking control of the meeting. "If you're planning on leaving, then we should set up a meeting with the baptized members of the congregation."

"I never said I was leaving. I love this community. Leaving it would break my heart." Hannah looked at each of them. "Who told you I was going to leave the church? Was it Barbie?"

The men shook their heads.

"But if it wasn't Barbie. . ." Hannah gasped when she realized who could've been talking about her. "It was Joshua, wasn't it?"

Both men averted their eyes.

Hannah shook her head while thoughts spun through her mind. *I should've known it was Joshua and not Barbie. He's always loved me, and he said he wanted to be with me after Gideon died. Of course he would report my relationship to the minister and the deacon. He's jealous!*

Melvin cleared his throat. "As Jonas was saying, if

you are leaving, and you'd like us to set up a meeting with the baptized members of the church, we can do it this Sunday. That way you can tell them you plan on leaving. Of course, you won't be able to stay in this *haus* since you rent it from your in-laws. You won't be able to do business with any Amish families once you're excommunicated."

Hannah shook her head. "No, I don't need you to set up a meeting. I told you, I'm not planning to leave the church."

Melvin nodded, and his expression softened. "I'm glad to hear that. We've been concerned about you. You know what a huge decision it is to leave the church. Just think of your *kinner*, Hannah. It would be difficult for them if you did leave the community. And it would break the hearts of all of our members. We don't want you to leave. You should really think through this relationship with the *Englisher*. It's in your best interest to stay in this community. You've been Amish since you were a child. Why would you want to leave?"

"He's right that we've both been worried about you. We only want the best for your family. We're glad to hear that you're not going to leave." Jonas folded his hands on the table. "It's not my place to judge, of course, but when I heard you were thinking of leaving, I thought of Gideon. He was the head of your household, and we all know Gideon had a very strong faith. He would be very upset if he knew you were considering taking your *kinner* away from the church."

"You're right. Gideon would be upset if I took our *kinner* away from the church." Hannah shook her head. "But I never said I was leaving, so you don't have anything to worry about." She wasn't sure what she wanted. She knew one thing for certain—she wanted everyone, including Joshua, Jonas, Melvin, and Barbie, to stop making assumptions about her and her future.

Jonas smiled. "I'm *froh* to hear we don't need to set up that congregational meeting for you."

"I'm *froh* too." Hannah stood as frustrated thoughts rushed through her mind. *I'm not certain what's in store for me right now. But I do know I want the community to stop making decisions for me before I've had a chance to make them for myself.* She walked toward the door. "*Danki* for coming by. Please tell your wives I said hello."

The two men made their way to the door.

"*Gut nacht.*" Jonas grabbed his hat from the peg on the wall in the mudroom.

Melvin nodded as he took his hat and followed him out the back door into the rain.

"Be careful on the way home." Hannah watched them jog through the rain to the waiting buggy. She shook her head. Why would they ask her if she was leaving the community if she hadn't expressed the desire to leave? And why did it seem as though Jonas and Melvin had a hard time believing her when she said she had no plans to leave? Hannah wondered if Joshua realized something she didn't. Perhaps he could sense her restlessness before she could. Maybe she did want to leave, but she hadn't admitted it to herself yet.

A streak of lighting lit up the sky followed by a clap of thunder.

"*Mamm?*"

Hannah looked back and found Lillian glaring at her from the doorway to the kitchen. "Lily? How long have you been standing there?"

Lillian's lip quivered. "I heard everything, *Mamm*."

"What do you mean?" Hannah took a step toward her, and Lillian stepped backward. "What did you hear?"

"Everything." Lillian shook her head. "You want to leave the church and that means we have to move out of our *haus*." She gestured around the room. "Where will we live? How can I be the teacher if I don't have a place to live? If you leave the faith for that *Englisher*, then I'm going to live with *Mammi*. I want to be Amish, and I want to be a teacher. I want to get baptized. I have goals for my life, and none of them involve being *English*. You can't ruin this for me, *Mamm*. It's not fair!"

"Just calm down. The last thing I want is for my family to be broken up into different homes. You and your siblings are the most important people in my life and that will never change." Hannah reached for Lillian's arm, but she pulled back. "I never said I was going to leave the faith. Jonas and Melvin assumed that, but I never said it."

"But they heard it from *Onkel* Josh. You told him you were going to leave!" Her voice was shrill as thunder shook the house. "*Onkel* Josh loves you, but you told him you love someone else. Right? Isn't that what happened?" Tears splattered down Lillian's pink cheeks.

"What?" Hannah shook her head. "Where did you hear that?"

"I heard *Onkel* Josh talking to someone yesterday at *Mammi's*. He was really upset. He said he was worried you were going to leave the church. He said *Dat's* heart would be broken because you'd break up our family. He's right, isn't he? We're going to lose our *haus* and the farm." Lillian sniffed.

Hannah shook her head. Why was Lillian over-reacting? Why was Joshua going around making assumptions and spreading gossip about her life? Why were things getting more and more confusing? It was too much to take in. There was too much pressure. She felt as if her head might explode from another migraine brewing in her temples.

"*Mamm!*" Lillian's voice quaked. "Please answer me. Are we going to lose everything when you marry Mr. Peterson?"

"Lily, please listen to me." Hannah took Lillian's hand in hers. "I never said I'm going to leave the church or marry Trey. I love this community. This is my home. I could never just walk away from everything I love. You're jumping to conclusions, just like everyone else in this community."

"I know what I heard." Lillian yanked her hand away and brushed away a tear from her cheek. "And I've seen how you look at Mr. Peterson. He's more than your *freind.* And what about *Dat?* How could you betray his memory like this? *Dat* wanted us to be Amish. He wanted us to live here." She gestured around the house. "This is the *haus Dat* chose for us. We're his family. This is where we belong."

"Lily, stop. You're not listening to me. I would never hurt your *dat's* memory."

Lillian lifted her chin as her scowl deepened. "I think

it's time you admit how you feel and be honest with us. We're your *kinner*. We deserve to know the truth."

Hannah leveled her eyes at Lillian as frustration boiled within her. "You're right. You're my *dochder*, but you have no right to talk to me this way. I always tell you the truth."

"Do you?" Lillian's eyes narrowed. "Did you really stay home yesterday or did you go out somewhere?"

Hannah studied her daughter. "What do you mean?"

"I saw new tire tracks in the driveway when we got home from *Mammi's* yesterday. Andrew pointed them out to me." Lillian gestured toward the window where the rain pounded the glass. "I could tell someone had been here in a car. I know it wasn't a customer because the farm is closed on Sundays. Did Mr. Peterson come to see you?"

"I don't think that's any of your business, Lillian."

"You have been seeing him in secret." Lillian shook her head. "*Onkel* Josh is right. We're going to lose our farm and everything. Where will we live? How will we make a living?"

"Lily, that's ridiculous! I only went to church with Trey and had lunch with him. That's it. We're *freinden*. I don't understand why everyone is jumping to conclusions about all of this."

"You're betraying *Dat's* memory by seeing that man." Lillian shook her head. "It's wrong to see him."

"Stop fighting!" Amanda marched into the room with her hands up. "This is ridiculous!"

"I can't just stand here and let *Mamm* disrespect *Dat's* memory by seeing Mr. Peterson." Lillian's voice rose over the rumbling thunder. "Our family is falling apart. If *Dat* were still alive, everything would be normal. We'd be like every other family in this community, and no one would be talking about us behind our backs."

Hannah placed her hand on Lillian's shoulder. "You just need to calm down. I've done nothing wrong. We are allowed to have *English freinden.*"

"No," Lillian said through gritted teeth. "I'm not overreacting. I'm only telling the truth. I'm going upstairs." She disappeared, and Hannah heard her feet stomp up the stairs.

Amanda touched Hannah's arm. "She'll be okay. You know how she overreacts about everything, and then she gets over it."

Hannah studied her blond daughter. "Are you upset with me too?"

Amanda shook her head. "No, I'm okay."

"Did you hear my conversation with Jonas and Melvin too?"

Amanda nodded. "*Ya*, I did. I hope you're not upset that Lily and I eavesdropped."

Hannah touched Amanda's prayer covering. "No, I'm not." She sighed. "I just don't know what to do. Sometimes I'm so confused about it all."

"You'll figure it out." Amanda smiled. "You're *mei mamm.*"

Hannah returned the smile. "I wish it were that easy."

A knock sounded on the back door.

"I'll get it." Hannah started for the door. "Would you make sure your *bruder* is getting ready for bed?"

"*Ya.*" Amanda hurried up the stairs.

Hannah opened the back door and found Josh standing on her porch, his clothing, shoes, and hat soaked by the driving rain. "Joshua! What are you doing here?"

He removed his hat and stepped into the mudroom. "I need to talk to you."

Her heart lurched as she thought of her in-laws. "Is everything okay? Did something happen to your parents?"

He shook his head. "They're fine. As I said, I just need to talk to you."

"Oh." She thought of her conversation with Melvin and Jonas, and her stomach tightened. Joshua was the catalyst for their visit, and now he was standing in front of her. Perhaps he was here to apologize? She pointed toward the kitchen. "Do you want to come in and sit down? I can get you a towel and make coffee."

"No, *danki.*" He fingered his hat and cleared his throat, and she wondered why he seemed so nervous. "I have something to ask you, and I think it's time to just come out and say it."

Hannah folded her arms over her bib apron and nodded. "Take your time." She prepared herself for his apology along with a confession.

"I've known you most of my life, Hannah." His smile was tentative. "I've always admired you, and it was difficult when you chose *mei bruder* over me."

Hannah frowned and then opened her mouth to speak.

"Wait." He held up his hand. "Please just give me a chance to finish." He gripped his hat and stared into her eyes. "Hannah, I've always loved you, and I've been trying to show you just how much I love you. I think I've been going about it wrong. So, I'm here to officially ask you to marry me."

Hannah gasped. *Could this day get any more confusing?*

"So, Hannah." He took her hand in his. His skin was cold and wet from the rain. "Will you marry me? Will you be my wife and build a life with me?"

Her eyes filled with tears as a myriad of emotions drenched her. "Joshua, I don't know what to say." Her voice trembled. "This is so unexpected."

"Please tell me you'll at least consider it. I can't bear your rejection." His eyes pleaded with her.

"Joshua, I'm confused." She pulled her hand away and wiped her eyes. "Jonas Chupp and Melvin Bender were just here to see me."

Josh's hopeful expression fell as all of the color drained from his complexion. "Hannah, I'm so sorry. I should never have talked to them."

"I don't understand why you did." Hannah shook her head as frustration bubbled through her. "Did you really think you could come here and propose to me after you told Jonas and Melvin that I'm going to leave the community and marry an *Englisher*?"

Josh shook his head. "I'm so sorry, Hannah. I was wrong. I wasn't thinking at all."

"Why did you tell them, Joshua? I don't understand."

"I thought maybe Jonas and Melvin would talk some sense into you." Josh gestured as if grasping for an explanation. "I hoped they would make you see that you belong here with the people who love you, including me."

Hannah blew out a breath and tried to sort through her perplexing feelings. She didn't know where she belonged. Should she be with Joshua and continue living the life she knew? Or should she consider a life with Trey, the man she loved, and risk losing Lillian?

"Hannah?" His eyes were hopeful. "Would you please forgive me for talking to Jonas and Melvin? I know it was a mistake, a huge mistake, and I'm so sorry. I never meant to hurt you."

She nodded. "I know, Joshua. I know you would never knowingly hurt me."

"So, what's your answer? Will you marry me, Hannah? I'll give you everything I have. I'll do my best to build a *gut* life for us and the *kinner*. I'll love you with my whole heart. Please, Hannah. Just give me a chance. You won't regret it."

The sincerity and desperation in Joshua's eyes tugged at her heart strings. She couldn't tell him no, even though she wasn't sure if she would ever say yes.

"Joshua, I'm really confused right now." She pressed her hand to her throbbing temple. "My head is pounding at the moment. Let me think about it, okay?"

"*Ya!*" His smile was electric, causing his face to glow with excitement. "Please think about it. I'll be anxiously awaiting your answer." He slipped his hat onto his head and started for the door. "I'll see you tomorrow." He disappeared through the back door.

TWENTY-TWO

Hannah closed the door behind Joshua and then leaned back against the cool wood. The evening's events swirled around her like a tornado and her heart pounded against her rib cage. She'd gone from telling the minister and deacon that she wasn't going to leave the community to arguing with her daughter, who threatened to move out. She then received a marriage proposal from her brother-in-law. She found herself drowning in all of the baffling emotions. Her pounding headache caused her stomach to sour.

Hannah needed her mind off her headache and the emotions battling within her. She looked toward the counter and found where Lillian had started making a shopping list. She rummaged through the cabinets, refrigerator, and freezer and tried her best to concentrate on what she needed to buy during her next trip to the market. Her thoughts, however, were focused only on Joshua's proposal and Lillian's threat to leave.

She leaned against the counter and cradled her pounding head with her hands. She couldn't help wondering if she should marry Joshua to save her family. The solution made sense. After all, she and Joshua were close friends, and they ran a business together. He loved her children, and they loved him. Yet she couldn't see herself happy with him. When she closed her eyes and imagined herself as Joshua's wife, her shoulders tightened. Her heart didn't warm at the idea of living as his wife. There was no spark, no attraction. He was only Joshua, her good friend. She wondered if he was correct and she would eventually learn to love him for the sake of her children. But how could she fall deeply in love with someone who didn't warm her heart?

She pushed the frustrating thoughts away and stared down at her shopping list. The sound of tires crunching on the rocks outside followed by headlights flashing on the kitchen wall drew her attention toward the window. She looked out the window and spotted Trey climbing from his car.

Her heart thumped in her chest as she rushed toward the back door and opened it.

"Good evening." Trey stepped up onto the porch and smiled at her. He looked handsome in a blue collared shirt and khaki trousers.

"Trey." She rushed out to him and embraced him. "It's so good to see you." His arms were strong and comforting. The embrace he returned was the perfect therapy for her pounding headache and anxiety.

"It's good to see you too." He rested his cheek on her head while he held her. "How are you?"

Hannah stepped back from his embrace and shook her head. "It's been a stressful evening."

Trey's eyes regarded her with empathy. "I'm sorry. What happened?"

Hannah told him about her visit with the minister and deacon and then shared her argument with Lillian. "I feel like everyone is making my decisions for me. I'm tired of the pressure." She lowered herself onto a bench, and he sat beside her.

"I'm sorry for causing all of this stress in your life." Trey sighed and shook his head. "I had no idea things would be this bad for you." He studied her. "Do the Amish believe in chastising their members to convince them to follow their rules?"

"No, it's not that. We believe in encouraging our members to follow the right path. We live a simple life focused on God and family. If a member strays, we encourage that member to come back to the fold. They're only doing what they believe is right for me."

He frowned. "It seems more like bullying to me."

"No, it's not really bullying. Jonas and Melvin are trying to remind me of our beliefs." She sighed as she thought of Lillian. "I'm just so upset about Lily. I don't want to lose her."

He covered her hand with his. "I don't want you to lose her either, and I don't want to be the reason your family falls apart."

"I know." She leaned her head against his arm and felt the tension loosen in her shoulders and neck. She wondered why it was so easy for her to relax and open up to Trey. She could never share her feelings with Joshua as easily as she shared them with Trey. She thought of Joshua's proposal and almost told Trey about it. She felt, however, that she should keep that conversation to herself for now.

"Maybe I should stay away if I'm causing too much stress for your family." His voice was unsure.

Hannah shook her head and looked up at his worried eyes. "No. I don't want you to stay away. I'll figure this all out. I can't give you up that easily."

"Good." He leaned down and kissed her head. "I'm glad to hear that."

Hannah peered up at the sky and found that the rain had stopped and the clouds were breaking up.

Hannah's gaze cut to Trey. "Thank you for listening."

Trey smiled. "I'm always happy to listen to you."

"I never got to ask you why you came over tonight. Was this just an impromptu visit, or did you have a purpose?"

"I actually got some good news today." He angled his body toward her. "The house was appraised Friday, and I finally found out the results. The bank was happy with the appraisal. It looks like I'm going to close at the beginning of July."

"Wow!" Hannah clapped her hands. "That's wonderful. I'm so happy for you."

"I thought about trying to reach you by phone, but then I decided I'd rather tell you in person." He shrugged. "Any reason to see you is a good reason, in my opinion."

She smiled at him, and warmth filled her. "I enjoy seeing you in person too."

"Would you like to take a ride out to see the house tomorrow? We didn't get a chance to walk the property. I'd love to show you the pond and maybe get your thoughts on where I could put a garden." He pointed toward her garden by the porch where vegetables stretched up toward the sky. "It's obvious you know a lot about gardening."

"*Ya*, I'd like to see the house. Can you come get me around nine?"

"Absolutely. I'll be here at nine."

Hannah looked toward the door leading to the kitchen. "I better go check on my children. Thank you again. I look forward to seeing you tomorrow."

"I can't wait either. Have a good night, Hannah."

"You too." Hannah stepped into the mudroom. She smiled as she remembered the warmth of Trey's arms. Being with Trey felt natural and right. She'd never experienced that when she'd considered marrying Joshua. If Trey proposed to her, she would strongly consider saying yes. But how could she fathom leaving the community she loved so much? And, most importantly, how could she risk losing Lillian, her precious daughter?

. . .

Trey watched as Hannah walked toward the back door. She turned back and waved, and his heart swelled with love for her. He lingered for a moment until she disappeared into the house.

He climbed into his car and navigated toward the main road. He contemplated his conversation with Hannah while he drove. Instead of going to the hotel, he absently steered into the church parking lot as if a magnetic force were pulling him there. He made his way into the empty sanctuary and sat in the front pew.

He stared up at the cross while all of the emotions from the day churned within him.

"Lord," he whispered, while bowing his head and folding his hands together. "I'm so confused. My love for Hannah feels pure, and I'm certain it is a gift from you. But my love is wreaking havoc on her family and her life. Yet at the same time, Hannah told me that she can't give me up that easily. How can a gift so wonderful be wrong if it came from you?" He paused and wiped a tear from his eye. "Please tell me what I should do, Lord. Should I pursue my relationship with Hannah or walk away with a broken heart? Please lead me on the correct path, Lord. I ask this in Jesus' name. Amen."

Trey looked up and stared at the cross as calmness filled his heart. "Thank you," he whispered with a smile.

• • •

Andrew stared up at his mother as she leaned over his bed later that evening. "I heard you and Lily arguing earlier."

Mamm frowned. "I'm sorry you had to hear that. Lily and I disagree about something, but we'll work it out. It's nothing you have to worry about."

Andrew thought about the argument and what he heard while he was hiding on the stairs. "It has to do with Mr. Peterson, right?"

Mamm sat on the edge of his bed and sighed. "*Ya,* it does."

"Lily doesn't want you to be *freinden* with him."

She hesitated and then nodded. "*Ya*, that's mostly the reason."

"And Lily said she was going to move in with *Mammi* if you stay *freinden* with him."

"*Ya*, that's what she said." Her eyes became shiny as tears filled them.

Andrew's stomach twisted. He hated seeing *Mamm* cry. He couldn't stand it when she was upset and he didn't want to make her cry. Seeing her cry would make him cry too. She seemed to be upset lately, and he assumed it all had to do with her friendship with Mr. Peterson. Andrew didn't want to make his *mamm* cry like Lily did, so he was going to do his best to be *gut*.

"I won't leave you." Andrew shook his head. "I won't go with Lily if she leaves us. I'll stay right here with you."

She rubbed his hand. "*Danki*, Andrew. That makes me *froh*." Relief flooded him when she smiled.

He wanted her to keep smiling, so he tried to think of something positive to say to make her happy. "I can be friends with Mr. Peterson too. He seems nice. He likes horses, so I know I will get along with him. He had a horse that looked like Huckleberry, which means we already have something in common."

"That's *gut*. Everything will be fine, so don't worry about it." She leaned down and kissed his forehead. "It's time to go to bed now. Don't forget to say your prayers. *Ich liebe dich, mei liewe*."

"I love you too, *Mamm*." He rolled over and yawned. "*Gut nacht*."

. . .

Hannah gently closed Andrew's door and heaved a deep sigh. She was thankful Andrew wasn't upset after the argument earlier. She worried he would feel caught in the middle between her and Lillian.

She stepped into the hallway and crossed to her daughters' room. She and Lillian hadn't talked since their argument. Although she couldn't stand the silence between her and her daughter, she wanted to give Lillian time to calm down. She hoped they could talk tomorrow.

Amanda was sitting on the bed reading a book. "Are you reading one of Lily's novels?"

Amanda looked up and panic crossed her face. "No, I was just looking at something." She placed the book on the bureau beside her. "Lily's in the shower."

"Oh, *gut*. That gives us a few minutes to talk. What's that?" Hannah craned her neck in an attempt to see what book her daughter had been perusing. "*The Veterinarian's Manual*?" She read the title aloud and then studied her daughter's worried expression. "Why are you reading that?"

Amanda's eyes widened with worry. "Because I want to be a vet," she whispered.

"You want to be a vet?" Hannah was stunned by the news. "I had no idea, Amanda." She sank into a chair by the bed. "Why didn't you tell me?"

"I was afraid to. I've only told one person." She cleared her throat.

"Who is that one person?"

Amanda hesitated.

Hannah folded her hands in her lap. "I'll listen without judgment."

"His name is Mike." She grimaced. "He's not Amish. He's a *bu* who comes into the deli."

Hannah nodded slowly. "And you have become *freinden*?"

"We have. He's become a very *gut freind*." She grabbed the book from the bureau and ran her fingers over the cover while she spoke. "He's leaving for college at the end of the summer. His uncle owns the bookstore across from the deli, and Mike plans to work at the bookstore this summer. Mike wants to be a doctor, and I told him about how I want to be a vet. I've always loved working with the horses and the rest of the animals on our farm. That's why I've become friends with the vet who lives across the street from us. I want to talk to him about where he went to college. I'd love to know what the classes are like."

"Amanda, you could've told me this. I want to know about your hopes and dreams, and I will never chastise you when you share them with me." Hannah suddenly recalled a brief conversation she'd had with Amanda on Sunday. "Does this have something to do with why you argued with Nancy?"

Amanda gnawed her lower lip. "*Ya*, it does. Mike and I talked one day outside while I was eating lunch, and I asked him about college. He explained that I could go, but I would have to get my GED first. He said I'd have to take a test to get my GED, and I would have to study a big book. I went to the bookstore to see what the book looked like, and Nancy heard me ask the bookstore owner about it."

"And she was upset that you wanted to find out about the GED." Hannah filled in the blanks.

"*Ya.*" Amanda frowned. "She and I had a terrible argument, but she promised not to tell her parents I'm thinking about getting my GED."

"So you are thinking about it?"

Amanda hesitated.

"You know it's your choice, *ya*?"

"Just like it's your choice to be with Mr. Peterson."

Hannah sighed. "*Ya*, you're right, but my choice is much more complicated than yours. You're not baptized, Amanda. You can do whatever you'd like, no matter what Nancy—or even Lillian—says. And I'll always love you and be your *mamm* no matter what you choose."

Amanda nodded. "*Danki.* I really like Mr. Peterson, *Mamm.* He's so kind and thoughtful. I don't blame you for being his friend."

"*Danki.*" Hannah was so touched by her daughter's support and understanding that tears filled her eyes.

Amanda pushed her long, blond hair back from her shoulder. "I want to buy that GED book and look at it. I'm afraid I'm not smart enough to pass the test, but I want to try. I can't shake this dream of owning my own vet clinic. I could help animals all day long."

"I believe you're smart enough, Amanda." Hannah smiled. "If that's what you want to do, and you feel the Lord is leading you down that path, then you should at least look into the possibilities."

Amanda stared down at the veterinary book. "But

I don't know if I'm strong enough to leave. This is the only life I've ever known. Would our family understand?" She looked up and tears glistened in her eyes. "I want to have my vet clinic, but I don't want to lose my family. Would *Mammi* and *Daadi* still love me? Would they come to see my clinic? Would they write me while I'm in college?"

Hannah reached over and took Amanda's hand in hers, hoping to ease her tears. "Of course they would still love you and they would support you. They may not understand why you want to go to college, but you're not baptized. They would still treat you like family. You could open a vet clinic nearby and we'd all visit you. It's your decision, Amanda."

"But since you're baptized, it wouldn't be as easy for you if you left."

Hannah shook her head. "No, it wouldn't be as easy for me. I could easily lose your sister, and I don't think that's something I can live with."

Amanda nodded. "I understand. You're in a much tougher position than I am."

"That's very true."

"You should pray about it." Amanda squeezed Hannah's hand. "You should see where God leads you."

Hannah studied her daughter's eyes. "I will. And you should do the same, *mei liewe*."

She said good night to Amanda and then headed downstairs to her bedroom. She stared at the ceiling and contemplated her situation while begging God to guide her in her complicated and heart-wrenching decision.

TWENTY-THREE

Amanda's supportive words echoed through Hannah's mind while she rode beside Trey in his car the following morning. She'd spent a good part of the night continuing to stare at the ceiling while praying and contemplating what to do about her relationship with Trey. In her heart she knew she loved him, and this relationship was exactly what her hopeful heart had craved ever since she'd lost Gideon. Yet she'd never expected a new chance at love to come in the form of a man who wasn't Amish.

During her prayers, she'd begged God to give her a sign telling her what to do. Was leaving the church the correct path for her? She was also stunned by the news that Amanda dreamed of becoming a veterinarian. She'd noticed that Amanda enjoyed talking with Cameron Wood, the neighbor vet who came to help Andrew when he was hurt. She'd found Amanda over at Cameron's house more than once when she was supposed to be doing chores. Hannah had thought Amanda was just being neighborly. She had never realized how much Amanda liked to talk to the man. She also wondered if Amanda's situation was the sign she needed to illustrate that choosing a different path was okay. Maybe a new start was just what her heart needed.

But when she considered leaving Lillian, her heart ached. How could she leave the community when it would hurt her other daughter? The painful distance between Hannah and Lillian was growing. Lillian had only given Hannah one-word responses to her questions before Hannah left this morning. She felt her precious daughter slipping away from her, and it was breaking her heart.

"You're awfully quiet this morning." Trey smiled over at her from the driver's seat. "Are you doing better today?"

"I am." Hannah ran her fingers over the seat-belt strap.

"That's good. I know you went through a lot yesterday." He steered onto the road leading to the house. "How's Lily?"

Hannah nodded. "She's still not talking to me, but I think she may need a day or two to sort through her feelings."

He gave her a quick sideways glance. "I've been thinking about your meeting with the minister and deacon and also your argument with Lily. I'm sorry if I've caused trouble for your family."

Hannah shook her head. "Don't be sorry. Being with you was my choice. I believe everything happens in the Lord's time."

"I agree." He turned into the driveway and steered up to the house. "Here it is. If all goes well, this will be my new home in only a matter of weeks." He turned off the engine and pulled the keys from the ignition. "Let's go poke around."

Hannah climbed out and met him at the front of the car. "I still think it's perfect. I'm so glad you're able to buy it." She scanned the large house. "I love the wraparound porch. My parents' house had a porch like that. I always wanted Gideon to expand our porch, but his parents didn't like the idea. Since they own the house and the property, we had to abide by their wishes."

"You rent the house from Gideon's parents?" Trey started walking toward the enclosed pasture, and Hannah fell into step beside him.

"*Ya*, we do. Gideon wanted to buy it from them, but he never got around to applying for the mortgage."

"I want to ask you something, but it's not my business." Trey stopped and leaned against the fence.

"You can ask me anything." She shaded her hand over her eyes to block the bright sun and looked back toward the house, taking in the large trees filled with chirping birds.

"You said the minister and deacon were trying to lead you back to the fold. Right now you're breaking rules by seeing me. Does that mean you have to leave the faith to be with me?"

"*Ya*, I would have to leave the church."

"And what would happen then?"

Hannah folded her arms over her chest. "If I were to leave the church, I would be excommunicated."

"Is that the same as being shunned?"

"*Ya*, it is."

"What happens when you're shunned?" His expression was full of worry.

"When you're shunned, you can't do business with anyone who is Amish. No money can exchange hands. That means I couldn't rent my house from my in-laws or stay in business with Joshua. I wouldn't even be able to shop in an Amish store, so I couldn't buy cheese at the deli where Amanda works."

Trey frowned, and she wondered what he was thinking. The intensity in his handsome face caused her pulse to race.

She glanced around the property to break away from his stare. "You asked me where I would plant a garden." Hannah pointed toward an area between the house and the fence. "I would plant one there and expand it all the way to those two big trees. You could grow peas, tomatoes, strawberries, eggplants, zucchini, raspberries, string beans, lima beans, peppers, cauliflower, broccoli, onions, asparagus, carrots, and herbs." She motioned toward the other side of the large yard. "You could even do potatoes and sweet potatoes too. And if you really wanted to be ambitious, you could do corn." She turned to him, and he raised his eyebrows. "What? You think I'm silly?"

"No, not silly, but ambitious may be the correct word. I would need help to do all of that work." He smiled, and her heart fluttered. "Come with me." He took her hand and urged her forward. His warm touch made her blood hum fast through her veins as they walked the length of the pasture together.

"This is beautiful." Hannah looked up. "Listen to

those birds singing to God." She looked up at him. "Have you thought more about a name for the bed and breakfast?"

"What do you think of A Slice of Paradise?" He gestured with his free hand. "Isn't it a perfect fit for this land? It is a little piece of paradise, isn't it?"

She nodded. "*Ya*, it is."

"Especially when you're with me." He squeezed her hand, and her heart thumped in her chest.

They stopped by a small pond surrounded by cement benches.

"I think the previous owner spent a lot of time back here." He led her to a bench and they sat together. "This is so soothing. I think after a long day of work, you could come back here and just sit and think or pray. You would just feel like you're surrounded by so much of God's beauty with the birds and the flowers." He pointed toward the rose bushes and tulips. "Isn't it just perfect?"

"*Ya*, it is. I could stay here all day and forget all of my worries."

"I know." Trey cleared his throat. "I need to be honest with you about a few things."

"Go ahead."

"I'm in love with you, Hannah. I've known it for a while, but it really hit home last night." He held both of her hands in his, and his eyes sparkled in the sunlight. "I've been thinking about what happened last night with the deacon and the minister and also your argument with Lily. I can tell our friendship has caused you a lot of heartache and stress."

"Trey, I told you not to blame yourself for this. It's my choice to spend time with you."

"Please," he began, "let me finish. I've wrestled with whether or not I belong in your life, and I even stopped by the church on the way home and prayed last night. I asked God to show me a sign that will tell me whether or not our relationship is a part of his plan for us." He paused and took a deep breath. "Last night I dreamt you and I were married here in this garden. And you were going to help me run this bed and breakfast."

Hannah gasped. "You dreamt that?"

Trey nodded. "I did, and it felt like the sign. We were happy in the dream. Your children were here, and they lived in the apartment with us. It was perfect. It was paradise." He cleared his throat again. "So, I want to ask you something."

Her heart thudded in her chest and her eyes filled with tears.

"Hannah, I love you." He lifted her hands and squeezed them again. "I want to build a life with you. I know we haven't known each other long, but I see my future when I look into your eyes. I believe the Lord brought us together to give us another chance at happiness. Would you do me the honor of being my wife and making me the happiest man in the world?"

Hannah gasped. She felt as if the world were spinning out of control right before her eyes. She looked back toward the house and imagined herself living there, running the bed and breakfast with Trey, as his wife. The idea warmed her heart, but could she walk away from the life she'd known and loved since birth?

Memories flashed through her mind as tears flooded her eyes. She remembered running through the pasture at the house where she grew up. She thought about sitting on her mother's lap during church services when she was a little girl. Her memories moved to the one-room schoolhouse of her childhood and then to the youth group gathering times she spent with her friends. When her thoughts moved to Gideon, and their courtship and wedding, the tears streamed down her cheeks.

Her Amish community was where she'd grown up and planned to raise her family. How could she leave it all behind? And where would this leave Lily? It all seemed too surreal.

"It's too soon, isn't it?" He let her hands fall from his grip. "I'm pushing you too hard. I shouldn't have asked yet."

Hannah took a deep breath and wiped the tears from her warm cheeks. "No, don't apologize." She cleared her throat in an attempt to strengthen her thin voice. "I'm really overwhelmed right now. I've thought about where this relationship could lead, but I never imagined getting there so quickly."

"I'm sorry. I don't want to hurt you." He shook his head and his frown deepened. "I should've kept my feelings to myself."

"No." She touched his arm. "That's not what I meant. I think of you constantly, and when we're apart, I find myself daydreaming about when I might see you again."

His smile returned. "I'm glad to hear you say that."

"I want to be with you, but I need some time to think

about all of this. By marrying you, I'll have to uproot my family. I've already told you I can't stay in my house if I'm shunned."

"I understand. And it will be devastating for the children."

"I'm just so worried because Lily has already threatened to move in with Barbie. She wants to become the schoolteacher where she's the assistant now. She also plans to be baptized, and there's a boy she hopes to date. My heart breaks when I think of her moving out. I never thought my family would be broken apart. Losing Gideon was difficult, but I can't imagine also being separated from a child.

"Andrew said he would go with me wherever I choose to go. Amanda's transition would be much easier than her sister's. She told me that she wants to get her GED, go to college, and become a veterinarian."

"Wow." Trey smiled. "That's an amazing dream. How do you feel about it?"

Hannah shrugged. "I would support my children in whatever they want to pursue. I just wish Lillian would support me and see that I don't want to lose her." Her eyes filled with fresh tears. She looked toward the house again and, to curb her threatening tears, imagined planting a garden there. She imagined herself helping Trey run the bed and breakfast. She would be living her dream of cooking and caring for the guests. But where would that leave Lillian?

"I need some time to think about it." She looked up at him. "Leaving my community will be very difficult. Do you understand?"

"Yes, I do." Trey leaned down and brushed his lips over her cheek, sending the pit of her stomach into a wild swirl. Her heart rate surged, pounding fast in her ears.

"I love you, Hannah. I'll give you all of the time you need."

"Thank you," she whispered. She touched her cheek where his lips had been and thanked God for bringing love back into her hopeful heart.

. . .

Trey sat in the hotel's restaurant Wednesday afternoon and sipped a mug of coffee while glancing through the paper. Although his eyes scanned the newsprint, his mind couldn't focus on the stories. He couldn't stop worrying about Hannah and praying for her ever since they'd parted ways yesterday. He wished she were enjoying a cup of coffee with him as they'd done only a few weeks ago.

When he'd dropped her off at her house, she was close to tears again, talking about how much she loved her community and how much she would lose if she chose to be with him. She promised to call him in a few days after considering his proposal. He'd spent most of last night glancing at his phone and praying he'd find a missed call, even though he kept the phone close by at all times. He knew it wasn't logical to expect her to make such a life-changing decision within twenty-four hours, but he prayed she would.

He'd hoped to run into her at the hotel today, and he'd even lingered in his room this morning to see if she would come by while cleaning. Yet he hadn't seen her at all, and he worried that something had happened. His mind ran wild with possible tragedies that had kept her away from him today. What if she'd been hurt in an accident or was at home with a sick child?

Trey finished his coffee and moved through the restaurant toward the elevators. He stopped when he spotted one of Hannah's coworkers coming out of one of the employee offices. The woman looked to be in her mid-sixties; she had graying hair peeking out from under her prayer covering. She glanced toward him and smiled, and he felt the urge to ask her about Hannah.

"Excuse me." Trey approached the woman. "I was wondering if you've seen Hannah Glick today."

She shook her head. "No, I haven't. She's not in today."

"Oh." Trey frowned. "Is she okay? Is one of her children ill?"

The woman tilted her head. "Are you Mr. Peterson?"

"Yes, I am." He held out his hand and she shook it. "I'm surprised she told you about me."

"I've heard quite a bit about you. I'm Ruth Ebersol." She motioned toward the office she'd just exited. "Come in here for a moment, and we can speak in private."

He followed the older woman into a break room that included a table, countertops, sink, refrigerator, and microwave.

She closed the door behind him. "Hannah decided to use her vacation time for the rest of the week."

Trey studied the older woman and tried to comprehend her words. "You mean she took the rest of the week off and won't be at the hotel at all?"

Ruth nodded. "That's right."

Worry gripped him. "Did she say why she needs the rest of the week off?"

She shrugged. "I didn't talk to her. She called our supervisor."

Trey wondered if Hannah wanted to be away from him so she could think. Or perhaps she needed her distance to let him down gently, without facing him, when she told him that she didn't want to be with him.

"You seem upset." Ruth's eyes were filled with concern. "Is there anything I can do to help you?"

"Yes." Trey tunneled his fingers through his hair while he debated what to do. He needed to respect her request to give her time alone, but he didn't want her to forget he cared about her. "Would you please get a message to Hannah?"

"I'd be glad to."

"Please tell her something. Tell her to remember that no matter what she decides, she has my heart."

Ruth nodded. "I'll tell her."

"Thank you." Trey watched Ruth leave the room, and he prayed the message would help Hannah make her decision.

. . .

Hannah sat on the porch Wednesday evening and sipped a warm cup of tea while listening to the crickets sing. She'd spent most of the day contemplating Trey's marriage proposal and wondering how she could make a life outside of the community she'd known her whole life. How would she know if she belonged in the *English* world?

Most of all, she struggled with her dual roles as a mother and as a woman. She knew her job as a mother was to nurture and protect her children. Yet she also felt the tug of a woman in love with a man who offered her the chance at a new life. Whenever she considered telling Trey yes, however, she felt the tug of her children pulling her back to her old life, the life of working at the hotel and running the horse farm without the joy of a soul mate.

The back door opened with a squeak, and Amanda stepped out onto the porch. "*Mamm*, I didn't know you were out here."

"Have a seat." Hannah patted the swing beside her. "I was just enjoying the sound of the crickets."

Amanda sank into the swing. "I was looking for you."

"Oh." Hannah pushed the swing, and it moved back and forth. "What did you need?"

"I just wanted to see how you are. You've been quiet." Amanda looked up at her mother. "Is something on your mind?"

Hannah frowned. She couldn't possibly tell Amanda what was on her mind without also telling Lillian, and she wasn't ready to share the news with both of them. "I've just been thinking about a lot of things." She touched Amanda's arm. "How was your day?"

"It was *gut*. Nancy isn't talking much, but it's okay." She settled back in the swing. "She wasn't as cold to me today as she has been since we argued. Maybe she's coming around to accepting my decision."

"That's *gut* news." Hannah sipped her coffee. "You know, if you want that GED book, I'll give you the money for it."

"You will?" Amanda's eyes widened.

"Of course I will. I just want you to be *froh*. You can pick it up on your way home tomorrow if you'd like."

Amanda's eyes narrowed. "You're acting different. Is there a reason you took the rest of the week off, *Mamm*?"

"I have a big decision to make, and I need time to think things through. Besides, I haven't had a vacation in a while."

Amanda stared off toward the road. "Whatever you decide, I'll stand by you."

"Are you certain?"

"*Ya*, I am. If you can support me getting my GED, I can support whatever you decide about Mr. Peterson."

Hannah studied her daughter. Amanda's continued support caused a surge of relief to fill her. She wondered if this was the sign she needed to go forward with a decision to choose Trey over Joshua.

TWENTY-FOUR

The following morning, Hannah heard a knock and rushed to the door. She wondered who could be dropping by to visit. Could it be Trey, even though she had told him she needed time? She pulled the door open and found Ruth smiling while holding up a covered dish.

"Ruth!" Hannah opened the door wide. "Please come in. What a nice surprise."

"I hope you're hungry. I brought cheese cupcakes."

"*Ach!*" Hannah clapped. "My favorite." She followed Ruth into the kitchen and gestured toward the table. "Please have a seat. I just made fresh coffee. Would you like some?"

"That would be nice."

Hannah brought plates, napkins, cream, sugar, and two cups of coffee to the table. "How have you been?"

"*Gut.*" Ruth gave her a knowing smile. "The question is, how have *you* been?"

"I'm fine." Hannah sat across from her. "I'm just enjoying a couple of days off. I needed a break. We work so hard at the hotel."

Ruth raised an eyebrow. "Is that truly why you're not coming to work tomorrow?"

Hannah pointed toward the platter of cheese cupcakes. "May I try one of those cupcakes? They smell *appeditlich*."

"No, you may not. Not until you answer my question." Ruth folded her hands and studied Hannah. "Does your sudden vacation have to do with a certain *Englisher*?"

"How did you know?"

"He talked to me yesterday."

Hannah hesitated a moment before asking, "What did he say to you?"

"He asked about you and told me to give you a message."

Hannah's heart fluttered. "What was the message?"

"He told me to tell you that no matter what you decide, you have his heart."

Hannah nodded and cleared the lump swelling in her throat.

Ruth placed a cupcake on Hannah's plate. "Hannah, please tell me what's going on. I'm very concerned about you, and I want to know the truth."

Tears filled Hannah's eyes, and she cleared her throat again. "Trey asked me to marry him and help him run the bed and breakfast he plans to open in Paradise."

"He did?" Ruth's eyes were wide. "What did you say?"

"I told him I need time to think, which is why I took time off from work. I need to think it all through and weigh my options. My heart breaks when I think of leaving the community and all of the people I've loved and who have loved me since I was a child. I can't imagine walking away from the home where Gideon and I raised our children. Yet I also keep thinking this new start may be what my heart has been craving since Gideon left me alone."

Ruth shook her head. "Hannah, are you certain your heart can't heal here in the community?"

"I've wondered that myself. Joshua also proposed to me. He loves me and he adores my *kinner*. He wants to keep running the business he and Gideon built."

"What?" Ruth gasped. "Both Trey and Joshua proposed to you?"

Hannah nodded.

"What did you tell Joshua?"

"I told him I have to think about it. But I don't love him." Sadness and regret filled Hannah's soul. "I care about Joshua, but that's not a feeling I can base a marriage on." She paused and considered how she felt about her options.

"If I married Joshua, it would only be a marriage of convenience on my part. I would be trying to cling to the life I've always known." She gestured toward the window. "Part of me feels I belong here, but, at the same time, I never really loved this horse farm the way Gideon did. I always enjoyed hosting dinners for *English* tourists when I was a girl. Running a bed and breakfast is a dream of mine too. I love talking to the tourists and telling them about our community. It would be a nice change and a fun new start. I feel very torn. It's not an easy decision." With her tears temporarily stopped, she bit into the cupcake and savored the rich cheese flavor while allowing Ruth to mull over her words.

"What do you want to do, Hannah? Where is your heart leading you?"

"In my heart, I want to marry Trey, but my life will change drastically if I do. I'm not certain it's fair to *mei kinner* to pull them away from the only life they've ever known." Her eyes filled with tears again as she thought of her daughter. "And Lily has threatened to move in with Barbie if I leave the community. I don't think I could live with that. I know it would break Gideon's heart if he saw our *dochder* move out. I don't think I could live with hurting Lily *or* knowing Gideon would be so hurt if he were here."

Ruth took Hannah's hand in hers. "So, then don't do it, Hannah. If it feels wrong, then it is wrong. Stay in the community. Once you're gone, you can only come back if you confess in front of the congregation. Is that what you want to do?"

Hannah wiped her eyes and considered her thoughts. "My feelings are a jumbled mess. My heart crumbles when I think of leaving the community, but at the same time, I keep thinking everything has led me to Trey. He showed me the property he's purchasing, and I could see myself planting a garden, cooking for the guests, and giving tours of the area. I could imagine Amanda and Andrew living in the little apartment and helping me with the chores."

Hannah managed to finish the cupcake and wiped her hands on a napkin. "When I'm with Trey, I'm a whole person again. I could even see myself worshiping with him at his church. It feels as if God is giving me a new chance, even though it's not what I'd imagined for myself. I thought I'd fall in love with an Amish man, possibly even a widower. Sometimes during church I would look around the room and wonder if any of the men there would be my future mate, but it never happened."

"But you just told me Joshua wants to marry you. He's the opportunity to rebuild your family here in our community." Ruth tapped the table. "Don't you see Joshua as God's way to keep you here?"

"No, Ruth, I don't." Hannah wiped her cheeks with a crumpled napkin. "Joshua wants to marry me, but I don't think I could be *froh* with him. He told me I would learn to love him, but I don't believe true love can grow like that."

Ruth shook her head as she took a cupcake from the dish. "I don't agree. My parents married as *freinden* and then fell in love after a few years. You may not love Joshua like that now, but you could love him later. Think of how much easier that would be on your *kinner*. If you married Joshua, then Lily wouldn't move out. You'd keep your family intact. Isn't that what Gideon would want?"

"I don't know." Fresh tears filled Hannah's eyes. "I'm so confused. I don't know what to do."

"If you're that confused, then you shouldn't do anything. Tell Trey you're not ready. Tell him that leaving your community is just too difficult." Ruth frowned. "Tell him that if he loved you, he would become Amish instead of making you leave the faith."

"He's not making me do anything. It's all my choice, and he said he'll wait as long as he has to."

Hannah glanced around the kitchen and her lower lip quivered. "This isn't an easy decision. It's a painful decision. I've cried so much that I'm surprised I have any tears left."

Ruth put down her uneaten cupcake and reached across the table to take Hannah's hand in hers again. "If it's painful, then it may not be the right decision. You've never wanted to leave the community before. I just don't think this is right for you, Hannah. You say you love Trey, but you have too much to lose."

"I know I'll lose Lillian." A tear trickled down Hannah's cheek, and she let go of Ruth's hand to swipe it away with the back of her hand.

"But you think your other *kinner* would support you?"

Hannah wiped away more tears. "I know Amanda would. Andrew said he'll go with me, but I think he'd have a hard time leaving the farm, especially his favorite horse."

Ruth hesitated and then spoke her mind in love. "You need to take a step back and think about how much this decision will hurt the people who love you."

"I have. I've been considering how it will affect every aspect of my life."

"I don't think you realize how much you'll hurt other people." Ruth's eyes glistened with tears. "When Aaron left, he took a piece of my heart with him. I've already told you that I miss him every day and some days are worse than others. I pray that the hurt will get easier with time, but it doesn't. In fact, the pain deepens every day that passes without hearing my son's voice. He's been gone fifteen years, and the wound is still fresh in my heart."

"I'm so sorry." Hannah shook her head. "Your pain must be unbearable, Ruth."

"Some days it is unbearable." Ruth swiped the back of her hands over her eyes. "Don't you see that you'll inflict the same pain on your family if you leave?"

Hannah paused and considered Ruth's words while guilt rained down on her. "I know you're right. I just feel so torn right now."

Ruth leaned forward and folded her hands on the table. "What kind of message do you feel God is sending you?"

Hannah shrugged. "I feel calm when I pray about it."

"Do you mean, like God is blessing your relationship with Trey?"

Hannah nodded while wiping more tears. "*Ya*, that's sort of how I feel. I can't really put my finger on it."

"I want to share a verse I read this morning during devotions. It's from the book of Hebrews. 'Let us run with perseverance the race marked out for us, fixing our eyes on Jesus, the pioneer and perfecter of faith.'" Ruth's expression was tentative but comforting. "I don't agree with your considering a decision to leave, but I think this verse applies to you, Hannah. If you believe you belong with Trey, then you need to accept the path God has put before you. You'll handle all of the bumps in the road, but you'll handle them with faith in the Lord."

Hannah couldn't stop the tears from flowing from her eyes. "I love him, Ruth, and I want to be with him,

but I don't know how to go about it. How do I walk
away from the life I've known since I was born?"

"Run with endurance. The Lord will lead you. Look
to Jesus for the answers, and he will provide them
for you." Ruth pushed the plate of cupcakes toward
Hannah. "Have another one."

"*Danki*, Ruth. You're a blessing to me." Hannah
picked up a cupcake and then wiped her eyes. She
knew the road ahead would be bumpy, but she'd keep
her faith close.

. . .

Friday morning, Hannah brought a platter of fried
potatoes to the table and set it next to the platters of
homemade bread, eggs, and bacon, along with a bowl
of oatmeal. She sat next to Andrew and across from her
girls before bowing her head for the prayer.

Once the prayer was complete, Hannah began to
fill her plate with potatoes, bacon, and eggs, even
though her appetite was nonexistent. She'd endured
another sleepless night of crying, praying, and worrying about how she was going to tell her children
that she had made the decision to leave their Amish
community.

Lillian bit into a piece of bacon and then looked at
Hannah. "Are you going back to work today, *Mamm*?"

Hannah shook her head and folded her hands on the
table. "No, I'm not going back today. I'm not certain
about next week either."

The twins shared surprised expressions.

"Did you get a new job, *Mamm*?" Andrew chewed a mouthful of bread.

"Andrew, chew your *brot* with your mouth closed." Lillian wagged a finger at him. "*Mamm*, why aren't you going back to work? Were you laid off?"

Andrew swallowed. "Were you fired?"

"No, I wasn't fired or laid off. I think I'm going to take my life in another direction." Hannah paused for a moment. "I've made a decision."

Lillian's eyes widened. "*Ach*, no."

"It was a very difficult decision, and I want you three to know I've prayed about it and agonized over it for quite a while. I didn't make this decision without weighing all of my options and considering how it will affect you all." She touched Lillian's hand and Andrew's arm. "You three mean the most to me. You're the most important people in my life, and I would never do anything to hurt you intentionally."

Tears trickled down Lillian's cheeks, and Amanda nodded.

"What are you talking about?" Andrew scrunched his nose as he looked up at her. "You're confusing me, *Mamm*."

"I'm sorry." Hannah touched his nose. "I didn't mean to confuse you. I'm talking about our life. We're going to have to live a little differently."

"*Mamm*, just come out and say it." Lillian's voice quavered. "You're leaving the church and then you're going to marry that *Englisher*." She pushed her chair back and stood. "I can't believe you're doing this to me!" She turned and ran from the kitchen, her footsteps echoing as she stomped up the stairs and shouted. "I'm leaving. I'm going to *Mammi's haus.*"

Amanda touched Hannah's hand. "Go talk to her. I'll talk to Andrew."

Hannah sniffed as tears filled her eyes. "*Danki.*" She made her way upstairs and knocked on Lillian's closed door. "Lillian, please let me talk to you."

"Just go away."

Hannah pushed the door open and found Lillian tossing her clothes into a large tote bag. "Lily, please stop packing. Please listen to me."

"I know what you're going to say." Lillian glared at Hannah. "You love him, and you can't live without him. So you're going to uproot all of us so you can live a new life that excludes our family."

"That's not true." Hannah sat in the chair next to the bed. "You know I love you and your siblings, but I can't go on pretending I don't love Trey. This wasn't what I expected at all. I thought I'd stay here the rest of my life and marry another Amish man or live alone after you and your siblings were grown and living your own lives. This wasn't part of my plan, but it seems like God has other plans for me."

Lillian opened another drawer in the bureau and began pitching more clothes into the bag. "I can't stay in a *haus* where the Amish faith is questioned. I'm going to live with *Mammi* and *Daadi.* They will understand, and they will take me in." She scowled at Hannah. "You told me you were going to stop seeing Mr. Peterson. You lied to me. You never stopped seeing him."

"Lillian, you're not being fair to me. I'm trying to

explain to you that I never meant to hurt you. When I told you I would stay away from Trey, I truly believed I could. But this was out of my control."

"But where does this leave me, *Mamm*? Where do I go from here?" Lillian faced Hannah with tears streaming down her face. "How can I be a teacher and get baptized if I'm living with you in your *English haus*?"

"You can." Hannah leaned forward. "There's enough room for you and your siblings in the *haus* Trey is buying. You and your *schweschder* can share a room, and you can still teach. Nothing has to change for you."

"Everything will change." Lillian gestured widely. "All of my *freinden* will feel sorry for me when they find out you've left the faith. They'll treat me differently. It will be as if everyone has to be extra nice to me. I don't want to be singled out. I want to be like everyone else."

Hannah sniffed and wiped her eyes. She knew Lillian was right. She'd seen how everyone treated her friend Rebecca after her mother chose to leave the faith. Rumors flew about the family and all of the young people were careful about what they said to Rebecca. Her friend was so embarrassed by the whispers and sad smiles that she too chose to leave the faith and go to public school. Hannah didn't want Lillian to be the object of the community's pity or rumors.

"I'm sorry, Lily. I never intended to hurt you." Tears trickled down Hannah's face. "You mean so much to me."

"If I mean so much to you, then why are you abandoning me?" Lillian's voice shook with anger. "You're leaving me. You're betraying *Dat's* memory. I don't understand why you're doing this to me. We're a family. We're supposed to stay together."

"I didn't plan this, Lillian." Hannah's voice was thin as a lump swelled in her throat. "I don't want to lose you. You're my *kind. Ich liebe dich.* I wish you would come with me. Losing you is breaking my heart."

"So, then don't go. Stay here with Amanda, Andrew, and me. You can marry *Onkel* Josh, and we'll be a family again." Lillian's voice trembled. "Please, *Mamm.* Don't change everything. We're doing fine here. It's been hard since we lost *Dat,* but we're doing okay."

Hannah's heart ached as she stared into her daughter's eyes. She'd thought she'd made the right decision when she decided to accept Trey's proposal, but now she wasn't so certain.

A knock sounded on the door frame behind them. Amanda stood in the doorway with Andrew beside her. "I don't mean to interrupt, but Andrew is ready to leave for school. He wants to say good-bye before he meets his *freinden* at the corner."

Hannah leaned down and touched Andrew's shoulder. "I don't want you to worry about this. I'll talk to *Onkel* Josh and make sure you'll always be able to help him on the farm. You'll be able to see Huckleberry no matter where we live."

Andrew gnawed his lower lip. "Okay."

Hannah opened her arms, and Andrew gave her a quick hug. "Have a *gut* day. We'll talk more later, okay?"

Andrew nodded. "Amanda told me we have a lot of things to work out, but everything will be okay."

"That's right." Hannah forced a smile despite her breaking heart.

Lillian wiped her tears and then waved to him. "See you later, Andrew."

"Bye!" Andrew ran down the stairs.

Amanda stared at her twin. "Lily, what are you doing? Why are you packing?"

"I'm leaving." Lillian spoke with emphasis. "I'm moving in with *Mammi. Mamm* wants to leave the faith, and that leaves me all alone. She's ruining my life and also betraying *Dat.*" She studied her sister. "I don't understand why you're so calm. Why aren't you upset? Don't you want to be baptized and stay in the community with me?"

Amanda glanced at Hannah as if asking her permission to tell the truth.

"Tell her, Amanda." Hannah gestured toward Amanda, in an effort to encourage her. "You can be honest with your *schweschder.* Just because your choices are different doesn't make them wrong."

"What are you talking about?" Lillian looked back and forth from her mother to her twin. "What are you both keeping from me now? Why does this family keep so many secrets?" Her voice rose again. "I feel like an outsider in my own family. Everyone is betraying me. It's not fair."

"Just calm down and listen, Lily," Hannah said.

"Lily, you're my twin. I would never betray you. Just give me a chance to explain myself." Amanda took a deep breath. "One of the customers who comes into the deli is a guy named Mike. He and I have become *freinden*. He's leaving for college in the fall, and I've been asking him about school. I want to try to get my GED. If I get a high school diploma, I could think about college too. I've always dreamt of becoming a veterinarian, but I've been afraid to tell you. I didn't think you'd understand."

"So you want to live with *Mamm* and be *English* too." Lillian's eyes glistened with tears. "That means Andrew and Amanda will live with you, *Mamm*." Lillian folded her arms over her middle. "I'll be the only one who stays Amish. You're all abandoning me."

"That's not true, Lillian. I love you, and I will never abandon you." Hannah reached forward to take Lillian's hand, but Lillian pulled away.

"*Ya*, you are abandoning me. You're leaving me." More tears poured down Lillian's cheeks. "*Dat* would never approve of this. He would take my side."

"*Dat* is gone." Amanda touched her sister's arm. "If *Dat* were here, then we wouldn't be discussing this. *Mamm* is trying to make a life now that he's gone."

Lillian glared at Hannah, causing Hannah to flinch. "If you leave the faith for that man, I won't give you my blessing. I won't come and visit you at your home either. If you want to see me, you'll have to come to *Mammi's*. I will never accept your decision to leave the faith or marry that man."

Amanda wagged a finger at her sister. "You shouldn't talk to *Mamm* that way. That's disrespectful."

"It's okay, Amanda. I will respect your sister's feelings." Hannah studied Lillian. "I don't want you to leave."

"It's too late." Lillian hefted her bag up onto her shoulder. "I'm going and you can't stop me." She marched out of the room and down to the kitchen while Hannah and Amanda followed her to the back door.

"Please don't go. You're my twin." Amanda's voice trembled. "I can't imagine being alone in our room."

Lillian faced them and her eyes were red and puffy. "I can't stay here. I don't belong here anymore."

"Ich liebe dich." Hannah said the words and then swallowed a sob.

"Lily, please." Amanda shook her head. "Please don't leave us."

Lillian turned and disappeared out the back door.

Hannah stared after her for a moment. She then lowered herself into a chair at the kitchen table as overwhelming grief crashed down on her. "I just lost my *dochder.*"

Amanda sat beside her and rubbed her arm. "She'll be back."

They sat in silence for a moment, and Hannah wondered if she was making the wrong decision. She'd prayed that Lillian would somehow understand and accept her decision to leave the community and start a new life with Trey. Yet she knew deep down that Lillian would never accept it. She'd known all along that this was inevitable. Yet it didn't make accepting Lillian's leaving any easier.

"We can't stay in this house when you're excommunicated." Amanda's voice was quiet and unsure. "When are we going to have to move?"

"I'm not certain about that yet." Hannah ran her

fingers over the wood grain in the table. "I need to talk to a few people first. I'm going to tell *Onkel* Josh tomorrow."

"Okay." Amanda nodded. "Remember, *Mamm*, I'll support you no matter what."

"*Danki, mei liewe*." Hannah blew out a deep breath and considered all of the planning she needed to do. First she had to tell the members of her community her decision and then she'd tell Trey. Her pulse raced at the thought of telling Trey she was ready to give him her whole heart.

Yet her heart was broken after seeing her daughter walk out the door. She hoped somehow she could convince Lillian to forgive her.

TWENTY-FIVE

Amanda gnawed her lower lip and stepped into the bookstore during lunchtime later that day. She smiled when she spotted Mike working at the front counter. His eyes met hers, and he grinned in return.

"Amanda!" Mike waved as she approached. "It's great to see you. How have you been?"

"I'm fine." Amanda fingered her wallet in her apron pocket. "How are you?"

"I'm doing great. I graduate next week."

"That's fantastic." Amanda clapped her hands together. "You must be so excited."

"I am." He gestured toward her. "I'm really surprised to see you in here. How can I help you?"

"I'm looking for a book."

He stepped out from behind the counter. "What kind of book are you looking for?"

Amanda pointed toward the far side of the store. "I believe it's located in the reference section."

"Okay. Let's head over there."

Amanda walked beside him as they made their way through the fiction and religion sections toward reference.

"Now, what kind of book would you like?" He pointed toward the books lining the shelves. "We have history books, language books, dictionaries . . ."

"I was looking for the GED preparation books."

He raised his eyebrows. "You're going to get your GED?"

"I'm going to try." She shrugged. "I guess we'll see if I pass."

"I'm certain you will. That's fabulous, Amanda. I'm so happy for you." He chose a book from the shelf and showed it to her. "Here you go."

"Thanks." Amanda examined the cover and wondered if she'd be intelligent enough to understand the contents of the book. "I'm going to look through it and see if I can learn it. It's been a couple of years since I was in school."

"I'm sure you can do it." He leaned against the shelf. "I'd be happy to tutor you, though. We can get together at lunchtime and talk about the book."

"I'd like that." Amanda hugged the book to her chest while imagining spending her lunchtime with him every day. She'd have to talk to Nancy about it and explain that he was helping her study so that Nancy wouldn't get the wrong idea. Maybe her *mamm* would have to talk to Nancy's parents about it too; she couldn't lose her job right now. But she would worry about that later. She smiled up at him. "I bet you're excited about your graduation."

"Oh yeah. I can't wait."

She thought about her mother's decision to leave the church and considered telling Mike. She glanced behind her to make sure no one was close to them and then lowered her voice. "Things are going to change for my family."

He stepped closer to her. "What do you mean?"

"My mom decided she wants to leave the church."

He frowned. "I'm sorry, but I'm not sure what that means."

"That means she doesn't want to be Amish anymore."

"She doesn't want to be Amish?"

Amanda shook her head.

"How do you feel about that?" Mike's eyes were full of concern.

"I'm okay with it."

He nodded. "How are your siblings taking this decision? Are they as understanding and supportive as you are?"

Amanda grimaced. "My sister isn't taking it well at all. She's having a hard time understanding why my mom wants to leave the church."

"I'm sorry to hear that. It'll be a big adjustment since you have to move and all."

"*Ya*. My sister wants to stay Amish, so she moved in with my grandparents. My brother and I will go with my mom." Amanda looked down at the book in her hands. "I don't think I want to be Amish either."

"What about your brother?"

"He's sad, but my mom promised he'll still see our uncle and help out on the farm. I'm certain he's most upset about leaving his favorite horse, but I'm sure my uncle will say he can visit Huckleberry anytime."

She thought of her farm. "It's funny. I've lived in this one house my whole life, but I'm not as sad as I thought I'd be about leaving. I'm looking forward to seeing where my life will lead."

"Do you have to leave Lancaster County after your mother is shunned?"

"No." Amanda shook her head. "We can stay close by. We just can't do business with other Amish families, so my mom can't keep the horse business."

"Oh. Where does your mom want to live?"

"I'm not certain, but I hope we'll be close to Paradise."

"That's good." Mike smiled. "We can still be friends."

"Mike!" a voice called from the front of the store. "Can you take over the register?"

"That's my uncle. I better get back to work."

Amanda looked up at him. "Thanks for your help finding the book."

"You're welcome. Let's go up to the front, and I'll ring it up for you real quick. I can give you the family discount."

She walked with him to the front of the store. Mike took his place behind the counter and rang up a customer before taking care of Amanda's book. She gave him the money, and he slipped the book into a bag and handed it to her.

"Thank you. See you later." Amanda gripped the bag and started toward the door. She couldn't wait to start studying for the GED.

Amanda hurried across the street to the deli. She

slipped into the break room and put the book into her tote bag.

"What are you doing?"

Amanda looked back and found Nancy eyeing her from the doorway. "I didn't hear you come in. I bought a book at the bookstore."

Nancy craned her neck. "What kind of book did you get? Is it a novel for your *schweschder*?"

"No, it isn't for Lily. It's for me."

"Does it have to do with the GED?"

Amanda nodded.

"Oh." Nancy frowned as she stepped into the room. "I had a feeling you'd want to do that. You're smart enough to pass a big test like that. I always wished I were as smart as you when we were in school."

Amanda's mouth gaped. "Nancy, I had no idea you felt that way."

"*Ya*, I always have. You've always been so much braver than I was." Nancy motioned toward the bag. "I'd never have the confidence to try to take a test like that." She looked back toward the doorway. "And my parents would never let me take the test. Does your *mamm* know you want to take it?"

"*Ya*, she does. In fact, she gave me the money for the book." Amanda hesitated. She considered telling Nancy that her *mamm* was leaving the church, but she decided it was up to her to decide when the community should know about her choice.

"Oh. That's *gut* that your *mamm* supports you."

Amanda bit her lower lip. "I hope you understand I still want to be your *freind*. God may be leading me toward a different path, but that doesn't change how much your friendship means to me."

Nancy smiled. "I understand our lives are going to be a little different, but I still want to be your *freind*. I'm really sorry for everything I said about you and your *mamm*. I didn't mean it, and it was terrible of me to accuse you of being a bad person." She hugged Amanda. "Even if you do get your GED and decide to go to college, you need to keep in touch with me."

"I promise I will. You're my best *freind*, Nancy."

"Best *freinden* forever." Nancy touched Amanda's arm. "Don't forget it."

"I won't." Amanda smiled and wondered where the possibility of a GED might lead her.

. . .

Later that afternoon, Lillian walked past her grandparents' pasture and studied the horses frolicking and grazing on the other side of the fence. She never dreamt she'd ever leave the only home she'd ever known and move in with her grandparents. Her grandparents had welcomed her with open arms and told her she could stay as long as she wanted. She was thankful for their love.

Yet betrayal and hurt filled her as she considered her *mamm*. Although she loved *Mamm*, Lillian couldn't understand why she would want to leave their beautiful farm and their church district.

Her eyes filled with tears when she thought of the farmhouse where she'd grown up. She'd no longer have the same little bedroom she'd shared with her twin their whole life. How would Lillian cope with being separated from her family?

"Lillian?"

Lillian turned and found Leroy King walking toward her. Her stomach fluttered with delight. "Leroy? I didn't know you were coming over today." She touched her prayer covering and then smoothed her apron.

"I was over at your house. Daniel asked me if I could come over and help shoe a few horses. I told him I wanted to learn how, so it was the perfect opportunity. I asked him where you were, and he said you'd gone to see your grandparents." He lifted his straw hat, smoothed his dark hair, and then placed the hat back on his head. "I hoped to see you."

"Oh." Lillian's heart thundered in her chest. "I'm glad you came."

"How are you doing?" He leaned against the fence.

"I'm doing okay." She placed her hand on the rung of the fence and frowned. "Actually, I'm not doing well at all."

"*Was iss letz?*"

"*Mei mamm* made a decision that's going to change my life, and I'm having a difficult time getting used to the idea." Lillian felt tears in her eyes, but she hoped she wouldn't cry.

"What happened?" Leroy's expression was filled with concern. "Is there anything I can do to help you?"

"If I tell you, will you promise to keep it a secret? I don't know when *mei mamm* is going to talk to the minister and the deacon."

His mouth gaped. "Your *mamm* is leaving the church?"

Lillian nodded as a tear trickled down her cheek. "You can't tell anyone."

"I promise I won't tell anyone."

"That means we can't live at our *haus* anymore because my grandparents own it. *Mei mamm* wants to be with the *Englisher*. I had a feeling this would happen, but I didn't think it would be this fast. I'm not ready for my life to change so drastically." A few more tears sprinkled down her hot cheeks.

He frowned. "I'm going to miss you."

"I'm not going with her." Lillian sniffed and wiped her eyes.

"What do you mean?" He raised his eyebrows.

"I'm living here with *mei mammi* now. I still want to stay here and be a part of the community. I don't want to be *English*." She wiped her tears from under her glasses. "I don't understand why *mei mamm* wants to leave, but her mind is made up. I feel as if she's abandoning me and she's also betraying my *dat's* memory. It's so unfair. How can she leave me like this?"

"But you'll stay in the district, so that means you'll still go to church and youth gatherings?"

Lillian nodded. "*Ya.*"

"That's *gut.*" Leroy smiled, but his smile quickly turned to a grimace. "I didn't mean it the way it came out. I'm sorry your *mamm* is leaving, but I'm glad you're staying." He shook his head. "Does that make sense?"

"*Ya*, it does." Her heart warmed, knowing he wanted her to stay in the community. Perhaps her dream of dating him would come true despite her mother's decision to leave the church. "I just hope people don't take pity on me. I don't want to be singled out. I just want to be the teacher and live in the community."

Leroy shrugged. "You can do that. Your *mamm* has made her choice, but you can make your own choice. And I'm glad you want to stay because I'm enjoying getting to know you."

"*Danki*, Leroy. I'm enjoying getting to know you too." She nodded toward her grandmother's house. "I made oatmeal raisin cookies earlier. Would you like to come in for a snack?"

"*Ya*." He smiled. "That sounds *gut*."

They walked together to the house. She looked up at Leroy and a weight lifted from her shoulders. Although she was hurt by her mother's decision to leave, she felt a sense of hope and excitement. She was going to be okay, and maybe, just maybe, her dreams would come true too.

TWENTY-SIX

The following morning, Hannah wiped her hands on a dish towel and forced a smile at Andrew as he made his way toward the back door to finish helping with chores. She'd spent most of the night thinking about Lillian and praying she would come home. Her daughter, however, never walked through the door. She knew Lillian's decision was permanent, and it shattered her heart. During the night she also contemplated how to approach Joshua with her news about leaving the church. She'd considered talking to him during breakfast and then decided to wait until she could get Andrew and him alone in the stable.

She hung up the dish towel and then walked toward the mudroom where Andrew was pulling on his boots. "I finished the breakfast dishes, so I was wondering if I could come outside with you this morning?"

Andrew put his hat on his head and then shrugged. "Sure. Are you going to help *Onkel* Josh and me with chores?"

"*Ya*, I can help, and I also want to talk to you both."

"Oh. Is this about the farm?" Andrew frowned. "Last night I talked to Amanda and I asked her if we can buy the farm from *Mammi* and *Daadi*. She told me that we can't. She said we have to move and we can't keep the farm anymore." His lip quivered. "What will happen to Huck?"

Hannah took her son's hands in hers and wished she could erase the sorrow in his eyes. "Andrew, I'm sorry, but your *schweschder* is right. We can't buy the farm from *Mammi* and *Daadi*." At that moment, it occurred to her that she hadn't asked Andrew what he'd wanted. She'd been so wrapped up in plans for her and the twins, but she hadn't once considered what Andrew had wanted. "Where would you like to live, Andrew?" She held her breath while hoping his answer wouldn't break her heart.

Andrew paused as if he were deep in thought. "I told you I'll always stay with you." He paused and frowned. "But part of me wants to live with *Onkel* Josh, and then another part of me wants to be with you. I just don't want to hurt anyone's feelings."

"Don't worry about my feelings. What do you truly want?"

He shrugged. "I always kind of wondered what it would be like to ride on a school bus and go to a big school. If we moved into Mr. Peterson's *haus*, would I get to go to a school like that?"

Hannah felt the tension ease in her shoulders and her expression relaxed. "*Ya*, Andrew, you would. You'll make all new *freinden*. Does that mean you want to live with Amanda and me?"

"*Ya*, I do, but what about Huck?" His frown returned. "What would happen to him?"

"Like I told you before, I'll ask *Onkel* Josh if you can

work with him on Saturdays, and you can take care of Huckleberry." An idea popped into her head, and she smiled. "Maybe you can work with *Onkel* Josh and Daniel all summer. What do you think about that?"

He nodded. "*Ya*, that might work. Let's go ask him."

Hannah followed Andrew out to the stable where Joshua was shoveling manure.

His gaze met theirs, and he leaned the shovel against the stall and wiped his brow with a handkerchief. "Is it snack time already?"

"No." Andrew shook his head. "*Mei mamm* wants to talk to us about the farm."

"*Ach.*" Josh frowned. "This sounds serious." He adjusted his hat on his head. "Let's walk outside."

Hannah walked out of the stable and prayed she could remember everything she'd planned to say.

Josh leaned against the stable wall. "What did you want to discuss with us, Hannah?"

"I guess you already know that Lillian went to live with your parents."

"She's staying there permanently?"

Hannah nodded.

"Oh. I didn't know it was permanent." He raised his eyebrows. "Why did she move out?"

She cleared her throat in an effort to sound more confident in her decision. "I'm leaving the church."

Josh's mouth gaped.

"We have to move out of our *haus*." Andrew pointed toward the pasture where the horses were. "I'd like to take care of Huckleberry. Would you please let me come over on Saturdays and help you? Please, *Onkel* Josh?"

"Are you joking, Andrew? I expect you to care for Huck. He's your horse, not mine." Josh smiled at Andrew, and Hannah's heart warmed. She was thankful Joshua's demeanor hadn't changed toward her children.

"Great!" Andrew clapped his hands together. "I'm so *froh*. I thought that when we had to move, I'd lose everything, including you and my horse."

Josh leaned down, leveling his eyes with Andrew's. "You, Lillian, and Amanda will never lose me. I made a promise when your *dat* died that I would always be there for you and your siblings. No matter where you live, I'll keep that promise."

"*Danki*." Andrew hugged him.

Josh motioned toward the stable. "Why don't you go help Daniel with the shoveling? I need to talk to your *mamm*."

"Okay!" Andrew ran into the stable.

Josh studied Hannah as a scowl formed on his face. "So, that's it. You're leaving the community." He gestured around the farm. "You're leaving all of this."

Hannah could only nod again as regret washed over her and stole her voice. She wiped her eyes and hoped she could stop her tears.

Josh frowned at Hannah. "We have a lot to talk about. Why don't we go sit on the porch?"

Hannah cleared her throat and was thankful to find her voice again. "That sounds *gut*." She climbed the porch steps and sat in the swing.

"So, you're leaving the church for him." Josh sat on a porch chair and folded his arms over his wide chest. "You're going to be shunned for that man."

"It's not just for him." Hannah sat up taller. "It's for me too. I've prayed about it, and this is the path God has laid before me. I'm going to do what I feel is right for myself and also for my family." She gestured around the farm. "You and Gideon loved this farm. This was your dream, but it was never my dream."

"What do you mean this was never your dream?" Josh looked confused. "You told Gideon you loved this place."

"*Ya*, I loved living here with Gideon, but I always wanted to do something more than raising horses. I loved hosting dinners for the *English* when I was a child. I was able to host a few before Gideon died, but then my life changed. I would love to work at a bed and breakfast and make dinners for the visitors."

Josh shook his head. "You never told Gideon or me that you didn't want to have the horse farm."

Hannah shook her head. "I never said I didn't want the horse farm. I love the horses, but it wasn't my dream. It was Gideon's dream."

Josh blew out a deep sigh. "That means you don't want to run it with me anymore. And it also means that you won't accept my proposal."

Tears filled Hannah's eyes as she nodded. "I'm sorry, Joshua. I'm honored you asked me to marry you, but I can't. I love someone else. It wouldn't be fair to you or me if I lived a lie. We'd wind up resenting each other."

"I was praying I could change your mind." He shook his head. "I can't imagine what Gideon would say."

"I'm going to start a new life, which is my decision. Gideon has nothing to say about it since he left this world." She stared toward the pasture. "You'll never understand why I'm making this choice, but I need you to respect my decision."

"Fine." He glowered. "I'll respect it, but I won't ever agree with it. I can't understand why you wouldn't just give me a chance. I would've given everything I had to you and your *kinner*. But I'm tired of pleading with you. Your decision has been made, and we need to discuss what happens now. Once you're shunned, our business no longer exists."

"I know." Hannah glanced toward the sign for Glick's Belgian and Dutch Harness Horses and tears filled her eyes again. It was Gideon's dream to own this business with his brother, and Hannah had kept his part alive for as long as she could. Now Joshua would take over, and she knew he'd keep that dream alive even though Hannah wanted to pursue another dream. "You'll have to buy my half of the business from me."

Josh nodded. "I know." He looked toward the front door. "I'm going to see if I can move in here after you're gone. It would make it easier for me if I were here on the property."

Hannah studied his frown, finding sadness there. "Joshua, you'll always be welcome in our *haus*. You're family, and the *kinner* want to spend time with you. That doesn't have to change."

"But everything else will, Hannah. I won't be able to see you all at church." He turned his eyes toward the pasture. "It will never be the same."

"You'll see Lily." Hannah watched the horses run in the pasture. Her thoughts moved to Lillian living with her grandparents while she, Amanda, and Andrew started over in a new home. Her heart broke every time she imagined not having nightly devotions with all three of her children. How had things changed so quickly in only a matter of a couple of months? She pushed the thoughts away and forced herself to concentrate on the present. "*Danki* for allowing Andrew to continue to work with you. I know it's his dream to work here as an adult."

"He can still do that if he chooses to. His *dat* started this business, and he's a Glick." He turned toward her. "How does Amanda feel about all of this?"

"She's comfortable with my decision. She wants to get her GED and possibly go to college. I found out recently she's always wanted to become a veterinarian. She'd never told me before."

Josh's eyebrows careened toward his hairline. "Amanda wants to be a vet? Now it makes sense that she likes going across the street to talk to Cameron Wood."

"I know. I never made the connection until I found her reading a book about veterinary medicine."

"How do you feel about that?"

Hannah folded her hands in her lap. "I'm going to let her make that choice."

Josh nodded and pursed his lips. He was silent for a moment, as if taking all of her news in and contemplating it. "I guess your *freind* is excited that you're going to leave our community for him." His frown softened. "He should know he's blessed to have your love. That's what I dreamed of for years. It's going to be difficult for me to let go, but I know I have to."

Hannah touched his arm. "*Danki*, Joshua. I never meant to hurt you, but God has chosen a different path for me. It wasn't something I ever expected." She paused. "And now I need to go see your parents."

He stood. "I need to get back to work. Let me know if you need me to hitch up the horse for you."

Hannah waved off the offer. "I can do it, but *danki*." She watched him lope down the steps, and she hoped her meeting with his mother would be as simple.

. . .

Hannah knocked on Barbie's door later that afternoon. She prayed Barbie would listen to her and not ask her to leave before she finished explaining her decision. She also prayed Lillian would speak to her.

The door opened with a loud squeak, and Barbie frowned at Hannah. "Well, I was wondering when you were going to come visit your *dochder*."

Hannah closed her eyes and held her breath to stop angry words from leaping from her lips. "May I come in?" she finally asked.

Barbie pushed the door open, and Hannah followed her into the kitchen where Lillian was rolling out dough.

"Lily." Hannah's heart twisted when her daughter glowered at her. "How are you?"

Lillian shrugged and continued rolling out the dough. "I'm fine."

Barbie stood in front of Hannah and folded her arms over her round middle. "I guess you're here to tell us about your decision to leave the community and abandon your *dochder*. I hope you've told Joshua. When Lillian came to us yesterday, Eli insisted we not say anything to Joshua so you could tell him yourself. You owed him that."

Hannah nodded. "*Ya*, I told him this morning. And I want to explain my decision to you and Eli."

Barbie made a sweeping gesture toward the kitchen table. "Sit. I'll call Eli in from outside."

Hannah sat at the table and watched Lillian cut out cookies. "How are you doing?"

"I told you. I'm fine." Lillian kept her back to Hannah.

"We miss you."

Lillian didn't respond.

Hannah felt tears fill her eyes, and she hoped she wouldn't cry. "Lily, I pray that someday you'll realize why I'm doing this."

Lillian faced her with anger shining in her eyes. "No, *Mamm*. I never will understand why you would choose to break up our family."

Hannah heaved a heavy sigh and wished she knew the correct words to heal her daughter's broken heart. She prayed God would someday remove the wedge between them.

Barbie returned to the kitchen. "Eli is on his way." Barbie turned to Lillian. "Why don't you finish those *kichlin* later? Bring the meadow tea to the table, and I'll get glasses."

Lillian rolled the dough back up, placed it in a bowl, and stuck it in the refrigerator. She then brought a platter of peanut butter cookies and a pitcher of tea to the table before sitting across from Hannah. Lillian grabbed a cookie from the platter. "These are my favorite."

"I know, *mei liewe*." Barbie smiled. "I was thinking of you when I made them."

"*Wie geht's*." Eli stepped into the kitchen and washed his hands at the sink. "*Gut* to see you."

"It's *gut* to see you too." Hannah's stomach clenched. Gideon had resembled his father. She prayed she could look into Eli's eyes and share her decision to leave the church without feeling as if she were disappointing Gideon.

Barbie and Eli sat across from Hannah, leaving her the only person on her side of the long table. She felt isolated and alone, and she wondered if that was what it felt like to be shunned.

Eli studied Hannah. "I had a feeling you'd come to see us." He palmed a cookie from the plate and bit into it. "Mmm. Very *gut*, Barbie."

"*Danki*." Barbie helped herself to a cookie.

Hannah took a deep breath and tried to remember the speech she'd prepared on her way over to her in-laws' house. She suddenly felt at a loss for words. "First, I want to thank you for taking in Lillian."

Barbie frowned. "Of course we welcome our *gross-dochder* into our *haus*. We would never turn away our *grandkinner*. In fact, we would never kick out our *kind* either."

Hannah scowled. "I didn't kick out my *kind*. She chose to leave."

"You left me no choice." Lillian's eyes filled with tears.

"Lily, that's not true." Hannah's voice trembled. She looked back and forth between her in-laws. "You already know I'm leaving the church. I'm here to tell you my reasons for my decision."

"Are you going to tell the bishop?" Barbie asked.

Hannah nodded. "*Ya*, I'm going to tell him later today."

"So you haven't changed your mind, even after your *dochder* left you?" Barbie's tone was accusatory.

Hannah paused and wished she had someone to defend her. She felt as if she were fighting an uphill battle with Lillian and Barbie. "No, I haven't changed my mind."

Eli frowned and shook his head. "I'm very sorry to hear this. Are you certain this is what you want to do?"

"*Ya*, I'm certain, but it wasn't an easy decision." She paused to prevent herself from crying. "I've prayed about it, and I've come up with the same conclusion each time—God is leading me to a new life outside of this community."

Eli fingered his long, white beard. "I don't know what to say, Hannah. This has been a shock to me." He gestured toward his wife. "Barbie told me you had a *freind* who was *English*, but I'd hoped it was an innocent friendship and not a relationship that would lead you away from the community."

"Believe me, I'm just as surprised as you are." Hannah picked up a paper napkin and began to fray the edges. "I've wondered why God has presented this path to me after I've spent my whole life in the Amish community. I love this community. It's been my home since I was born, and I never imagined leaving it. It doesn't make sense, but I can't deny myself the opportunity to live the life God wants me to live."

Barbie shook her head. "This isn't right, Hannah. You can't take our *grandkinner* away from us. They're all we have left of Gideon." She sniffed and wiped her eyes. "You're breaking my heart. And I know this would break Gideon's heart as well. He would never want this for his *kinner*."

"I'm not taking your *grandkinner* away from you, Barbie. I'd never keep my *kinner* from their family." Hannah looked at Eli. "You know they love you both dearly, and they will want to see you as often as they can. Joshua too. He said this morning that he wants to stay in the children's lives. You may have heard that Trey is opening a bed and breakfast here in Paradise, so we'll be living close by."

"But this is wrong." Barbie tapped the table with her finger. "Gideon built that horse farm with his heart and soul. He wanted to have a *gut*, steady income for his *kinner*. You're betraying his memory by taking his *kinner* from that farm." She gestured toward Lillian. "What about Lillian? You're abandoning her. How can a *mamm* abandon her *kind*?"

Lillian nodded with emphasis. "*Mammi* is right. If it weren't for her, I'd be homeless."

"*Ach*, of course you're welcome here, Lily." Barbie wiped her eyes with a napkin and then turned to Eli. "We love having her here, don't we, Eli?"

"Of course we do." Eli's eyes glittered with tears. "You're always *willkumm* here." He turned to Hannah. "I don't understand why you would break up your family like this, Hannah. Have you really thought this through? You'll be shunned, and your *kinner* will be caught in the middle between you and the community."

Hannah took a deep breath and prayed she could respond to their accusations with grace and respect. "My *kinner* will not be caught in the middle. Amanda and Andrew are going with me, and Lily will be fine here. I want to see her as often as she'll see me."

Lillian glared at Hannah and then wiped her tears.

Hannah cleared her throat before she continued speaking. "I know what will happen when I leave the community, but I have to follow my heart. I've prayed about this, and I do have my *kinner's* best interests in mind."

"But you're breaking our hearts." Barbie shook her head as tears flowed from her eyes. "I know I've been hard on you over the years, but I always thought you did the best you could with the *kinner*. I never imagined you'd do something like this. I don't understand, Hannah. This is nonsense. Gideon wanted his *kinner* to be Amish. He would never give his blessing for this, Hannah."

"Gideon isn't here anymore, *Mamm*. I have to do what I think is best." Hannah's voice shook with emotion. "I'll let you know when I'm ready to move out of your *haus*. Joshua said he wants to move in. He's going to buy my portion of the horse business from me."

Barbie wiped her eyes with a crinkled napkin. "Do you realize what you're doing? You're uprooting your *kinner* for purely selfish reasons, Hannah. How can you do this with a clear conscience?"

"*Mamm*, I told you. I've prayed about this, and I've struggled with all of the consequences of my decision." Hannah wiped her eyes with a napkin and then paused to gather her thoughts. "I believe Gideon would want me to be *froh*. This is the path that will make me *froh*. And I've always wanted to work in a place like a bed and breakfast, so I know I will enjoy being with Trey in the one he's opening here in Paradise. I'm not betraying Gideon's memory. I'm doing what I believe is right for my family and me. Lillian has asked to stay in the community, and she wants to be with you. I hope you'll allow Amanda and Andrew to visit you often and be a part of your lives. Even if they aren't members of the church, they're still your family. They still need to know what it means to be Amish, and you can show them. They are a part of Gideon, and they want to continue to be close to you both."

Eli pulled at his beard. "I don't agree with what you're doing, but, of course, we will welcome them into our *haus*."

Hannah nodded. "*Gut. Danki, Dat.*"

Barbie nodded stiffly. "I won't punish my *grandkinner* for your horrible decisions." She regarded Lillian with a sad smile. "We're *froh* you're here, Lily."

Hannah stood. "I hope you all will understand my decision someday." She turned to Lillian. "*Ich liebe dich, mei liewe.* I hope you will visit us. We all miss you."

Lillian shook her head while still frowning. "I need some time to sort this out."

"I respect that." Hannah said good-bye and then started toward the front door.

As Hannah stepped outside, she sent up a little prayer to God, asking him to heal her broken relationship with her daughter. She climbed into the buggy and guided the horse as fresh tears sprinkled her warm cheeks.

. . .

Hannah stopped the horse at the end of the driveway in front of the bishop's two-story white house. She wiped her tears and then prayed for the right words before making her way up the front porch steps and knocking on the door.

Elmer opened the door. "Hannah. I was expecting a visit from you." He pointed toward the chairs on the porch. "Would you like to sit down?"

"*Danki*." Hannah sat on the chair and looked toward her waiting buggy. "I'm certain you know Melvin and Jonas came to see me. They were concerned I was going to leave the church, and they asked me if I wanted a meeting called with the baptized members of the congregation."

Elmer leaned back in the chair. "They told me you said you weren't planning to leave. Have you now made a decision otherwise?"

Hannah nodded. "After many prayers, I truly believe God is leading me toward a new life. I plan to leave the church."

"I'm sorry to hear that." Elmer frowned. "You'll be missed at church. You and your family are a part of our community and that makes you our family." He paused a moment. "Do you know what this means, Hannah? Have you really thought about the consequences of your decision?"

"I have." Hannah nodded. "I've thought about it, I've cried about it, and I've prayed about it. I know this is the path God has chosen for me. You have to understand, I didn't come to this decision easily. It's the most difficult decision I've made in my life."

Elmer pulled on his long beard. "You were born into this community. Your ancestors were Amish. I knew your parents and your grandparents. You've always had a strong faith, so I don't understand how you can give up the only life you've ever known. I'm not judging you, but I want to understand your decision."

She paused to gather her thoughts. "I never imagined I would leave the community, but Gideon left me with a broken heart. I thought I would marry another Amish man, but I never found the right person. When I met Trey Peterson, my heart came alive again, and we are going to build a life together. We plan to open a bed and breakfast, which is actually a dream I've always had. Trey is a good Christian man, and he will be a wonderful role model for my *kinner*. He also lost his spouse tragically—as well as his daughter—and we understand each other well."

Elmer heaved a deep sigh. "Your *kinner* will have a difficult time adjusting to life outside their community. Have you considered how this will affect them?"

"I have." Hannah explained how Lillian had moved in with her grandparents, while Amanda was considering going to college someday. She also told him that she planned to move out of her house and sell her business to Joshua.

"This will be a huge adjustment for you, Hannah. You're going to face some challenges." He tapped the arm of the chair. "Just remember you'll be welcome to come back at any time after you confess in front of the congregation. We all pray that our members who have left will return."

"*Danki*." Hannah stood. "I need to get home to my *kinner*. I appreciate your time."

"Good-bye." Elmer waved.

Hannah headed toward the buggy and felt as if she were starting out on a new and exciting journey.

TWENTY-SEVEN

Hannah guided the horse back to the barn. She'd spent the ride back to her farm considering the bishop's words and wondering what to do next. Now that she'd made her decision public, she felt lost and a little confused. She prayed again that Lillian would someday forgive her and respect her decision to leave the faith.

Hannah unhitched the horse and walked it toward the stable. She felt as if she were walking through a dream. The decision to leave the church had her reeling. Yet saying the words aloud to the bishop made it all feel concrete. She knew the choice to leave had come from God, and she was following both her heart and the path he had laid out for her. Now she needed to tell Trey that she'd made her choice.

She stowed the horse and then glanced toward the room where the phone was. She wondered where Trey was today. She longed to see him and tell him that she was ready to start her life with him.

Her heart thudded in her chest as she made her way to the phone. She wanted to meet him somewhere special when she told him the news. She smiled as she lifted the receiver and dialed her driver's number. After she set up her plan with Phyllis, she would call Trey and tell him where to meet her.

. . .

Trey's iPhone rang in his pocket as he crossed the grocery store parking lot. He balanced his bag of groceries in one hand while pulling the phone from his pocket with the other. "Hello?"

"Hi, Trey. How are you?" Hannah's voice was soft on the other end of the line, and his heart skipped a beat. He'd been praying for her and hoping she'd make a decision about his proposal. Of course, he wanted her to accept the proposal, but he'd tried to prepare his heart for a rejection just in case she didn't say yes.

"Hannah. I was hoping to hear from you." He weaved through the sea of cars toward his sedan parked in the back. "I'm fine. How are you doing?"

"I'm well."

"I've missed you at the hotel. Ruth told me you'd taken a few days off." He unlocked his car and climbed in, placing his bag of groceries in the seat beside him. "Is everything okay with you and your family?"

"*Ya*, we're fine. I just needed a few days off to think about everything."

"Oh." He thought about his conversation with Ruth. "Did you get the message I sent through Ruth?"

"I did." She hesitated, and he held his breath, hoping that she wasn't calling to reject him. "It's a beautiful day out, *ya*?"

"Yes, it is." He looked up at the bright blue, cloudless sky through his windshield and wondered if she was stalling. *Is she trying to figure out the right words to say good-bye to me?*

"I was wondering if you could meet me out by your new house in about ten minutes. I've called a driver, and she's coming to get me."

"Oh." Hope swelled within him. *Maybe this will be good news.* "You don't have to hire a driver. I can pick you up."

"That's not necessary. I'll meet you out there. I'll see you in a few minutes."

"Sounds good. I just have to stop by the hotel and drop off my groceries." He disconnected the call and prayed Hannah wanted to meet him to accept his proposal and not to shatter his heart.

. . .

Hannah fingered the ties on her prayer covering while standing in the driveway at Trey's new house. She'd tried to gather all of her thoughts during the ride over in Phyllis's car. After she paid Phyllis and thanked her for the ride, Hannah found herself staring at the house and wondering what she was going to say.

Trey's shiny car steered into the driveway, and her stomach fluttered. Her life was going to be changed forever after today, and she felt dizzy with excitement, not fear.

"Hannah." He climbed from the car and walked over to her. "I was really glad to hear from you."

She gestured toward the backyard. "Would you take a walk with me?"

"Of course. How's your family?"

"They're all well. Amanda and Andrew are doing chores right now. Lily is at her grandparents' house. She moved out yesterday."

Trey's eyes widened. "Lily moved out?"

"She wanted to stay with her grandmother, and I had to let her go. It was her decision."

"Hannah." The concern in Trey's expression warmed her heart. "Are you okay with her leaving?"

"It was difficult, but I've accepted it. It will be okay. I'm going to continue to pray that someday she'll forgive me. Only the Lord can repair the distance between us, and I have faith that he will." She pushed back her sad emotions and looked up at the house. "Do you have a closing date?"

"Yes, it looks like it's going to be July 1." He smiled. "I can't wait."

"Have you decided on a name?" She stopped by the pasture fence.

He shook his head. "No, I haven't had any real inspiration."

"What do you think about the Heart of Paradise?"

Trey rubbed his chin. "I think I like that. That's really catchy."

"I've been thinking about this bed and breakfast." She gestured toward the backyard. "I was wondering what kind of vegetables you'd like me to plant in your garden."

His eyes rounded. "You're going to plant a garden?"

"*Ya*." She nodded. "Also, I can put together a menu

for you to give to your guests. They can have one authentic Amish meal included and then be charged for additional meals." She then pointed toward the stable. "Joshua said Andrew can work for him on Saturdays, and he can take care of Huckleberry there. But if you want to have a horse on the property, we can bring Huckleberry with us."

"Hannah." Trey took her hands in his. "Are you saying what I think you're saying?"

Hannah removed her prayer covering and unpinned her hair, which fell in waves past her shoulders. She smiled up at his shocked expression. "Yes I will marry you. And Andrew, Amanda, and I would like to help you run your bed and breakfast."

He breathed out a deep gasp and shook his head. "This is music to my ears, Hannah. Are you certain you want to leave your community for me?"

Hannah nodded. "I've spoken to my family, Joshua, Barbie and my father-in-law, and the bishop. I've told them all I have to follow my heart and also God's plan. I think I belong with you." She reached up and pushed a lock of hair back from his eyes. "I see my future when I look into your eyes, and I feel like I'm home when I visit this house. It will be difficult since not all of my family agrees with this decision, but I know we can build a life together."

"You've made me the happiest man on the planet." He leaned down and kissed her lips. "I will do my best to give you all of the happiness you've brought to me. I love you, Hannah. I will cherish you and your children for the rest of my life."

"I love you too, Trey."

He opened his arms, and she stepped into his warm embrace. Closing her eyes, she thanked God for bringing love back into her life and giving her a second chance at happiness.

DISCUSSION QUESTIONS

1. Hannah finds love in an unexpected place. Although she's always felt at home in her Amish community, she considers following her heart and leaving. Have you ever longed to make a big change in your life? If so, did you follow through with that change? How did your family and friends react? What Bible verses helped you with your choice? Share this with the group.

2. Amanda finds herself caught between two worlds. Although she loves her family and her community, she feels drawn to the possibility of getting her GED and going to college. She keeps her aspirations a secret until later in the story. Have you ever faced a crossroads in your life? If so, which road did you choose? Share this with the group.

3. Ruth quotes Colossians 4:5–6. "Be wise in the way you act toward outsiders; make the most of every opportunity. Let your conversation be always full of grace, seasoned with salt, so that you may know how to answer everyone." What does this verse mean to you?

4. Lillian struggles with where she fits in the family when she learns that both her mother and sister

are considering leaving the church. She has to find her own path and follow her heart despite what her family members choose to do. Take a walk in her shoes. What path would you choose?

5. Josh dreamt of having a romantic relationship with Hannah and taking care of her children after his brother died. He's heartbroken when he learns Hannah is falling in love with Trey. Although he's angry, he can't deny his love for Hannah. Think of a time when you felt lost and alone. Where did you find your strength? What Bible verses would help with this?

6. Gossip, even in a community that is supposed to be Christlike, can hurt people and lead to misunderstanding. Do we do this in our own church communities—judge and gossip about our fellow Christians without considering the consequences? If so, why do you think that is?

7. The verse Ephesians 4:32 is mentioned in the book: "Be kind and compassionate to one another, forgiving each other, just as in Christ God forgave you." What does this verse mean to you? Share this with the group.

8. Lillian is convinced that her mother is being selfish and is betraying her by leaving the Amish community. Do you agree with Lillian's feelings or do you believe Hannah is justified in her decision to leave and pursue a new life outside of the Amish faith? Share your thoughts with the group.

9. Which character can you identify with the most? Which character seemed to carry the most emotional stake in the story? Was it Hannah, Trey, Amanda, Lillian, Joshua, or even Andrew?

10. What did you know about the Amish before reading this book? What did you learn?

Acknowledgments

As always, I'm thankful for my loving family, including my mother, Lola Goebelbecker; my husband, Joe; and my sons, Zac and Matt.

I'm more grateful than words can express to my patient friends who critique for me—Stacey Barbalace, Margaret Halpin, Janet Pecorella, Lauran Rodriguez, and, of course, my mother. I truly appreciate the time you take out of your busy lives to help me polish my books. Thank you also to Bobbi Kendrick for her help with the horse research.

Special thanks to my special Amish friends who patiently answer my endless stream of questions. You're a blessing in my life.

Thank you to my wonderful church family at Morning Star Lutheran in Matthews, North Carolina, for your encouragement, prayers, love, and friendship. You all mean so much to my family and me.

To my agent, Mary Sue Seymour—I am grateful for your friendship, support, and guidance in my writing career. Thank you for all you do!

Thank you to my amazing editors—Sue Brower, Becky Philpott, Jean Bloom, and Becky Monds. I appreciate your guidance and friendship. I'm grateful to each and every person who helped make this book a reality.

To my readers—thank you for choosing my novels. My books are a blessing in my life for many reasons, including the special friendships I've formed with my readers.

Thank you most of all, God, for giving me the inspiration and the words to glorify you. I'm so grateful and humbled you've chosen this path for me.

ABOUT THE AUTHOR

Amy Clipston is the award-winning and bestselling author of more than a dozen novels, including the Kauffman Amish Bakery series and the Hearts of the Lancaster Grand Hotel series. Her novels have hit multiple bestseller lists including CBD, CBA, and ECPA. Amy holds a degree in communication from Virginia Wesleyan College and works full-time for the City of Charlotte, North Carolina. Amy lives in North Carolina with her husband, two sons, and four spoiled rotten cats.

. . .

Visit her website: amyclipston.com
Facebook: Amy Clipston
Twitter: @AmyClipston

Enjoy Amy Clipston's Hearts of the Lancaster Grand Hotel series!

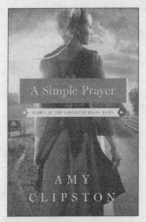

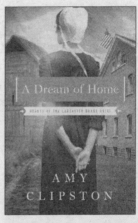

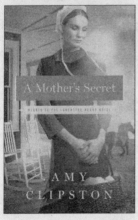

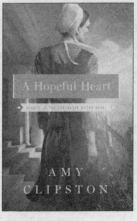

Available in print and e-book

The *Kauffman*
Amish Bakery Series

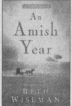

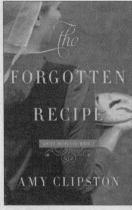